PRAISE FOR MICHELLE PAVER

'Paver is the mistress of suspense.'
The Times

'Terror on a grander scale.'
The Guardian

'Just fantastic.'
The Daily Mail

'A heart-freezing masterpiece.'
The Observer

'A tale of terror and beauty and wonder.'
The Financial Times

'A chilling period piece.'
The Independent

'This vivid ghost story reads like a classic.'
The Sunday Mirror

'A tense and strangely beautiful narrative.'
Metro

'Spellbindingly creepy.'
The Sunday Express

Wakenhyrst

MICHELLE PAVER was born in Central Africa
but came to England as a child. After gaining a
degree in Biochemistry from Oxford University she
became a partner in a city law firm, but eventually
gave that up to write full time. She is the bestselling
author of the adult gothic novels *Dark Matter* and
Thin Air and the prize-winning children's series
Chronicles of Ancient Darkness, which has sold
over three million copies worldwide.

Wakenhyrst

MICHELLE PAVER

HEAD
of ZEUS

First published in the UK by Head of Zeus in 2019

9 7 5 3 1 2 4 6 8

A catalogue record for this book is available from
the British Library.

ISBN (HB): 9781788549561
ISBN (XTPB): 9781789540604
ISBN (E): 9781788549554

Jacket art and illustrations © Stephen McNally

Printed and bound in Great Britain by
CPI Group (UK) Ltd, Croydon CR0 4YY

Head of Zeus Ltd
First Floor East
5–8 Hardwick Street
London ECIR 4RG

WWW.HEADOFZEUS.COM

Wakenhyrst

1966

The Mystery of Edmund Stearne
by Patrick Rippon
Only in *The Sunday Explorer Magazine*

Like a witch's lair in a fairytale the ancient manor house crouches in its tangled garden. I can't take my eyes off the ivy-choked window above the front door. It was from that window in 1913 that 16-year-old Maud Stearne watched her father set off down the steps with an ice-pick, a geological hammer – and murder in his heart.

We've all heard of Edmund Stearne. We've marvelled at his works and shuddered at his crime. Why did he do it? Did he confide his secrets to a notebook? *Why won't his daughter reveal the truth?*

For more than 50 years Maud Stearne has lived the life of a recluse. I'm the first outsider who's met her and been inside Wake's End. What I've learned blows her father's case wide open.

Maud was the only witness

Strange to think that until last year Edmund Stearne was unknown except in the sleepy Suffolk hamlet of Wakenhyrst. Locals remember him as a rich landowner and respected historian, a man of spotless reputation – until one summer's day when he slaughtered the first person he came across in the most bizarre and horrible way.

Maud was the only witness. She spoke briefly at his trial, then never again. Maud, Maud. It always comes back to Maud.

Her father spent the rest of his life in an asylum, where he devoted every waking moment to creating three astonishing paintings which have taken the world by storm. These days they're everywhere. Athena sells more of his posters than all the Impressionists put together. Yet on his death they were sold for a song to the Stanhope Institute of Psychiatric History.

For years they languished in obscurity until last year a lady academic stumbled on a dusty tea chest in a storeroom. 'My hair stood on end,' shrills Dr Robin Hunter, 36, a mini-skirted redhead in white vinyl boots. 'I knew I was onto something big.'

The rest is history. The paintings went on show and they caused a sensation. Edmund Stearne was an Edwardian gentleman but his work is strangely modern: it fits our era of beatniks, hippies and LSD. But what really caught the public's imagination is the *mystery*.

That's what I went to Wake's End to solve.

Rendezvous in the Fen

'Wake's End bain't on the road to nowhere,' warned the barmaid at the Eel Grigg in Wakenhyrst. 'You only goes there if you're going there.'

I was. I'd been invited by Maud Stearne herself.

From the village I drove across the Common and past the church. Wake's End is less than a mile from St Guthlaf's but it stands alone. Nestling in a bend of a willow-fringed stream, it's cut off at the front by a 10 foot hedge which bristles with hand-painted signs: PRIVATE PROPERTY! NO SHOOTING, EEL-BABBING OR TRESPASSING! KEEP OUT!

But it's not just the hedge that makes Wake's End a place out of time. It's Guthlaf's Fen.

These days what we call 'the fens' are windswept fields criss-crossed by drainage dykes. But the watery wilderness that guards Wake's End is the *real* fen: the last stretch of the ancient marshes that once drowned the whole of East Anglia. It's said to be the oldest, deepest, rottenest fen ever. Here lived the dreaded 'fen tigers': savage folk who doctored their 'ague' with home-brewed opium and feared nothing but the spirits that haunt the meres.

On a previous recce I'd ventured in. In 10 paces I was lost. The reeds stood tall and dead: I had the oddest feeling they wanted me gone. The light was failing. I caught a swampy smell of decay. Behind me something rustled and I saw the reeds part for some unseen creature. I thought: No wonder Maud's mad. All her life in a place like this?

But *is* she mad? Everyone describes a different Maud.

'Typical spinster, unhealthily devoted to her father,' opines her sister-in-law Tabitha Stearne, 66.

'Miss Maud hated her dad,' mutters a yokel in the pub.

'She walks the fen by night,' says another. 'Thass summat we *nivver* does.'

Tabby Stearne again: 'I'm afraid the poor old dear's quite batty. I gather that small dead animals have been found hanging from trees.'

So who is the real Maud Stearne?

A historic meeting

Maud Stearne is 69 and spare, with a tall woman's stoop. Dressed in shabby jersey and slacks, ancient gumboots and mac, she has her father's strong bones but not his staggering good looks. As she stands in the doorway of Wake's End her eyes avoid mine, moving restlessly as if she's watching something only she can see.

She won't shake hands, I'm just a grubby little hack who should have used the tradesman's entrance. 'I'm orff,' she barks in a cut-glass accent. 'Cook will show you raynd.' Before I know it she's striding towards the back of the house, over a rickety foot-bridge and into the fen.

'What do the paintings mean?' I shout after her.

'Never seen 'em!'

She's never seen the paintings? If my theory's right, she's at the heart of them.

No one ever forgets the paintings of Edmund Stearne. Your first impression is an explosion of colour like shattered stained glass. Leaning closer, you become aware of tiny malevolent faces leering at you. You want to pull back but you can't. Against your will you're drawn deeper into the murderer's twisted world.

All three are untitled and share the same mysterious design. At the dark heart stands a woman in a long black dress. You only see her back and her rippling fair hair, while around her swarms a vortex of otherworldly creatures. They're the stuff of nightmares, painted in such obsessive detail they could be alive. Grotesque, bewitching, even evil... No wonder Stearne is compared to that medieval master of the macabre, Hieronymus Bosch.

But what *are* his creatures? Elves? Imps? Fairies? Do they hold the key to the murder? Who is the unknown woman?

Inside Wake's End

'Cook' is a mountainous woman in overalls who exudes power and violence like a jailor. She could be anything from 50 to 75 – marcelled hair, pinched scarlet mouth – and the look she gives me is arctic. In these parts if you weren't born in Suffolk you're from 'up the Sheres'. In other words, you're a Martian.

She's no talker but as she shows me round I gather that she and 'Miss Maud' hate each other with the kind of loathing it takes decades to perfect. My 'tour' feels oddly stage-managed: I'm being shown only what Maud wants me to see. I wonder if that will include the fabled notebook.

There's no money at Wake's End, that's for sure. Thick medieval walls are blistered with damp; mouldy furnishings are pre-World War I. Time stopped in 1913.

'The Master's study' feels weirdly as if Edmund only just left. On a washstand two silver-backed brushes are tangled with strands of fair hair. On his desk lies a stack of yellowed typescript: *The Book of Alice Pyett (1451–1517), Mystic. Translation & Exegesis by E.A.M. Stearne, D.Phil. Cantab.* He was working on that before the murder.

But still no notebook.

Maud's desk is in the library across the hall. It overlooks a shaggy lawn with trees and what resembles a wishing-well: round stone wall, bucket on a rope. That's the well where they found Edmund after the murder. That's the orchard where he did it. This is what Maud looks at year after year.

On her desk lies a blue china wing (yes, a wing) and a large red book stamped with gilt initials: *E.A.M.S.* Edmund Algernon Montague Stearne. My mouth goes dry. That's it. That's his notebook. Maud has always refused even to confirm its existence, yet now she's left it here for me to see. What's she playing at? More to the point, can I take a look?

'Five minutes,' growls Cook. 'Thass all you got.'

I'm too excited to argue. His writing shouts at me from the page: 'Edmund Stearne – Private, 1906.' Seven years before the murder.

At first it's just jottings, then nothing for five years. From 1911 every page is crammed. His writing is small and illegible but here and there the odd phrase leaps out. And some are very odd indeed.

... a long, narrow passage tiled in oxblood ceramics; hot to my touch, and repellently glossy...

... the fleshy mound on her upper lip...

There are angels, but not as many.

She was brought in horribly changed.

Deft little sketches appear: grotesque medieval faces, a bat, a toad, a magpie. Each is disturbingly life-like and oddly threatening.

I know what you did.

It is only a picture. It can't do me any harm...

... a high thin cry on the fen...

I shall find the answer in Pyett.

The last page is blank except for a single scrawled sentence underlined twice: '*Dear God, I hope I'm wrong.*'

Murder in the orchard

Why didn't Maud give the notebook to the police? What is she hiding?

At the trial she said that on the day of the murder she was upstairs and when she glanced through the round window at the end of the passage she saw her father heading down the front steps with an ice-pick and a hammer.

She shouted at the boot-boy: 'Fetch help! The Master's gone mad!' Then she raced to the orchard. Too late. Edmund was already kneeling over a corpse.

The coroner said the first blow was lethal, the ice-pick piercing the eyeball and brain. Let's hope so, because Edmund chiselled back the scalp, hacked out a chunk of skull and dug around in the grey matter as if he was looking for something. And Maud saw the whole thing.

What followed next is one of the great mysteries of the case. Somehow Edmund ended up down the well, screaming in terror as he fought off a squirming mass of live eels.

Maud *said* she didn't see it happen as she was staring at the corpse. Next thing she knew, the housemaid burst onto the scene. The maid didn't see the body in the long grass but she heard her master screaming and ran to help.

'Leave him!' shouted Maud, damning herself in the eyes of the public. The Press dubbed her 'callous and unfeminine'. It didn't help that she was plain.

But her father's guilt was beyond doubt. When the police hauled him out he calmed down and confessed: 'I did it. But I did nothing *wrong*.'

He never said *why* he did it and there was no ill-will between him and the victim, he'd simply slaughtered the first person he met. In his pockets the police found shards of green glass matching the ones embedded in the victim's eyeballs, ears and tongue, as well as four leaves from a plant named Solomon's Seal. Three more were crammed down the victim's throat.

All this proved his guilt – but to me it means far more. Because for centuries, Solomon's Seal has been used in witch-craft.

He didn't do it

What have witches got to do with Edmund Stearne? Every-thing. Because I think he was innocent.

He didn't scream down that well because he was mad. He'd had a horror of eels since he was a boy. His doctor in Broadmoor wrote: 'His behaviour is perfectly rational. His sole indication of mania is that he is terrified of the tiny beings he feels compelled to paint, and yet he seems quite unable to desist.'

His *sole* indication of madness! Edmund wasn't mad on the day of the killing, he went mad *afterwards* in the asylum.

As for the murder, *we only have Maud's word that he did it!* And her evidence is full of holes.

Why did she shout 'The Master's gone mad' when all he'd done was leave the house with an ice-pick and a hammer?

Why send the boot-boy away? He was a strapping lad of 16, he could have stopped Edmund himself.

How did Edmund end up down the well? Did someone else push him – *before* the murder, to get him out of the way? Did someone else plant those items in his pockets, then toss in the weapons and eels?

But what's all this got to do with witches?

It's not just the Solomon's Seal, it's that glass. I found it in Wakenhyrst's tiny museum. Experts say it's medieval and bears traces of urine and deadly nightshade, both common ingredients in a 'witch-bottle'. That's an ancient charm against the evil eye.

And it can't be coincidence that one of Edmund's ancestors was a 'witch-pricker', someone who inspects the accused for tell-tale warts. Or that John Stearne was in cahoots with the notorious Witchfinder-General, who in 1645 hanged 40 people at Bury St Edmunds. (Another judge ended up in Salem, Massachusetts, the most famous witch trial of them all. Film people call that 'an American angle' and it's got Hollywood panting for Maud's story.)

Finally the clincher: *Wakenhyrst sources claim that Maud Stearne thinks she's a witch.*

I'm not saying she is, mind. But back in 1913, *believing* she was, did she commit the murder and frame her father – who, to protect her, nobly took the blame?

Why did she do it? All is revealed in my book. But everything fits and it solves the mystery of Edmund Stearne.

His paintings are coded messages pointing to Maud's guilt. The woman at the heart of each one is a witch. The creatures swarming around her are her evil familiars.

And the witch is Maud.

Murder in the Orchard by Patrick Rippon,
published by Titan.
For reader discount see p 48.

Letter from Maud Stearne to Dr Robin Hunter,
14th November 1966

Dear Dr Hunter,

An anonymous 'well-wisher' sent me Mr Rippon's preposterous article and since I decline further contact with that dreadful little man I am writing to you. Am I to be libelled as a madwoman and a murderess? Of course Mr Rippon knows that I can't afford to sue.

Cook is behind these lies about witches. She and my sister-in-law wish to put me in a 'home' and sell the fen. When I was a girl it stretched beyond the church, but that part was common land and sold after the War. I may be poor, but I will *never* allow *my* fen to be drained and turned into fields for pigs.

Naïvely, I had supposed that by allowing one interloper into Wake's End I might be rid of the lot. I shan't repeat that mistake. *If you badger me again I shall burn the notebook.* Lest you dismiss that as an idle threat, I enclose a page ripped out at random. That is all you will ever see. I will never tell you or anyone else my 'story'. I must be left *alone*.

Maud Stearne

Letter from Dr Robin Hunter to Miss Maud Stearne,
16th November 1966

Dear Miss Stearne,

Please forgive me for troubling you again and I *beg* you not to harm the notebook – but I've just been inside St Guthlaf's for the first time since it was renovated and what I found was so astonishing I had to write.

I'd heard of the medieval painting known as the Wakenhyrst Doom, discovered under remarkable circumstances in 1911 – but I'd never seen it until today. As you'll know it's a typical Last Judgement, in that Hell is far more convincing than Heaven. What makes it extraordinary is the link with your father's paintings.

I know you don't wish to hear about them but a detail in Painting No. 2 is crucial. Three of its creatures have become justly celebrated. Dubbed 'The Three Familiars', they are now known as 'Earth', 'Air' and 'Water'. It is the hideous 'Earth' who sparked my epiphany in St Guthlaf's.

I had stood before the Doom for hours and it was only as the vicar was turning off the lights that I noticed a scaly little devil in one corner. He is naked, squatting with legs indecently splayed, and though he has hooked a female sinner with his spear, he isn't leering at her, but at *us*.

That was when I happened to glance at my working file, the cover of which bears a copy of 'The Three Familiars'. 'Earth' met my gaze with his lecherous wink. I glanced back to the devil in the Doom. He too is winking, and his toad-like grin is very similar to that of Earth.

In fact it's identical. That was when I knew. The creatures in your father's paintings aren't fairies or elves, and certainly *not* familiars. *They are devils.*

Forgive my incoherence, it's 3 a.m. – but *please* don't ignore this letter. I'm desperate to know what you think.

Yours very sincerely,
Robin Hunter Ph.D.

Eastern Daily Press, *20th November 1966*

Storm Damages Historic Home

The storm that battered Suffolk yesterday night caused considerable damage in the parish of Wakenhyrst. Worst hit was historic Wake's End, erstwhile home of famous artist Edmund Stearne. The roof is said to be close to collapse, and experts estimate the cost of repairs at many thousands of pounds.

Letter from Maud Stearne to Dr Robin Hunter,
24th November 1966

Dear Dr Hunter,

Come to Wake's End the day after tomorrow at two o'clock and we will discuss the sale of my 'story'.

Yours &c,
Maud Stearne

60 Years Earlier

'Those who can make you believe absurdities
can make you commit atrocities.'

VOLTAIRE

One

MAUD started awake with the cry ringing in her ears. She lay in the dark, listening to her brother turn over in the other bed and Nurse's snores rumbling through the wall. She didn't know if the cry had been real or in a dream.

There it was again. Her stomach clenched. It was coming from downstairs: from Maman. It meant the groaning had begun. *Please please* don't let her die.

Every year Maman got the same illness and it often ended in a baby. Her middle swelled so that she couldn't wear stays, and Dr Grayson made her take constant nips of brandy, which she loathed. Then came the terrible time the servants called the groaning, when Maman's middle would burst and Maud would huddle in the nursery and stop her ears.

The best way for a groaning to end was with a bloody chamberpot, as that was soonest over. Second-best was a dead baby and worst was a live one, because Maman cried when it died – which it always did. Maman was careful never to cry in front of Father, as he didn't like it.

Now that Maud was nearly nine, she knew it was her task to save her mother. She had to do something to keep the babies away. She'd tried praying but it didn't work, probably because it was God who sent the babies.

Her gaze drifted to the windows giving on to the fen. The fen had power. Maybe it could help.

Father hated the fen. He forbade Richard and Maud to cross the foot-bridge and venture in, and all the windows overlooking it – which meant almost all of them – had to be kept shut always. Cook was under strict orders never to serve fish or fowl from the fen, especially eels. Father said eels were unclean as they fed on dead things.

Nurse didn't like the fen either. 'Don't you nivver go near un,' she'd say, thrusting her spongy face close. 'If'n you do, the ferishes and hobby-lanterns ull hook you in to a miry death.' Strangely, though, Cole the gardener disagreed. He often went in to catch a tench for his dinner. He said if you watched what you was about, the fen couldn't do you no harm.

Secretly, Maud sided with Cole. To her the fen was a forbidden realm of magical creatures and she longed for it with a hopeless passion. In summer the scent of meadowsweet drifted across the Lode and the reeds rang with the *eep-eep* of frogs. In winter Maud could hear the ice cracking on the Mere and the skies were alive with vast skeins of geese. One afternoon they'd flown right over the garden, and the beat of their wings had lifted Maud as if she were flying. It was the grief of her life that she couldn't open the windows and listen to the wings.

For her seventh birthday, Cole had brought her a present

from the fen: a viper's sloughed-off skin. Maud kept it behind the loose piece of wainscot under her bed. It was her most precious thing.

Now as she listened to her mother's moans, she knew that the time had come to use it. If she climbed on the chair by the window, she could see the fen. She could pray to it on the viper skin to keep Maman safe.

Scrambling out of bed and keeping one eye on horrid Richard, she prised the wainscot loose and extracted her treasure. Her brother went on sleeping, so she crept to the chair, hitched up her nightgown and climbed on, ducking beneath the curtains and peering round the edge of the blind.

She stopped breathing. There was an owl on the windowsill.

At first all she saw was its wings folded over its back. Then it swivelled its head right round and she saw its moonwhite face and deep black eyes.

Nurse said that a bird tapping on your window means death. But the owl wasn't tapping the pane, it was staring at Maud.

Please keep Maman safe, she begged it silently. *Please keep the babies away.*

The owl turned and glided off into the night. The fen was flooded with blue moonlight. Along the Lode the willows stood motionless, the reeds as still as planted spears.

Nurse said owls bring bad luck, but Cole said that's only if you shoot one. Maud knew that this owl was a messenger from the fen. It had perched on the windowsill opposite *her* bed, not Richard's – and it had looked at *her*.

Did this mean that her prayer had been heard, and Maman was safe?

Maud wasn't allowed to leave the nursery during a groaning, but she *had* to find out if Maman was all right.

The passage on the top floor wasn't too frightening because apart from Richard and Maud, only the servants slept up here. The stairs down to the first floor were scarier. Maud avoided the creaky step and eased open the door at the bottom.

At the other end of the passage, the doors to her parents' bedroom were open, and Father stood in the yellow lamplight, a column of crimson in his dressing-gown of Chinese brocade.

Fortunately his back was turned, and he was speaking to someone Maud couldn't see; she guessed it was old Dr Grayson. She couldn't make out what Father was saying, but he sounded calm. Surely he wouldn't be so composed if something were wrong? Seeing no servants, she assumed that Daisy and Valerie were with Maman in the dressing-room, where the groanings took place. Greatly daring, Maud crept along the passage.

It was indeed Dr Grayson talking to Father. 'I'm beginning to think it's an inherited flaw…' he said in a low voice.

'Inherited?' Father said sharply. 'There's never been anything like that in our family.'

'My dear fellow, I mean that of Mrs Stearne.'

'Ah. But she can have other children?'

'To be sure. Although perhaps... a spell of rest?'

Maud could tell by Father's silence that he was displeased. So could the doctor, but just then he spotted Maud. 'See there, we have an audience.'

Father turned his head and Maud nearly fainted. 'What are you doing downstairs?' he said brusquely. 'Where's your nurse?'

Now he was looming over her. His face was as severely beautiful as the alabaster knight in church, and the pupils of his eyes were black holes in icy pale blue.

When Maud still didn't move, he put his hand on her shoulder and gave her a little push. 'Off you go, you'll catch cold.' It was the first time he'd ever touched her, and although it didn't hurt, she was awed by the strength in his fingers.

But not even Father could stop her from finding out about Maman, so instead of climbing back upstairs, she hid on the bottom step.

Presently she heard a rustle of skirts, and saw Daisy emerge from the dressing-room. The old housemaid was frowning and carrying a covered chamberpot.

Ducking out of sight, Maud heard Daisy rustle into the bathroom. Then came the gurgling roar of the water closet, and Maud caught a sweet, coppery smell, like on the day they killed the pig.

She sagged with relief. The fen had heard her prayer. Maman's illness had ended in the best possible way: with a bloody chamberpot.

Next morning before breakfast, Father sent for Nurse. Nurse returned to the nursery with a face like thunder and gave Maud a thrashing with the stiff-bristled brush. Her eyes were red when she went down to the breakfast-room for morning prayers.

As Father began the reading, her thoughts drifted to the owl. If she stole a mouse from the traps in the pantry, maybe she could lure it back.

'*Thy will be done*,' intoned Father. To her relief, his gaze passed over her and settled on the servants' bench. 'Steers,' he said to the butler. 'Ada is improperly dressed.'

There was a gasp behind Maud, and Ada began to cry. With the distant curiosity of the saved for the doomed, Maud saw that a lock of the kitchen-maid's hair had escaped her cap. It was a pity. Maud had liked Ada. But Ada knew the rules: no loose female hair at Wake's End. That was why Nurse plaited Maud's so tight that it hurt. Her plaits hung to her waist and horrid Richard liked to pull them. Maud wished she could chop them off but that was also against the rules.

The rules governed every moment of Maud's day and there were two different kinds. One sort belonged to the lower orders: it was called superstition and Father detested it, which meant that the servants observed their rules behind his back. Thus Daisy left a dish of bread and milk for witches outside the boot-room door, and Cook avoided bad luck by hanging a hagstone from her bedpost. (Even Father did that, although his stone was merely a childhood memento.)

The other rules were Father's – and much stronger, as he had God on his side. They included never running about in the garden and always being silent downstairs. The rule Maud hated most was the one against animals. Father tolerated Blossom and Bluebell as they were needed for the carriage, but dogs were banned from Wake's End and Jessop had orders to drown any cat that strayed into the grounds.

What made these two sets of rules so dangerous was that you got punished if you mixed them up, but you couldn't always tell what kind of rule it was. If you spilled salt, you had to toss a pinch over your left shoulder; but was that to blind the Devil, as Nurse said – or was it because Judas Iscariot spilled salt at the Last Supper?

Maud pictured the two sets of rules as a pair of gigantic thorny walls leaning over her. She knew exactly what St Matthew meant when he said: 'Narrow is the way, and few there be that find it.'

Two

LIKE the house at Wake's End, St Guthlaf's Church was part friend and part foe.

The outside was mostly foe. The tower had slitty eyes and there were monsters snarling from the gutters. Worst was the stone crow near the porch. It perched on the head of a howling man with its talons sunk in his eyeballs.

Inside, what Maud feared most were the devils. They were carved on the font, the columns, even the ceiling. Father said that in olden times they would also have been painted on the walls, but they'd been whitewashed by the Puritans. Maud thought the stone devils were quite bad enough.

The Sunday after the groaning, she felt horribly at risk without Maman. As she followed Father up the aisle, she nodded a particularly polite greeting to the bench-ends: the unicorn, the mermaid, the wodewose, the Seven Deadly Sins. She was counting on them to keep her safe.

Things improved when she reached the family pew. The kindly old chest against the wall had stumpy little legs in case of floods and was made of bog oak from the fen. Its carvings helped Maud stay awake during Mr Broadstairs' sermon. She didn't care for St George but she adored the dragon. She *knew* that the very next moment it was going to bite that spear in two and fly away.

She also loved the frogs carved along the bottom. Cole called frogs 'fen nightingales', but Cook said a frog in the house is a witch in disguise. Last week she'd found one in the scullery and flung it on the fire. Nurse said it had gone all blistered and twitched for ages.

Maud began to feel sick. She wished she'd been allowed to see Maman, but she never was after a groaning, not for weeks. Maman made church bearable. She protected Maud from the devils, while Maud helped her mother past the family vault and the effigy.

The vault was in the churchyard near the path. It had a granite monument on top and slimy stairs leading down to a cobwebby darkness beneath; Nurse said you could see the coffins through the grille. Maman always averted her eyes when she walked past.

Maud rather liked Sir Adam de Braunche, the alabaster knight who slept in the aisle with his alabaster skeleton on a plinth underneath. But for some reason the skeleton *horrified* Maman. Maud would take her hand and thrill with pride when her mother murmured, 'How brave you are, *ma petite Mode.*'

At last the sermon was over and they stood up to sing. As the organ began, Maud swayed. Suddenly she knew why Maman was frightened of Sir Adam and the family vault. It was because she thought she was going to die.

Black spots swam before Maud's eyes. She pictured the bloody chamberpot and the frog twitching in the flames.

Nurse pinched her arm.

Father turned his head and stared.

As Maud pitched forwards, the dragon lifted off the chest and flew towards her.

Nurse wanted to thrash her for making a fuss in church, but Father summoned her to his study to explain herself.

Maud had only been there three times before. It lay behind not one but *two* pairs of double doors, so that Father could work undisturbed. When you opened the first pair, you were trapped in a nasty shadowy gap where you had to wait, dreading what was to come.

As Maud waited in the gap, she tried to think up something to tell Father. She couldn't say that she'd fainted because of Maman and the bloody chamberpot, then he would know that she'd disobeyed him on the night of the groaning.

At last his voice said, 'Enter,' and she opened the inner doors.

He was seated at his desk, writing. The scratch of his pen was loud in the silence. 'Tell me,' he said without raising his head. 'Why do you think you are here?'

Maud swallowed. 'Because I fainted in church.'

'Because you interrupted the prayers of others and neglected your own.'

'Yes, Father.'

She watched him clean his pen with the pen-wiper Maman had embroidered for him last Christmas, then align his notebook with his green Morocco blotter. The notebook was bound in scarlet and stamped in gilt with his initials. Maud longed to know what he'd written.

'Why did you faint?' he said quietly.

Her mind went blank. 'Um. I was looking at a frog.'

He frowned. 'You're not telling the truth.'

'I was looking at a frog, Father, it's carved on the chest and it reminded me of...' She broke off. If she told about the burned frog, that would get Cook in trouble and then she would pinch Maud under her lung protector, where it didn't show. 'It reminded me of a dead toad I saw in the garden,' she lied.

'You ought to have been praying.'

'Yes, Father.'

He adjusted the notebook a fraction. 'Do you enjoy looking at the carvings?'

Maud was startled. Father rarely spoke to her and he never asked what she enjoyed. 'Yes, Father,' she mumbled doubtfully.

'And why do you imagine they are on that chest?'

'Um – because frogs are God's creatures and will go to Heaven?'

'What on earth makes you say that?'

She took a breath. 'Because Miss Broadstairs says animals can't go to Heaven as they don't have souls but I know for a *fact* that she's wrong, I found proof.'

'Indeed. And where did you find this proof?'

'In the Bible. Where Isaiah says about creating new heavens and the wolf and the lamb feeding together and not hurting each other on the holy mountain.'

Father wasn't frowning any more. Two lines had appeared on either side of his moustache. He was *smiling*. 'But Isaiah only meant that figuratively. Do you know what that means?'

She nodded, although she didn't, not really. She couldn't believe she was having a conversation with Father. She wanted it to go on for ever.

'In the same way,' he continued, 'those carvings aren't intended merely to portray God's creatures. The frogs are symbols of wickedness. Do you know what a symbol is?'

'Yes, Father,' she said eagerly. 'Like in the Book of Revelations: "I saw three unclean spirits like frogs"?'

His eyebrows rose. 'How old are you, Maud?'

'Eight and three-quarters. I shall be nine on the twenty-sixth of May.'

'And do you enjoy reading your Bible?'

She nearly told the truth and said that she only read the Bible because she had nothing else and please *please* could she be allowed in the library? Out of caution, she simply nodded.

'Your knowledge of Scripture is impressive, but you mustn't show off. Intellectual conceit is unattractive, particularly in females.'

'Yes, Father,' she said happily. *Impressive*. He'd called her impressive.

Taking up his pen, he opened the red notebook. 'You may go. You will write out one hundred times that it is wrong to look about you in church instead of attending to your prayers.'

'Thank you, Father.'

She left the study floating on air. She'd escaped a thrashing and impressed Father. And another thing: it looked as if he'd written today's date in his notebook. Was he keeping a diary, like Miss Broadstairs, whose journal had a beautiful little gilt lock?

Maud was desperate to know if he'd written anything about her.

Three

AUD once heard Lady Clevedon remark that as Maman's people were Belgian and in trade, poor Dr Stearne had had to work miracles to teach her good taste. Maud had hated Lady Clevedon ever since.

Strangely, though, Maman seemed to agree. 'Your father did a wonderful thing in marrying me,' she told Maud. 'I owe him everything. It's my duty to make him proud.'

This meant looking beautiful all the time. When Maman's middle was so swollen that she couldn't wear stays, she wore the most gorgeous tea gowns. When she was well again, she spent her days changing her clothes: breakfast gown, walking dress, afternoon gown, evening gown.

She was ideally suited to the fashions of the time. Her bust never needed enhancing with hidden flounces, and her swan neck was perfect for boned collars reaching to her ears. Years later, Maud realised that Maman could only have achieved her hourglass figure by savage tight-lacing. She must have lived in almost constant pain.

Sometimes Maman came to the night nursery to kiss

them when they were in bed. Maud would hear the rustle of her skirts and breathe the milky scent of her skin and the smell of the little sachets of violet powder sewn into the underarms of her gowns. '*Dors bien, ma petite Mode*,' she would whisper, and they would exchange butterfly kisses with their eyelashes. Plain as Maud was, Maman really did seem to love her back.

Another part of making Father proud was obeying his every word. Maman never disturbed him by playing the piano, and she never kept any mementoes of the dead babies because he didn't approve. He said it was right and proper to pray for them and engrave their names on the family monument, but mementoes were for Catholics, and it was better not to dwell on one's loss.

It didn't occur to Maud that her mother might disagree with him until one afternoon in April when he was away in London doing research.

Valerie was downstairs pressing a bodice for the evening and Maman was in the dressing-room, while Maud was in the bedroom, playing with her mother's jewellery casket for a treat. In one of the little rosewood drawers, she found a small oval box that she hadn't seen before. It was dark-blue enamel inlaid with silver roses, and inside were seven tiny locks of fine hair. Each was tied with a yellow ribbon minutely embroidered with tiny letters. Maud recognised the names of the dead brothers and sisters for whom she had to pray every night.

'Promise you won't tell Father,' Maman said calmly from the doorway.

'I promise,' said Maud. 'Or Richard or Nurse or anyone.'

'There's my good girl. Now put it back where you found it.'

Maud did as she was told. 'But how did you *get* them?' she breathed. Maman was never allowed to see the dead babies. Dr Grayson always had them taken away before her sleeping draught wore off.

'That was easy,' her mother said drily. 'I bribed the monthly-nurse.'

'But – doesn't it make you sad? Being reminded, I mean.'

Maman made a little gesture of impatience. 'Of course it does. But this isn't something one can simply put out of one's mind. Nor do I want to.'

Maud looked at her with new respect. She had disobeyed Father not once, but *seven times*.

A few days later, Maud and Maman were taking a drive on the Common when the carriage came to a halt and Maud was surprised to see Biddy Thrussel approach Maman's window. Biddy was the village wisewoman, a large moon-faced cottager who kept one fingernail filed to a point to 'break the waters', whatever that meant. Maud watched her bob a curtsey, then hand Maman a small bottle of greenish liquid. Slipping it into her reticule, Maman pressed a shilling in Biddy's palm and told Jessop to drive on.

Maud asked what was in the bottle.

Maman hesitated. 'A herbal tonic.'

'What's a tonic?'

'It keeps me well.'

'Does it taste nice?'

'I don't know, I've never tried it. But I thought I would.'

When they were nearly home, Maman said, 'Your Father

wouldn't like me accepting things from Biddy, so we'll say no more about it. *Entendu, ma petite?*'

'*Entendu, Maman.*'

'There's my good girl.'

Maud forgot about the herbal tonic until after Easter, when Maman was ill again. This time it wasn't a proper groaning, merely an indisposition that lasted a few days, and it ended in a bloody chamberpot.

But Maud didn't begin to suspect that the question of babies might be more complicated than she'd been led to believe until she finally had a chance to read Father's notebook.

It was early May and the damp weather was making washing week a trial. Lady Clevedon said Maman ought to ask Father for money to pay an outside laundress, but she never did. This meant that every six weeks the servants were bad-tempered and the house stank of bleach.

The smell had given Father a headache, and he'd gone to Ely to buy books. Dr Grayson was upstairs with Maman, and Nurse was with Richard, who had whooping-cough.

Maud was downstairs in the passage. Father's study doors were open, as Sarah had just sprinkled the rug with damp tea-leaves and was sweeping them up. Maud was hanging about by the side-table. This was covered in an Indian shawl on which stood a glass dome full of stuffed bats. Her grandfather had caught them before she was born, and they'd lived on the side-table ever since. Maud liked them because they were the only animals allowed in the house.

At the end of the passage the green baize door opened

and Daisy called Sarah to come and help with the mangle. When she'd gone, Maud peeped into the study. Father's notebook was lying on his desk.

No no, she *couldn't*.

Could she?

He'd only written a few paragraphs and his writing was so tiny she couldn't make out much: '… the chancel arch is a disgrace, we *must* have it re-plastered… old Clevedon's so damnably mean…' Maud blinked. Father had written a rude word.

A few paragraphs down, she spotted her name. 'Maud is much more intelligent than Richard. What a pity she isn't a boy.' She flushed with pleasure. She'd often thought the same thing.

Over the page the writing was slightly easier to read: 'Grayson has been badgering me about steps to prevent conception. I told him such measures are revolting, unnatural and wrong. I doubt he'll raise the matter again.'

At that moment, Maud heard a carriage in the drive. Her mind darted in panic. Father was back.

Slamming the notebook shut, she sped to the doorway. Already she could hear him climbing the steps.

Steers hurried past her on his way to the front door. The instant before he opened it, Maud lifted the Indian shawl and shot under the side-table.

She heard Steers take Father's hat, cane and gloves and help him off with his ulster. 'No thank you, Steers, I'll unwrap the books myself.' The Indian shawl didn't quite reach the floor: Maud could see the glossy tips of Father's boots. Silently, she begged the bats to protect her.

Steers told Father that Dr Grayson was with Mrs Stearne, and Father headed for the stairs, while Steers returned to the back offices. Maud was about to flee when Sarah rustled past to set the study to rights.

Voices upstairs. Dr Grayson was leaving and Father was walking him to the door. In an agony of suspense, Maud heard them come downstairs and halt at her hiding place.

Dr Grayson was so close that she could hear him breathing through his whiskers. 'Mrs Stearne needs rest,' he said in an undertone. 'Rest, that's the ticket. So perhaps – not *every* night? Eh?'

'Whatever can you mean,' Father said coldly.

Maud could tell from Dr Grayson's flustered apology that he'd made the most awful mistake.

Soon afterwards, she escaped to the day nursery. Dr Grayson was not seen at Wake's End for several weeks.

The wet weather continued. In the churchyard the sexton had to remove pails of water when he dug a grave, and at Wake's End the Lode began to creep across the lawn.

In the day nursery, Maud puzzled over what she'd read in Father's notebook. Conception was when God gave a lady a baby, she'd read that in Isaiah: 'Behold, the virgin shall conceive and bear a son.' Was that why Father was angry with Dr Grayson for suggesting how to prevent it?

Maud remembered a conversation she'd overheard between Nurse and Cook.

'If he so much as *sees* Master Richard or Miss Maud I

gets a warning,' grumbled Nurse. 'How's it my fault if he don't like his own childer?'

Cook sniggered. 'He likes making en, though, don't ee?'

Nurse snorted one of her rare laughs. 'Gah! You terror!'

Maud felt uneasy and confused. Surely it was God who sent the babies. What did Father have to do with it?

Four

*S*OON after Maud's ninth birthday, Father took Maman to Brussels to visit her uncle – and amazingly, Richard and Maud went too.

At first Maud was beside herself with excitement. She'd never been further than Bury St Edmunds. But 'abroad' proved to be a huge disappointment. She didn't see the sea at all as it was dark, and Brussels turned out to be the same as home, because Nurse and the rules came too.

Afterwards, three things stood out in her memory: Great-Uncle Bertrand, the dragonfly pendant and the porcelain wing.

Father said Great-Uncle Bertrand was vulgar. Maud liked him because he let Maman play the piano. It was the first music Maud had heard apart from hymns and she found it confusing. But she was extremely proud of her mother.

The dragonfly pendant was a late birthday present from Maman. It was blue enamel set with peridots, and Maud's very first jewel. She was thrilled that Maman had remembered that she loved dragonflies.

Maud found the porcelain wing one afternoon when Father was away in a library reading about a lady named Alice Pyett, and Maman had taken Richard and Maud to a park where she had played when she was a little girl.

The park was a dusty expanse of hard brown grass, but next to it was a churchyard shaded by the most beautiful trees. While horrid Richard was throwing a tantrum and being fussed over by the grown-ups, Maud squeezed through a gap in the fence and explored.

She was entranced. This churchyard was nothing like St Guthlaf's. Every headstone bore a dear little oval portrait of the person buried underneath, and the children's graves were adorned with wreaths of lilies studded with small porcelain angels. Maud was enchanted by their wings. They were ruby, sapphire and emerald, like the butterflies in the drawing-room pictures at home.

Maud met a girl of about her own age and learned in broken French that her mother was tidying the family grave. Maud had never cared for dolls, but she was intrigued by the ones this girl had with her. Her mother couldn't afford to buy her real dolls so she'd rescued some of the angels from the wreaths and knocked off their wings with a hammer.

Maud found a snapped-off wing in the grass. It was a glossy sky-blue with darker lines marking the feathers. It made her think of the geese flying over the fen.

She had just slipped it in her coat pocket when Nurse's spongy red face loomed over her. 'So *that's* where you been!'

Maud was hustled back to Great-Uncle Bertrand's in disgrace. Even Maman was displeased. 'We *won't* tell Father,' she said sternly. 'He'd be appalled if he knew you'd been playing in a Catholic cemetery.'

Maud was in despair. And Maman didn't even know about the wing. Later when she was in bed, she laid the wing on her pillow, where Maman would see it.

Her mother glanced at the wing and then at Maud. 'Do you want this *very* much?'

Maud nodded.

Maman smoothed back Maud's hair from her forehead. 'Then I didn't see it,' she whispered.

'But I *stole* it,' whispered Maud. 'I found it in the—'

'Don't say it! Talking about things makes them real. I never saw this. We don't speak of it. It never happened. *Entendu?*'

'*Entendu*,' Maud said doubtfully.

She was a thief. She had broken one of the Ten Commandments. But according to Maman, it hadn't happened.

That night before she fell asleep, Maud wished on the wing that Father would remain in the library for the whole of next day.

Her wish was granted beyond her wildest dreams. Father decided to stay abroad for his research, and sent them home without him.

It got even better. Soon after they returned to Wake's End, Richard fell ill with rheumatic fever. Within weeks he was out of danger, but he needed constant nursing. With

Maman and Nurse fully occupied, all Maud had to do was keep out of their way.

It was the wildest, happiest time of her life. Maman wasn't ill once, and as long as Maud did her ridiculously easy lessons and appeared promptly at meals, she was free. *Free.*

She helped Cole in the garden and he taught her how to put four seeds in every hole: *One for the rook, one for the crow, one to rot and one to grow.*

She took to haunting the Lode at the edge of the grounds, and one memorable day she spied a bittern in the reeds. It stared at her with a baleful yellow eye, and she knew that she'd encountered the spirit of the fen.

She'd always loved how Wake's End looked from outside. Its bumpy roofs were splashed with orange lichen and its dormer windows poking from the attics looked like eyebrows over its shaggy green ivy-clad face. The ivy kept Maud safe, and now she befriended the creatures that lived in it: wasps, spiders, whole families of sparrows. She would lie in bed watching the rustly green light filtering through the leaves and listening to magpies stomping about on the roof. The old house was home to thousands of wild creatures. Not even Father could evict them.

Spring turned to summer, and still he stayed away.

As the weather grew hotter, Maud passionately envied the village children who ran about barefoot. Dr Grayson said it was good for children to perspire, so she was always bundled up in a tight leather lung protector, two flannel petticoats, a worsted skirt, jumper, jacket, stockings, buttoned boots, and a black straw hat whose varnish went sticky and smelled.

One particularly hot day when she was out of sight of the house, she daringly removed her hat. When nothing happened, she unravelled her plaits and raked her fingers through her hair. The breeze cooled her scalp. Father and Dr Grayson would have been appalled.

The following day she unlaced her lung protector and stuffed it behind a bin in the harness-room. Henceforth she would wear it only for meals. Her stockings went next. The grass between her toes was the most delightful feeling she'd ever experienced.

A week later she started stealing fruit. She and Richard were never allowed much fruit as Dr Grayson said it was too acid for children. Now Maud raided the orchard and the kitchen garden. Apples, pears, currants… She especially loved the gooseberries' taut skin and squidgy green insides. If Cole noticed any of this, he turned a blind eye.

Autumn went by in a flash. Even in winter, Maud haunted the grounds and watched the geese flying overhead. One day she found the wing-prints of an owl in the snow. She could see the pattern of its outstretched wings, every feather as sharp as a knife-cut. Cole said it was a tawny and that it had been hunting mice, but Maud knew that it was *her* owl, the white messenger of the fen.

Sure enough, that evening brought the stupendous news that Father would remain abroad until at least the following spring. This gave Maud the courage to do what she'd been longing to do for months. She ventured into the library. She didn't dare touch Father's books, but she found a shelf of volumes that had belonged to *his* father. She liked Audubon because of the pictures, and found Lyall on fossils difficult

43

but fascinating. She was also astonished to read that thousands of years ago, the fen had been a forest, and that bog oak was the remains of ancient trees.

But the book she loved most was *Robinson Crusoe*. She read it again and again. She envied Robinson his parrot and dreamed of surviving on her own in the wild. Her favourite bit was when the dog jumped out of the shipwreck and swam after Robinson to be his faithful companion.

Even more than the books, what she loved was being alone. Until now she'd lived in the nursery with Richard and Nurse and she'd been lonely. In the library she was solitary and happy.

But it never occurred to her that she could live like this all the time. Not until the following year, when she met Jubal Rede.

Five

MAUD still hadn't ventured into the fen, but now that Richard slept in the day nursery and she had the night nursery to herself, she spent hours gazing at the forbidden realm.

One night she heard a high thin cry and glimpsed a shadowy creature slipping through the reeds. Another time she spotted a man skating the frozen Lode with long sure strides. When next she saw him he was walking under the moon with a spear over his shoulder and a knot of black eels wriggling at the end. Maud shivered with awe. This must be Jubal Rede, the wild man who lived in the fen.

According to Cook, Jubal had webbed feet. 'Though I never seen en,' she chuckled. 'Old Jubal never wash without he fall in a dyke.'

'He'm not old,' said Daisy. 'Why, they say he were boot-boy here at the Hall when Master were a lad.'

'I never seed a better man arter snipe,' remarked Cole.

'Got a mouth on him, though,' sniggered Jessop. 'Blister the tar off a barn, can Jubal.'

'That's enough,' snapped Nurse, who'd spotted Maud. 'Jubal Rede is a wicked bad man and you mun't nivver go near en!'

So of course Maud was desperate to do just that.

Summer came and still Father remained abroad. Richard caught scarlet fever, which kept the grown-ups busy. Maman had never been so well, and Maud knew that this was due to the fen. She swore on the viper skin that before she turned ten, she would cross the foot-bridge and thank it in person.

The day before her tenth birthday, she kept her word.

Her heart hammered in her chest as she crashed through a tunnel of sedge as sharp as knives. She was *inside* the fen, inhaling its swampy green breath. Gnats whined in her ears. She heard the squawk and splash of moorhens. She was running barefoot at the edge of the Lode. If she fell in, she would drown.

The fen was nothing like what she'd expected. It didn't care about her. It didn't want her. She knew that. But still she ran.

The Mere wasn't quite two miles from the house, but the path to it seemed endless. Then suddenly she was out in the glare and there it was, a reedy wilderness of water glinting wickedly in the sun. The scent of meadowsweet was dizzyingly strong. Reeds hissed and swayed, swifts screamed overhead. Their village name was develin, and that's what they sounded like, devils.

The Mere was utterly forbidden, the haunt of ferishes

and will-o'-the-wisps that dragged you to a miry death. And yet Maud felt drawn to the edge. She leaned over. Fish fled her shadow. In the deep green murk she saw the skeletons of drowned weeds.

'*Git away from thar!*' roared a voice, and strong hands yanked her off her feet.

Squirming out of his grip, Maud fell backwards. A shaggy red dog trotted over and sniffed her toes. Its master spat a stream of brown liquid into the Mere and glared at Maud.

'Frit me half to death you did. Din't nobody nivver tell you to stay away from the Mere?'

Jubal Rede was small and wiry and he stank of the fen. His skin was as brown as if he'd been cured in peat-water and his hands were tougher than bog oak. His beard was clotted like a sheep's behind and his hair grew through the rents in his cap, which he never took off. He dressed in layers of grimy sacking tied on with eelskins to ward off the rheumatics. Maud never found out if he had webbed feet, as he kept his boots on day and night.

From a wary distance she watched him wedge his punt in the reeds, unwrap a leathery dried fish from a filthy handkerchief, and share it with the dog. Maud forgot to be scared. She was face to face with the fabled denizen of the fen.

'How do you do,' she said politely. 'My name is—'

'I know who you are,' growled Jubal. His eyes were black and fierce and swimming in red. They took in the whole of her at a glance.

She sucked in her lips. 'What's your dog's name?'

'Nellie.'

'May I stroke her?'

'I an't stopping you.'

Nellie was friendlier than her master. Soon she was licking Maud's feet and letting her fondle her matted ears. 'Is she your faithful companion? said Maud. 'Like in *Robinson Crusoe?*'

'Who's that?'

She told him, but Jubal was unimpressed. 'So you'm a scholard, like the Master.' From under his sacking he drew a pigskin flask and took a long pull.

'What are you drinking?' asked Maud.

'Ager mixter,' he gasped, baring a foetid ruin of yellow stumps. 'For the shakes.'

Maud had heard of the shakes. Her people called it malaria. It was rife among the villagers, who called it the ague. Desperate to keep Jubal talking, she asked what the mixture was made of.

'Paigle tea, poppyheads and frogskin wine.'

She blinked. 'Surely you don't make wine out of *frogs?*'

He barked a laugh. 'Dyke water, you lummock!'

'Oh. May I try some?'

He shook his head. 'Don't want you seeing things, now do we?' Tucking the flask back in his sacking, he pulled out a large clasp-knife and a lump of tobacco.

'I think you're frightfully brave to live in the fen,' said Maud.

'Why's that?'

'Most of the villagers daren't go in after dark.' She stood on one leg. 'Have you ever seen the hobby-lanterns?'

With a scowl he cut a chunk of tobacco.

'Have you?' she persisted.

'Once or twice,' he said with his mouth full. 'Flyen up and down.'

'What about ghosts?'

'What about en?'

'Have you seen one?'

He hesitated. 'I seen lots of rum things in the fen.'

'Father says that when you die your soul goes straight to Heaven or Hell and there's nothing in between, so ghosts can't possibly exist and it's wicked to say that they do.'

'Well he oughter know about sin,' snarled Jubal with startling savagery. 'Master's a great one for godly doings, an't he? Me, I don't hold by none of it. There's many a wrong thing done by godly folk.'

Maud was fascinated. No one had ever spoken to her like this. 'What about witches? Don't you believe in them either?'

'Moonshine,' he spat. 'When I were a lad, a woman lernt me the old charms. Most of en don't work. You're better off without.' He squinted at the sun. 'Sky's greasin up. We shall have a downfall soon, an you with no covering. Best run along home.'

'Oh. Please may I come again?'

He hesitated. Then he bared his rotten stumps in a grin. 'Can't hardly stop you, now can I?'

It didn't occur to Maud to wonder why he'd answered her questions so readily, but years later she remembered the way he'd looked at her: those sharp, appraising stares. Perhaps even at that first meeting he'd been wondering how much to tell her, and when.

She didn't have time for a proper wash, so she got a thrashing. It was worth it. After that she slipped off to see Jubal almost every day.

He showed her how to burn leeches off her skin, and he let her watch him spear the giant pike in the Mere. He taught her to know the fen as it truly was. She had been right when she'd sensed that it didn't care about her. The fen didn't care about anything human. It wasn't some enchanted realm full of magical creatures. It was wild, and she loved it all the more.

Jubal lived in a hut on an islet in a clump of chattering poplars. It had a sedge roof with a hole to let out the smoke, and its peat walls were two feet thick, with a tiny window made of horn and a door so low that even Maud had to stoop.

Inside, she found herself in a fishy-smelling gloom amid an upside-down forest of dangling eels and tench. Jubal slept on a trestle of grimy sheepskins with Nellie underneath, and his peat fire had been smouldering since he was a lad, and had run away to live in the fen. He'd been here ever since. He never went up-village except twice a year to barter eelskins for tobacco and laudanum. 'Out here I'm my own master,' he growled. 'Thass how I likes it.'

When he needed to, he sold a puntful of reeds to a thatcher, or did a day's mole-catching for a farmer. And if some cottager's pig strayed into the fen, well then of course it never came out. For the rest, Jubal lived by his gun, his nets and his eel glave, a seven-foot spear with vicious hooked tines. He knew the fen like nobody else, and he knew every creature that haunted it. He knew more than Maud ever imagined – and some of it turned out to be lethal.

But in his way he was kind to her, and without knowing it he helped her find a path through those twin banks of thorns, the rules of the village and those of the Church. Above all, he showed her it was possible to be free.

But that was after the coming of Chatterpie, when at last *she* had something to show Jubal.

Six

*I*T was a warm afternoon in October and Maud was reading under a pear tree where she couldn't be seen from the house. Suddenly she heard a strange echoing splashing coming from somewhere nearby. It sounded as if some creature was drowning.

Flinging down her book, she raced to the horse-trough. Nothing there. The splashing went on, panicky and trapped.

She rushed to the well – and there he was at the bottom, flapping his wings and so covered in muck that she could hardly tell he was a magpie. Another minute and he would drown.

Frantically, Maud cranked the handle to let down the bucket. She managed to scoop him up, then tore off her pinafore and flung it over him. The magpie didn't struggle. He froze. All she could see was his big dagger-like beak.

Clutching her precious bundle in her arms, she stumbled through the orchard to Cole's cottage. The magpie was alarmingly light and he wasn't moving. She was terrified that she'd squeezed him too tight. 'You're safe now,' she told him, her voice shaking with emotion. 'I'll look after you!'

She found Cole smoking his pipe on his doorstep. '*Promise* you won't tell on me,' she panted.

The gardener scratched his whiskers. 'Now what be you wanting with a chatterpie, Miss Maud?' Like all villagers, he hated magpies.

'*Swear* you won't hurt him,' she commanded.

He snorted. 'What, an bring bad luck to me an mine?'

She pestered him into giving her a pail of water and a trug to house her treasure. Tenderly, she dabbed slime off the magpie and patted him dry with a scrap of sacking. Throughout this ordeal, Chatterpie – as she'd already named him – kept rigidly still, clutching her pinafore tight in his claws.

Even after she'd finished, he clung on grimly. His grip was like iron, though his legs were as thin as matchsticks. They looked so dreadfully fragile, and one was oozing blood where he'd scratched it down the well. Maud tried to tug her pinafore free, but Chatterpie wouldn't let go. She let him keep it. She would make up some story about dropping it in the Lode.

Putting Chatterpie in the trug with the sacking over the top, she staggered with him to the compost heap. She found a piece of wood for a lid and headed back to Cole's cottage, where she set the trug in the sun.

'I'll be back *at once*,' she told Chatterpie. Magpies ate fruit, didn't they? She would find worms for him later.

When she raised the lid and slipped an apple in the trug, Chatterpie flattened himself on the bottom and tried to peck her hand. She made to replace the lid and he stared up at her with eyes as bright as blackberries. Something twisted in her chest. It was love. Pure, fierce, obliterating love. She would do anything for him. She would kill to keep him safe.

'I'll look after you,' she whispered, trembling with elation and fear. Where to hide him? She thought of cats, rats and servants. She swore she would never let them harm him.

She would never let anyone hurt Chatterpie.

Maud hid him in the hayloft for three days. Three days of terror, adoration and feverish deception.

He always knew when she was coming. As she climbed the ladder she would hear the scratch of his claws in the trug, and her heart would clench with love.

He treated her offerings of fruit and worms with lordly disdain and he never ate while she was watching. But that was his right, because he was wild.

Everything about him was perfect. He had a cape of dazzling white, and his wingtips were deepest black with glints of amethyst and sapphire, like Maman's shot-silk evening gown. His stiff black tail was sheened with emerald and bronze, and his breast was brighter than the brightest snow.

At night Maud lay awake, worrying. Chatterpie had recovered. The only trace of his ordeal was a grey scar on his leg. But in the hayloft he was at risk. She couldn't keep him much longer – and yet she couldn't bear the thought of letting him go. She didn't know what to do.

She took him to Jubal.

'A young un,' he muttered.

Chatterpie gave a hoarse squeak, like a rusty gate.

'How d'you know he's young?' Maud said crossly. Chatterpie never made any noise with her.

'Short tail,' said Jubal. 'Brownish cast to un.'

Nellie was sniffing the trug. Maud pushed her muzzle aside. 'Nurse says magpies are cursed by God because they didn't put on full mourning for Jesus. But that can't be right, or why wouldn't geese be cursed too?'

Jubal spat. 'Some say if you meets a chatterpie you've to bow down and tell it a greeting. Moonshine. Only thing I opinion true about chatterpies is they're sharp as vinegar, and if one chatters at you from a treetop, you'll see a stranger by and by.' He unfolded his clasp-knife. 'D'you want I should clip his wings so he can't fly off?'

'*No!*' shrieked Maud.

He shrugged. 'You could tame un. Lern un to talk.'

A tame magpie. Like Robinson Crusoe's parrot... But it was out of the question, because then Chatterpie would no longer be wild. 'No,' she repeated. 'I'm going to set him free.'

Again Jubal shrugged. But he was grinning.

She didn't free Chatterpie immediately. After leaving Jubal, she headed back along the Lode with the trug in her arms.

The wind had veered round to the north, and the

afternoon was cold. Winter was in the air. The dogwood was beginning to be tinged with red. Maud barely noticed.

According to Jubal, Chatterpie was of the age when young magpies start learning to live on their own. Nevertheless, she was determined to reunite him with his parents. She thought she'd seen them on the day of the rescue, hopping about on the edge of the well. They'd disappeared into one of the churchyard yews, the one by the lych-gate. Maud decided to free Chatterpie when she was opposite St Guthlaf's. Then he would only have to fly across the Lode to be home.

Chatterpie kept very still, as if he knew what was going to happen. Maud drew level with the church and halted under a willow tree that overhung the Lode. The tree would make him feel less exposed; and she hoped – oh, how she hoped – that he might perch on a branch, to thank her.

It was nearly dusk. She had just enough time to set him free, then race back and wash. She'd become adept at such calculations.

As she set the trug on the ground, her eyes began to sting. 'It's time, Chatterpie,' she said in a strangled voice. 'G-goodbye. I'll always always love you. Remember to stay away from cats.'

When she raised the lid, the magpie flattened himself on the bottom. His beauty pierced her heart. She longed for one last special look from him, although she was crying so hard she could barely see; but he didn't hesitate for an instant. No hopping on to the edge of the trug to get his bearings, no perching on a willow branch to chatter his thanks. Like an arrow he shot across the Lode and vanished into the yew tree. He knew exactly where he was going and he didn't look back.

From inside the tree came a clamour of magpie voices: *Where have you* been? Maud gulped and tried to smile, but her mouth was stretched in a howl of grief.

She stayed there sobbing, hoping against hope that he would return, while the fen hushed and the sky turned a deep, luminous blue.

She knew Chatterpie didn't love her, and that was as it should be because he was wild. But she also knew that for three days she had *mattered* to him – because she had fed him and kept him safe. Now all that was over, and once again she was on her own. Only this time it was worse – because he'd been so close, and now he was gone.

Maud couldn't face returning to the house straight away. Nurse could thrash her as hard as she liked. What did it matter, when Chatterpie was gone?

The light was dying and the wind had dropped. The fen was utterly still. Maud heard a warbler in the reeds, and from the Common, a dog's distant barks. In the churchyard, Chatterpie's yew had fallen silent.

Something swept over Maud's head with a soft rush of wings, and she saw a flock of starlings skimming the reeds. Sniffing and wiping her cheeks, she watched them fly off towards the Mere. Her head was throbbing. She felt exhausted and empty.

The wavering bank of birds swung round and sped back towards her. Again they skimmed the reeds, and this time as they sped skywards, more starlings flew up from the fen to join them.

Each time Maud thought they were gone, they returned, the flock growing larger with every sweep as it picked up more birds, and always changing shape: now contracting to a dense cloud, now stretching to a long, wavering ribbon.

Suddenly they were swooping very low over her head, netting the sky with their wings. In that torrent of birds she made out their small black cross-shaped bodies and heard their terse, signalling calls. They were so close she could have touched them, and her pain lifted a little, for she felt as if she too were flying.

She watched until the first stars came out and the birds finally settled to roost. She felt calmer. The starlings had been a visitation and a reward: the fen's gift to her for looking after one of its own.

Dimly, an idea took root: the notion that one day, maybe she too could be free. Like Jubal and Chatterpie and the starlings.

Jubal was right about magpies foretelling the coming of a stranger.

The day after Maud freed Chatterpie, she saw him perched on top of his yew tree. The branch was too weak to take his weight, and he was wobbling and dipping his tail to keep his balance. He was also chattering a warning.

Two days after that, Father came back.

Seven

*F*ATHER returned in mid-October, and by December Maman was pregnant again.

It was a bitter winter with black frosts and Arctic winds. Maud was barely allowed out. She missed Chatterpie savagely, but though she put food on her windowsill, he never appeared. Sometimes she glimpsed Jubal skating along the Lode, and at night she heard distant, mysterious cracking noises. It was the ice on the Mere. It belonged to another world.

Once again, the library was forbidden. 'No you can't borrow my books,' scoffed Richard, pompous after his first term at boarding school. 'You wouldn't understand them, you're only a girl.'

Felix was born in July, five weeks after Maud's eleventh birthday. When he didn't die in the first few days, she became uneasy. He was bound to die sooner or later and the longer he left it the worse it would be for Maman. But Felix clung on. In fact, he thrived.

As the weeks went by it dawned on Maud that he was

going to live. She tried to be glad for Maman but she wasn't. She was angry. Now she had two younger brothers who would look down on her always.

It was a wet summer, and Maud's worries about Maman, forgotten when she was free, came surging back. In September when her mother resumed poor-visiting, Maud went with her to keep her safe.

Wakenhyrst was three miles away across the Common. As well as the Rectory it had a stonemason, a wheelwright, a blacksmith and a shop in the back room of the Eel Grigg. The post-office was four miles off at Carrbridge, where the village children trudged to school when they weren't in the fields picking stones. According to the servants, Lord Clevedon never did anything for his tenants, who had to make do with outside earth-closets and water from the pond. As Maud perched on a stool in a tiny cottage parlour, she struggled to ignore the stink of the pigsty and the chamber-pot under the cot.

Maman sat beside an old carter who was dying. She was praying, but everyone else just wanted him to die. Mr Broadstairs had rattled through his prayers and left, and the carter's sons were out in the fields cutting corn. His sour-faced daughter stood in the doorway with her arms crossed. Next week was harvest horkey and she had brewing to do.

'Not long now,' said Biddy Thrussel.

'Not before time,' muttered the daughter.

The dying man was sucking in horrible rattling breaths. Maman took his hand in hers. Maud nearly vomited.

'Best be drawing the pillow,' said Biddy. Heaving herself to her feet, she pulled the stained pad from under the old man's head. Maud thought how awful it must be to feel your pillow yanked from under you, and to know that you'd been given up for dead.

But it worked. The dreadful rattling ceased.

A bee bumped against the wall. Maman crossed herself and pressed the dead man's hand to her breast.

Biddy was rolling up her sleeves. 'You can send to pass the bell now, Sal. I'll make a start.'

Briskly, the daughter turned the mirror to the wall while Biddy put a saucer of salt on the old man's chest, to stop him walking.

Maud was disappointed. The face of the corpse was the colour of candlewax and bore no trace of the heavenly peace that Miss Broadstairs had described.

Maman was still clutching the dead hand. Maud tugged her sleeve. 'Maman, *don't!*'

That was the last time Maud went poor-visiting. Shortly afterwards, Ivy arrived, and Maud learned the truth about the dead hand – and babies.

Village girls went into service at eleven, but Ivy was thirteen when she started as scullery maid at Wake's End. The eldest of ten, she'd been needed at home until pond pox had lessened her mother's load by taking off three.

From the beginning, Maud was wary because Ivy was pretty. She looked like a gypsy, although if you'd said that to her face she'd have scratched your eyes out. She was dark and thin, with a snap and a sparkle that even then caught men's attention. 'An early-ripe,' sniggered Jessop.

What you noticed first was her mouth. It was small but extremely full, the upper lip peaking to a swollen cushion of strawberry flesh. Some years later, Maud learned that this put Father in mind of how a groom tames a horse by twisting its lip in a rope.

Daisy said the cottage where Ivy grew up was the poorest in Wakenhyrst. 'Lousy as a cuckoo she were,' said the house-maid disapprovingly. 'We had to dunk her in kerosene afore we'd let her in the door.' Maud later learned that until Ivy came to Wake's End, she'd never seen water from a tap, or had milk in her tea. It was also said that during her mother's frequent confinements, she'd been expected to 'take on' her father. Had Maud known all this earlier, things might have been different between them.

Ivy was sly, with a knack for sniffing out weakness. The first time she met Maud, she sized her up at a glance.

It was in the back yard, and Ivy was scrubbing the door-step. Somehow, she'd learned that Maud liked starlings. 'My dad hates starlings,' she said boldly.

'Indeed,' Maud replied with glacial disdain.

'He'm a thacker, an starlings break the reeds so they'm no use. He nets en by the score for starling pudden.' She shot Maud another glance. 'Ma twists off their heads. Says it takes off the bitterness.'

'You made that up,' Maud said shakily.

Ivy grinned. But later, Cole told Maud that it was true.

It never bothered Ivy that she was only a skivvy while Maud was the Master's daughter, and Maud accepted her dominance without question because Ivy was two years older, and pretty. She didn't like Ivy, but she wanted Ivy to like her.

In November Felix went down with croup. When Dr Grayson pronounced him out of danger, Richard was furious: until Felix was born, he'd been the precious only son. Maud was relieved. She'd become used to the idea of Felix remaining alive and if he were to die now it would be the most dreadful shock for Maman.

'You're nivver a mother till you've lost one,' said Ivy, coming on Maud in the larder, stealing bacon rinds for Chatterpie.

'Then Maman is indeed a proper mother,' Maud said loftily, 'for she has lost seven.'

Ivy snatched a bacon rind and crammed it in her mouth. 'Master's been busy, then, an't he?'

Maud was puzzled. 'I – suppose so,' she said uncertainly.

Ivy pounced. 'You dun't know what I'm on about.'

'Yes I do.'

'Go on then, tell.'

'Why should I?'

'You dun't know!' crowed Ivy.

The following Sunday, Ivy showed Maud what she meant.

Nurse was in the kitchen chatting to Cook when Ivy grabbed Maud's hand and dragged her outside. She pointed through a gap in the hedge at two dogs playing in the mud. At least that's what Maud thought they were doing.

'Thass how you get babbies,' sniggered Ivy. 'The man sticks his thing up you and squirts slime. They all does it. Even the quality.'

The dog on top had glazed eyes and a lolling red tongue. It was jerkily pumping its hindquarters. The dog underneath was baring its teeth but making no attempt to escape. Eventually the big dog jumped off. Maud glimpsed a sharp red sausage between its hind legs with a cloudy droplet at its tip. She felt prickly and hot.

People did that? Father did *that* to Maman?

For weeks afterwards when Maud was in the presence of a man, an image would flash into her head of the sausage between his legs. Her cheeks would burn with shame and she would try to reassure herself that nobody could possibly know what she was thinking. But she was certain that it showed.

There must be something dreadfully wrong with her, or this wouldn't be happening. And the worst of it was that it did simply *happen*. It didn't matter who it was: Dr Grayson, Mr Broadstairs, Cole, Steers, Jubal, even Father. She pictured that moist red sausage in its secret nest of cloth.

Towards Christmas the images grew less frequent. By the time the bells of St Guthlaf's rang in 1909, they'd ceased. But by then the damage was done. Maud was observing her parents with new eyes.

When she knew she wasn't being watched, she would stare at her father without comprehension. He looked so handsome and well groomed – and yet he did *that* to Maman.

And he did it a lot. Maud remembered what Dr Grayson had said to him when she was hiding under the side-table. 'Perhaps not *every* night, eh?'

'I wish you weren't always ill,' Maud said to Maman.

'So do I, *ma chérie*,' said Maman, stroking Maud's hair. It was a sleety afternoon in January, and with Father in London and Richard at school, they were having tea in the drawing-room.

Maud sat on the rug beside Maman's chair, grinding a speck of soot under her thumb. 'Couldn't you – ask Father not to?' she mumbled.

Maman's hand stilled. 'Not to what?'

She squirmed. '… so you don't have babies.'

'*What?*' Maman sat up. 'Maud, look at me. Who's been talking to you?'

'No one. It's just – you're always so fearfully ill and I *hate* it!'

Maman gave her a penetrating stare, then turned away. 'The Bible says: "In sorrow shalt thou bring forth children." It's not for us to question these things.'

That evening, Maud heard Daisy and Valerie discussing an old country cure which they called the Dead Hand. Valerie said it turned her stomach. Daisy said yes but it was a proper good way of blighting a woman's parts.

Suddenly Maud remembered Maman clasping the dead carter's hand. She hadn't been holding it to her breast, but to her belly. She'd been trying to blight her parts, so that she wouldn't have babies.

A fortnight later, Maud found out that the Dead Hand hadn't worked. Maman was pregnant again.

'Master's been busy,' said Ivy with a grin.

'I don't know what you mean,' Maud said coldly.

With Ivy's laughter ringing in her ears, she rushed upstairs and flung herself on her bed. Now Maman would have to endure months of sickness and the agony of the groaning – and for what? For a bloody chamberpot or a bawling scrap of flesh that would probably die anyway.

Father could have spared her all that – but he'd chosen not to. *Not* every *night, eh?*

Maud's days of obedience were over. With Nurse she was sulky and recalcitrant. With Miss Broadstairs she was the nightmare child who wouldn't learn her catechism. She was even unpleasant to Maman, for she blamed her too. Why hadn't she made Father stop?

One Sunday in Bible Class, Maud answered back to Miss Broadstairs. The rector's daughter burst into tears and complained to Father, who summoned Maud to his study.

As before, he kept her waiting in the gap between the doors; and as before, he was writing. But this time, Maud wasn't scared.

'Miss Broadstairs tells me you were uncivil. Do you deny that?'

'No,' she replied.

He rose to his feet. 'Then you know what to do.'

Determined to show no emotion, she turned her back to him and rolled down her garters and stockings. Raising her skirts above her calves, she took her bottom lip between her teeth. Father administered ten stinging blows with the strap. She didn't utter a sound.

By the time she'd adjusted her clothing, he had resumed writing. It wasn't his notebook. She hadn't seen that for years.

'You may go,' he said without raising his head.

There was a soughing in her ears. She pictured Maman's exhausted face and swollen belly. She saw the dogs pumping and shuddering in the mud. She remembered what Father had written in his notebook about preventing conception: 'I find such measures revolting, unnatural, and wrong.'

She wanted to dash the inkpot in his face.

That night, a patch of skin between her thumb and fore-finger began to itch. The more she scratched the worse it itched. By morning it was oozing and swollen. It was the start of the eczema that would plague her all her life.

Two days later she was going downstairs when she noticed that the door of her parents' bedroom was ajar. Inside, she saw Father's childhood memento hanging from the bedpost. It was a flint with a hole in it: what villagers called a hagstone.

Maud took it.

Eight

MAUD was still standing by the bedpost clutching the hagstone when she heard Father coming upstairs. She froze like a trapped hare. He never came upstairs in the afternoon. He worked in his study, always.

Already he'd reached the landing. She darted behind the chaise longue.

She heard him pause in the doorway. She heard the hiss of his indrawn breath. 'What? *What?*' he muttered. Floorboards creaked as he strode to the bed.

Maud's world tilted. Father was kneeling on the bed like a housemaid, groping behind the headboard. Now he was flinging pillows aside. Father, who detested unseemliness, was tearing off blankets and throwing them on the floor. He was lifting the mattress and peering underneath.

Maud was horrified. She had hoped to disconcert him – but this turned everything upside-down.

From behind the chaise longue, she heard him stride to the bell-pull. 'Daisy!' he roared. It was the first time Maud had ever heard him raise his voice.

Holding her breath, she listened to him interrogate poor Daisy. He sent her off with orders to search the house till the stone was found and Maud thought he'd gone too, but when she risked another look he was still there.

She was shocked. Father had fine dry skin, and even on the hottest days he never perspired. Now his face was shiny with sweat. His hair was disarranged and when he touched his lips, his fingers shook.

It flashed across her mind that if losing his hagstone could upset him so much, he must believe in its power. Father, who loathed superstition: who forbade Maman to tap a hole in her eggshell at breakfast. Father had lied. He had said that the hagstone was merely a memento, but he was no better than a cottager. He truly believed that it kept him from harm.

The servants must have been too terrified to come near him because no one came upstairs and Maud heard him search the dressing-room himself. Should she flee, or stay where she was? He settled it for her by running downstairs.

When she was certain he was gone, she crept out from her hiding place. She had to replace the stone on the bed-post and get out.

But even though she knew this was the one thing that could save her, she didn't do it. Instead, with a feeling that this wasn't really happening, she slipped the stone in her pocket and left the room.

She couldn't have said why she did it. She only knew that some part of her was enjoying this. She had wanted to punish Father for making Maman ill, and at last she'd found a way.

Now she wanted to see what happened next.

What happened next was that Father questioned the servants one by one in his study. He started with Steers and worked down the hierarchy, ending with Ivy – on whom, as the newest member of staff, he placed the blame.

Maud had not anticipated this, but she knew at once what she had to do. She couldn't let Ivy take the blame. She had to confess.

When she tried to imagine how Father would punish her, her mind went white. And yet the idea of sacrificing herself for Ivy had enormous appeal. She pictured Ivy humbled by her courage and for ever in her debt.

By now events had spiralled so far beyond the everyday that Maud scarcely knew what she was doing. As if in a dream she walked downstairs, opened the two pairs of study doors, and marched in.

'I took it,' she said, placing the hagstone on Father's desk. Then her courage evaporated and she nearly blacked out.

His light-blue eyes were empty and cold. 'Why,' he said.

'I don't know.'

'Look at me.'

Not since she fainted in church had she met his stare. Then he'd viewed her as a child. Now he seemed to see her as an adult. Perhaps as an adversary. Dimly, Maud sensed that she had released forces which she didn't understand.

Father didn't thrash her after all. He didn't say another word to her. He rang for Nurse and gave orders that Maud was to be locked in the night nursery and left to consider the consequences of what she'd done.

It wasn't long before she found out what those con-sequences were. The following morning, Maman went into labour.

Afterwards, Daisy told Maud that Maman was in labour all that day and the following night. But Maud could only ever remember disjointed images: being locked in the night nursery and hearing Maman's cries and the sounds of running feet.

She remembered hammering at her door and shouting to be let out. She couldn't break down the door but in the end she managed to force the one that opened into the day nursery.

The day nursery was empty; she learned later that Nurse had taken Felix to the Rectory, but at the time all Maud knew was that she was alone on the top floor. When she raced down to the first floor, she found that the door at the bottom was locked. She hammered but no one came. She rushed back upstairs.

The servants' rooms were deserted. Nurse's room was directly above her parents' bedroom, so Maud flung up the sash and leaned out of the window. It was dark, and below she saw a yellow glow of lamplight. The blinds were up and the window was open, flouting Father's rules. Maud found that shocking.

She knew that Maman would be in the dressing-room, but she could hear no cries from below. From the open window beneath, she saw little twists of smoke and the red sparks of cigars. There were gentlemen down there, smoking at the bedroom windows. Maud saw a white cuff and a mottled old hand tapping ash on the sill. She recognised the voices of Dr Grayson, Mr Broadstairs and Father.

Afterwards, she knew that she must have stood there listening, but in her memory everything was out of order. The next thing she knew she was waking hours later, curled on the rug at the foot of her bed. It was a hot June dawn and very windy. The wind was keening in the chimney. The green light filtering through the ivy was trembling.

Maud padded barefoot past the servants' rooms and down the stairs. This time the door to the first-floor landing was ajar. No one had raised the blinds at either end of the passage. It was bathed in a strange fiery glow.

Her parents' bedroom doors were also ajar. The bedroom was empty, the great bed neatly made up. The sashes were down and the air was thick with a coppery, sickly-sweet smell. Maud went through to the dressing-room.

Biddy Thrussel was bending over Maman, who lay on the divan in a vast scarlet stain that spread on either side of her like monstrous wings. Maud knew at once that she was dead.

The voices she'd heard the night before came back to her.

'… an unenviable choice, my dear fellow,' Mr Broadstairs said quietly.

'And I fear that you must make it forthwith,' said Dr Grayson. 'There is a chance that Mrs Stearne's life could be saved. But then the child would surely die.'

'And if you save the child?' said Father.

'Then I fear, no hope for Mrs Stearne. And who knows but the child might not survive for long after being baptised—'

'But long enough for that,' cut in Father.

'Oh yes, I'd imagine so.'

This time it was Father who tapped ash on the windowsill. Maud saw his signet ring. 'Is it a son?' he said abruptly.

'My dear fellow,' said Dr Grayson. 'We shan't know that till it's born.' He cleared his throat. 'I'm afraid I must press you. What is it to be?'

More smoke hazed the air.

'Save the child,' said Father.

Nine

MAUD remembered lying by the Mere, watching a beetle crawl up a reed. She was cold; her nightgown was soaked in dew. She deserved it. She had stolen Father's hagstone and now Maman was dead.

Later she saw a dragonfly like the pendant Maman had bought her in Brussels. Then Nellie was licking her toes and Jubal was lifting her and carrying her back to Wake's End.

Maman died on the 9th of June. The baby, baptised Rose, died the following night. The next day Miss Broadstairs moved into Wake's End to run the household and order the mourning attire. The brooch she wore at her throat held a tiny plait of her dead sister's hair. This gave Maud an idea. Before the coffin was closed, she crept in and stole a lock of her mother's hair.

What lay in the coffin didn't look like Maman. It didn't smell like her and it felt cold and hard. It wasn't Maman. It couldn't be. The kiss Maud planted on its cheek felt oddly insincere.

All Wakenhyrst attended the funeral, and tradespeople came from Ely and Bury. Great-Uncle Bertrand was in America and couldn't be reached in time and Lord and Lady Clevedon were in Italy; they sent their carriage as a mark of respect.

Being a girl, Maud wasn't allowed to go, but she watched from the round window at the end of the first-floor passage. When they carried the coffin into the family vault, she knew that she oughtn't to have let Maman go down there on her own. But she couldn't *feel* it. She couldn't feel anything.

Father never mentioned Maman again. Every Sunday he put flowers for her on the family monument, and several times Maud saw him writing in his notebook. She wondered if he was doing so out of grief, or because he felt bad about having chosen Baby Rose instead of Maman.

Why had he done that? How could baptising a baby who'd lived less than a day matter more than Maman?

'I know it's hard, my dear,' said Miss Broadstairs in a hushed voice. 'But we are all born in sin, even poor little Baby Rose. So she *had* to be baptised, or she couldn't go to Heaven. You do understand?'

Maud nodded without comprehension. She began to feel vaguely sorry for Father, who'd been faced with such a terrible choice.

That was all she could manage: a cloudy grey sorrow. Everything was grey, as if she was living in fog.

Months passed and the fog didn't lift. Nurse was busy with Felix, and although Miss Broadstairs returned to the Rectory, she often came and set exercises for Maud.

Maud spent hours alone in the library at the writing table that became her desk. Before Maman's death, she would have thought this was Heaven; but it was part of her self-imposed punishment that she mustn't open a single book.

She worked obediently at her exercises, and ate her meals with Felix in the day nursery. She took sedate little walks around the carriage-drive and down the elm avenue. But she never watched the geese, or gazed out of her window at night. And she never crossed the foot-bridge into the fen.

Her thirteenth birthday came and went; then the anniversary of Maman's death; then Harvest Festival and Christmas. As Father didn't wish to engage a housekeeper, Maud and the servants managed on their own. The accounts were easy enough, as Maman had always needed Maud's help to balance them. For ordering Father's meals, Maud used the menus which she'd found in her mother's desk. They were written on ivory notepaper in Maman's graceful foreign-looking hand, and they smelled of violets. Maud copied them into an exercise book for use with Cook, and hid the originals in her handkerchief drawer.

She wondered why the servants could cry so readily, while she couldn't cry at all.

On Twelfth Night, she woke with a stomach ache. She felt sticky between her legs. Lighting her candle and throwing back the bedclothes, she saw a red stain on the sheet. She screamed.

Nurse burst in and slapped her till she stopped. Nurse said the blood was Maud's 'courses'. They would happen every month and while Maud had them she must stay out of the kitchen or she'd spoil the meat and turn the wine sour. Also she mustn't ever wash while she had her courses or she would surely die.

Miss Broadstairs had other names for them: the spinster's curse and the married woman's friend. She gave Maud a pad filled with sawdust and a canvas harness to hold it in place.

'But why does it happen?' said Maud.

Miss Broadstairs' horsey face turned red. 'It isn't nice to talk about, dear. I believe it's simply that girls grow faster than boys, so they need to get rid of the, er, excess.'

Maud hated what was happening to her. She hated her new breasts and the hair between her legs. She wondered if the latter was normal and felt too ashamed to ask.

Mercifully, Father noticed nothing; but he wrote and engaged a governess, a Miss Lark, to start after Easter – Miss Broadstairs having timidly reminded him that Maud would soon be fourteen.

Fourteen? How had that happened? In the grey fog, every day was the same.

Until, that is, the second coming of Chatterpie.

It was a blustery March morning at the start of Lent, and Maud was working at her desk. Today's exercise was harder than usual, a précis from a book on medieval history. She wanted to get it right, as it concerned Father's own period, the fifteenth century.

The fire in the grate hissed, and outside the rain had stopped. Maud glanced up – and there was Chatterpie bobbing his tail to keep his balance as he swung back and forth on the well-bucket.

Maud hadn't forgotten him, but he belonged to the time before. As she watched him hop down on to the wall and clean his beak on the moss with confident swipes, she wondered if he remembered the day four years before when he'd nearly drowned.

But was it even him?

As if he knew what she was thinking, he made a graceful swooping glide on to the lawn and landed right in front of where she sat. At that moment the clouds parted and sunlight transformed him into a bird in a stained-glass window, ablaze with sapphire, emerald and amethyst. Maud saw the grey scar on his leg. His black eye met hers. *Oh yes it's me all right.*

Did he remember that she had saved him? Or did he only recall the horror of the well – and perhaps even blame her?

With his familiar squeaky cry, Chatterpie flew off across the orchard – and as Maud watched him go, something inside her changed. The grey fog lifted. She could feel again.

And she wanted Chatterpie back.

To the right of the French windows, a clump of laurels hid the stables from view. In a fork of the nearest shrub, Maud tucked a rind of cheese.

Within ten minutes it was gone. She hadn't seen Chatterpie take it, but she knew it was him, she saw the flicker of his wings as he fled to an apple tree.

It might take weeks to gain his trust, but she relished the task. Her aim was not to tame him. She just wanted to bring his wildness closer.

She left more food, always in the same fork of the same laurel and always at the same time: after breakfast, and again after tea. Chatterpie was cunning and fast and he *hated* being watched. When Maud was at her desk, he wouldn't come at all unless she kept her head down. She was never able to glimpse him from the corner of her eye, and no matter how stealthily she turned, he'd always gone. It was the same if she hid behind the curtains, or opened the French windows and listened. He would outwit her with scornful ease, and all she would see was the dip and sway of branches springing back into place.

She made Daisy buy her a looking-glass in the village, which she propped on her desk at an angle, so that she could keep watch without Chatterpie knowing. It was a momentous day when she saw his reflection cast about shiftily, before making off with the cheese.

He came and went so swiftly that Maud had to watch the mirror all the time, or she would miss him. Her favourite moment of each visitation was when he first flew in, because he would stretch his neck and peer at her, to make sure that she wasn't looking.

She felt as if she had entered a secret world. She greeted him silently on her way to church, and in her room she listened for the thud of his feet on the roof and his harsh cry echoing down the chimney. When she broke her prohibition against books, she was delighted to read that magpies build their nests with roofs, to keep out the rain.

One morning halfway through Lent, Maud entered the library and saw to her horror that Chatterpie's laurel had been butchered. The magpie was in the orchard, clattering with alarm, and the under-gardener was dumping the severed branches in his wheelbarrow.

Maud flung open the French windows. 'What have you *done*!' she shouted. 'How *dare* you!'

The boy dropped an armful of branches and snatched off his cap. 'S-sorry, Miss. Mister Cole said to tidy up.'

'You should have *asked*!'

'I dun't mean to frit your chatterpie, honest I dun't!'

'Well you did, didn't you?' To her horror, she was close to tears. 'Be off with you! And don't you dare cut another twig!'

The next afternoon she was startled to see that a stake had been planted in what remained of the laurel, with a cross-bar nailed to the top. It wasn't exactly a bird-table, but since it was less obtrusive, it might entice the supremely wary Chatterpie.

Maud found the under-gardener in the kitchen garden, hoeing potatoes behind the glass-house. 'Did you put that stake in the shrubbery?' she said sharply.

A strawberry stain rose up his neck as he stared at his boots. 'Yes, Miss,' he mumbled. 'Did I do wrong, Miss?'

'How do you know it'll work?'

'My mam liked birds, Miss. It'll bring your chatterpie, you'll see.'

She looked at him suspiciously. 'You're new, aren't you? What's your name?'

'Clem Walker, Miss.'

'Why did you do it?'

The blush spread to his cheeks. 'I dunno, Miss. You was upset. I felt bad.'

Maud blinked.

He looked to be a few years older than her. Sturdy and raw-boned, he wore a gardener's green baize apron over the labourer's uniform of corduroy breeches, waistcoat and jacket. A blue and white spotted kerchief was tied around his brown neck, and his thick straight hair was the colour of straw. He cast her a shy glance and she saw that his eyes were grey.

He was kind to her. That was all it took.

Ten

SPRING gave Maud plenty of excuses for chancing upon Clem Walker. The looking-glass helped too. From now on she wasn't only spying on Chatterpie.

To his face she called him Walker, but in her head he was Clem. He was handsome, but not like Father. Clem's beauty lay in his kindly expression and in the slow flush that warmed his smooth brown skin.

Maud loved watching him mow the lawn in front of the library. Once when he wasn't about, she tried pushing the mower herself, and was thrilled when she couldn't budge it an inch.

She had conversations with him in her head. She pictured him being involved in some minor accident and her coolly coming to his aid and loosening his neck-kerchief.

She knew she was being ridiculous. She wasn't even fourteen, and the gulf between them couldn't be bridged. In her wildest imaginings she never went further than respectful admiration on his part, and distant friendliness on hers.

But his presence lent a secret glow to her existence. She dreaded the arrival of the new governess, Miss Lark.

She also spent long, despairing sojourns before her looking-glass. Those tiny eyes and that heavy jaw. Her only tolerable feature was her thick brown hair. She took to washing it in salad oil and borax, and brushing it for hours.

What to do about her clothes? Even at Wake's End, the revolution in fashion was being felt. Gone were the leg-of-mutton sleeves and hourglass silhouettes that had ruled Maman's life. Maud longed for one of the new hobble skirts and a petticoat that didn't rustle. She wanted a corset that made her hips disappear and reached halfway down her thighs, with a pair of cord fetters around her knees to make her take dainty steps.

But maybe Clem didn't mind that she was plain? She was greatly encouraged after Miss Broadstairs lent her *Jane Eyre* and *Pride and Prejudice*. Clearly some men could see past plainness to what lay underneath. Perhaps looks didn't matter as much as she'd feared.

However, in her darker moments she knew that all her efforts were doomed – because of her eczema. Years of scratching had given her scaly patches on her hands and forearms. 'These aren't fingers,' she would hiss in a frenzy of loathing. 'They're claws. Disgusting lizard claws.'

Miss Broadstairs gave her Sulpholine Lotion with a commiserating smile that set Maud's teeth on edge. The lotion made no difference. Maud begged Biddy Thrussel to bring her something stronger, and swore her to secrecy. While she waited for the wisewoman to prepare the potion, she swallowed her pride and donned the Nottingham lace gloves which Lady Clevedon had given her when she was confirmed.

Her worst fear was attracting Ivy's mockery. Eating her fill in the Wake's End kitchen had transformed the scrawny village girl into a plump, big-breasted beauty. When Sarah left to get married, she'd been promoted to under-housemaid and now dimpled becomingly when Dr Grayson chucked her under the chin. The female servants hated her, but Ivy laughed them to scorn, secure in the slack-jawed admiration of Jessop and Steers. Even Felix seemed fascinated by her, probably because she never made a fuss of him like the rest of the staff.

To Maud's relief, Clem regarded Ivy with alarm, while Ivy acted as if he was beneath her notice. Cook muttered darkly that Ivy had other fish to fry.

One day, Maud learned from Daisy that Clem's mother had died of pond pox last summer. She pounced on this as common ground.

'Does your father speak of her often?' she asked when he was raking the gravel in the elm avenue.

He scratched his head. 'Can't say as he do, Miss.'

'It's *exactly* the same with me! Father never speaks of Maman. I can't understand it.'

He gave his slow shrug. 'Mebbe he can't, Miss.'

'What do you mean?'

He reddened. 'Well. I can't talk of Ma. Cuts too deep.'

Maud looked at him. How wise you are, she thought.

You have seen what I did not: that Father *can't* speak of it. It cuts too deep.

Full of contrition, she thought of her father's frequent headaches, and of the little brown bottles of laudanum which Dr Grayson prescribed. Father *was* grieving. But privately. In his own way.

On Easter Sunday, Maud dined downstairs with him for the first time.

Nurse wouldn't let her put up her hair, but Maud thought that her new lime-green poplin was not unbecoming, and as her eczema was currently in abeyance, Father might not even notice if she kept her hands in her lap. She was horribly nervous. She reminded herself that he was grieving. She must show all her sympathy and tact.

To her surprise, he seemed in need of neither. 'I'm in an excellent humour,' he declared as he carved the joint. 'In fact, superlative.'

Maud stared at him. Father never spoke like this. He looked intimidatingly handsome in his dinner jacket and his eyes were more alive than she'd ever seen them: that light, astonishing crystalline blue.

'Miss Broadstairs showed me one of your watercolours,' he said. 'It was really quite tolerable. Should you care for painting lessons?'

'I – don't know, Father.'

'I had a fancy to paint when I was a young man. My pater was against it, but I took lessons at Cambridge all the same, and then in Italy. If one persists, one can always achieve one's desires.' He compressed his lips, as if at some pleasing private recollection. Maud felt a burst of sympathy. He and Maman had toured Italy on their honeymoon; he must be thinking of her.

Shyly, she asked if his headaches were any better. When he said that they were, she mustered her courage. 'Father, I wondered... we have so many books in the library, I could easily educate myself... with Miss Broadstairs' supervision, of course. So would you – *could* you put off Miss Lark? I mean, cancel her?'

He tasted his claret. 'I quite forgot to tell you. I cancelled the governess a fortnight ago.'

'Oh, *thank* you, Father!'

'That précis you prepared – the chapter from Moore and Blackthorne. It was surprisingly competent.'

She flushed with pleasure.

'You seem quite taken with the English mystics.'

'Yes, Father.' In fact, the only one she was remotely interested in was Alice Pyett, and that was only because Father was. Even then, Alice Pyett's mysticism struck her as faintly ridiculous. She had been the wife of a prosperous merchant until she'd had a vision of Hell, and developed a habit of sobbing noisily for hours. At the time people thought she was either blessed by God, or troubled by demons. Towards the end of her life she had dictated her experiences to a monk. But *The Book of Alice Pyett*, although known to history from references in other works, had been lost for centuries.

Maud had been a little startled on reading all this. Alice Pyett didn't seem quite worthy of Father's attention. Surely she might simply have been mad?

'Perhaps you'd care to help me in my work,' he said after Ivy had cleared the table. 'Copying, preparing indices, that sort of thing.'

Maud was so overcome she couldn't speak. Her mind flew to the engraving in the Rectory drawing-room. *Woman's Mission: the Helpmeet of Man* showed a pretty woman pouring tea for a scholarly gentleman bent over his books. Maud saw herself ministering to Father and assuaging his grief.

Next morning she sought Clem in the kitchen garden. 'You were right about Father!' she cried.

He broke into a sheepish grin. 'Wor I, Miss?'

He was in shirtsleeves. She saw the little gold hairs on his forearms, and a tiny scrape of blood on his jaw where he'd cut himself shaving.

You are so beautiful, she told him silently. A perfectly beautiful young man.

Eleven

*F*ATHER took Maud to Hibble's bookshop in Ely and bought her a black and red Remington typewriter. She mastered it in a week, and he set her to typing his monograph for the Society of Antiquaries.

Hitherto, 'Father's Research' had formed the backdrop to her life, but she hadn't had the least idea what it was about. As she embarked on the astonishingly intimate task of deciphering his handwriting, the purpose behind all those visits to libraries over the years was revealed. He'd been trying to track down the last surviving copy of *The Book of Alice Pyett*.

With the zeal of the convert, Maud became intensely keen on the fifteenth century.

'The Black Death was a recent and terrible memory,' Father wrote in his Introduction. 'This meant that fear of the Devil was at its height. Were we to attend a church service in Pyett's time, we would behold a ceremony quite unlike our own. There would be wavering rushlight and clouds of incense masking the stench from the graveyard outside. Every effigy in our church, every column and saint, would be picked out in brilliant colours. Only the priests would sing, and only in Latin. As for the congregation, being mostly illiterate, they would imbibe the lessons of Scripture from the vividly painted pictures on the walls...'

With each page that Maud typed, Father's quest for Alice Pyett became hers. His search had taken him from London to Paris, then all over the Continent and back across the Channel to the archives of an old Catholic family, the Butler-Parrys.

Astonishingly, their seat lay not far from Wake's End, just across the county border in south-west Norfolk. A fortnight ago, Father had written to Sir Julian Butler-Parry, seeking permission to examine his papers; so far, with no response.

Every morning, Maud watched his face when the post brought nothing from Norfolk. She felt for him. His cause had become hers.

Happily, Chatterpie seemed to find the clatter of her typewriter reassuring, and these days he went on eating even when she looked straight at him. As the weather grew warmer she took to opening the French windows a crack. When she paused in her typing she would listen for the faint yet audible snap of his beak.

One afternoon, Father came in and saw the magpie. 'Good Heavens,' he exclaimed as Chatterpie fled shrieking to the orchard. 'Have you acquired a tame bird?'

'Oh no, he's quite wild,' Maud said proudly. 'But he

tolerates me. If I'm late putting out his food, he taps on the windowpane. Sometimes I delay it on purpose, just to make him do it.'

'"Chattering pies in dismal discords sung,"' murmured Father as he scanned the pages she'd just typed.

'"Pie" means noisy, doesn't it?' she ventured. 'Do you think there might be a link with the name "Pyett"?'

He nodded without raising his eyes from the page, although whether at her typing or her idea, she couldn't tell.

I am happy, she thought, watching him return to his study. I want this to go on for ever.

With her new-found confidence, Maud made two improvements to the household.

First she obtained money from Father to pay an outside laundress – thereby earning the gratitude of the entire staff. It was so easy that she wondered why Maman had never done it. Hadn't she dared? Or hadn't she cared?

The second change was precipitated by Felix. Now a beautiful, chubby three-year-old with blue eyes and flaxen curls, he was the darling of the servants; Maud felt nothing for him except vague dislike. The week before, he'd developed chickenpox, and Nurse had bandaged his hands to stop him scratching. Having dosed him with Quieting Syrup, she told Maud to watch him for an hour while she did the darning; they both knew this meant taking a nap.

'You watch him,' Maud said coldly. 'I have work to do.'

Nurse blinked. 'Dun't you take that tone with me, my girl. Work, indeed! An him your own brother—'

'—and you're a servant, so do your job.'

Maud watched the spongy features pucker with outrage. Nurse snatched her darning and glared at her. Then she sat down heavily beside the sleeping child.

No more meals upstairs, Maud promised herself as she went downstairs. From now on I shall eat with Father. The reign of Nurse is at an end.

In late August, Father received the long-awaited letter from Norfolk. He was jubilant. Sir Julian had invited him to stay and examine his family archives at leisure.

'You're rather young to be left in charge,' said Father as he shrugged on the ulster Maud was holding out. 'Still, I daresay you'll manage.'

'I'm sure I shall,' she said, feeling extremely grown-up.

'Wish me luck!' he called as he ran down the steps to the carriage. She trembled at the intimacy of the remark.

For three days she heard nothing from him. Then a telegram arrived: PYETT FOUND! MS V FRAGILE STOP SIR J WONT LEND STOP AM STAYING TO MAKE COPY SEND FOUR QUIRES PAPER PENS SPARE SPECS. Bursting with excitement, Maud rushed into his study to collect what was needed. She couldn't help noticing that his notebook was missing from its drawer. Poor Father. He must have taken it with him so that he could confide his grief to its pages.

Two weeks went by without a word from him. She tried not to feel left out. She slept badly and her eczema flared up. To her horror, Clem noticed. He called it 'the huff', and suggested a cure. You said a charm and buried an eel's head in the ground; as the head rotted, so the huff disappeared. Clem offered to catch an eel for her and she said she would think about it. In fact, she was busy collecting what she needed for Biddy's potion. She already had cinders from a blacksmith's forge, and Biddy had the other ingredients. It only remained for Maud to gather some old man's beard an hour before dawn on the night of the full moon.

In the third week of Father's absence a telegram finally arrived, instructing Maud to send Jessop to Ely in the dog-cart to meet the 2.50 p.m train.

By seven that evening, Maud was seated opposite Father at the dinner table. It was the first time she'd put up her hair, in two braids coiled at her ears, but Father was too preoccupied to notice. His face was pale from overwork and glowing with a fervour that made her think of medieval monks.

The Book of Alice Pyett was written in something called Middle English. Maud gathered that this was an entirely different language and that before Father could begin to study *The Book* in detail, he must prepare a translation.

'Will that be immensely difficult?' she asked shyly.

'What, the translation? Good Heavens no. But obviously as *The Book* is so long it will take time. No, the real meat will be the interpretation, the exegesis.'

'I'll do everything to help,' she said.

He didn't reply. His pale-blue eyes were moving from side to side as if following something on a horizon only he could see. Clearly he relished the task ahead.

Maud pictured the day when he revealed his discovery to an astonished world. She saw herself – much slenderer, and free from eczema – accompanying him on lecture tours.

Not even in her imagination could she make herself pretty, but she fancied that in a well-cut tunic-jacket and narrow skirt she might achieve a certain distinction.

They would travel the globe together, Father giving lectures to learned societies, and she seeing to his every need. On trains and in hotels they would have long, intimate discussions about *The Book*, and he would listen respectfully to her ideas.

'Such a bond between them,' people would murmur admiringly. 'He thinks the world of her, you know.'

That was the night of the full moon, and as Maud set out her coat, galoshes and muffler for her early morning foray to gather the old man's beard, she floated on dreams of glory. A spark flew off her candle. She knew it was a sign that something momentous would happen tomorrow.

And to think that back in the spring, she had thought her life was empty! How rich it seemed now, how crammed with incident and possibility. Chatterpie, Clem, Alice Pyett, Father. Above all, Father.

She doubted if she would sleep a wink.

She woke when it was still dark. Plenty of time to collect the final ingredient for Biddy's potion.

She was tip-toeing past Father's bedroom on her way downstairs when she heard him cry out. Then a laugh: sly, muffled. Unmistakeably Ivy.

Maud stood listening at the door for some time. An

image came to her of the two dogs copulating in the mud. She wondered how long this had been going on.

She remembered Father's 'superlative' good humour on Easter Sunday, and the way he had pressed his lips together as if at some pleasant private memory. 'If one persists, one can always achieve one's desires.' That had been five months ago.

It seemed important to know the worst, so Maud made her way quietly down to Father's study and took his notebook from its drawer. She opened the curtains and raised the blinds.

Then she seated herself in his easy chair and began to read.

Twelve

MAUD skipped the first few pages, which she'd seen when she was a child. After that Father had written nothing for five years. Nothing about Maman. He had passed over her death without a word, and had only resumed writing in January this year.

15th January 1911

Last night I had the dream again. *Why?*

It's eighteen months since Dorothy died, and things have been going so well. That's not to denigrate the poor darling, it's simple fact. She made an excellent wife, but I was never destined to be a paterfamilias. She was such a typical *woman*: passive, emotional, no conversation beyond the kitchen and the nursery. What could she give a man like me?

The truth is, she held me back. There. I've said it. When God took her it wasn't only a release for her, but for me too. At last I was free to pursue my work. I hate to think of the time I've lost; of the accolades that might now be mine.

So why these dreams *now*?

It's always the same. I am breathless and terrified, forcing my way through a long, narrow passage tiled in oxblood ceramics; hot to my touch and repellently glossy. I'm frightened, yet unspeakably excited. I *mustn't* put my hand on those tiles – yet I always do. The feel of that thick, wet, bloody glaze... I wake entangled in bedclothes in a state of self-pollution.

I don't understand why this is happening.

2nd February (Candlemas)

No dreams, but bad headaches. This is too frustrating. It would be dreadful if my health broke down now, just when I'm on the brink of finding *The Book of Alice Pyett*.

Miss Broadstairs dropped another 'little hint' about a governess for Maud. To silence her I've written to an agency and engaged a suitable female – but to commence only after Easter. I *must* have peace until then.

13th February

Tea with old Grayson proved surprisingly helpful. He advises against wasting myself in clerical work and suggests hiring a secretary. The idea has merit. Miss Broadstairs would do it for nothing, but I couldn't stomach that dog-like devotion, not to mention that wart. And yet were I to retain a stranger, I'd have two of them, a secretary *and* a governess twittering about the house. Insupportable. There must be another way.

More importantly, Grayson pointed out that as Dorothy's death deprived me of regular connection, it is this which poses the greatest threat to my health. When a strong constitution finds no outlet this causes a congestion in the blood, resulting in headaches and other disturbances. Grayson suggests re-marriage, but I see no necessity. Thanks to Dorothy's settlement I have no financial need, and as regards my bodily requirements, there must be some other way that won't impede my work.

Meanwhile, the good doctor advises countering the urge to self-pollute with cold sponge baths and oatmeal porridge. He also suggests shunning 'lewd pictures' – which is rather rich, coming from him. I'll try the sponge baths, not the porridge; I can't abide the stuff.

14th March

This past month has been a trial. Dreams frequent, sponge baths useless. The only thing that helped was the trip to London – i.e. Piccadilly: of doubtful cleanliness, but at least my needs were met.

It also cleared my head, and on the train I had an idea that might make hiring a secretary unnecessary. To test my hypothesis, I've instructed Miss B. to set a précis for Maud.

25th March

I was right: no need to retain a secretary *or* a governess! At one stroke I've solved both problems and saved a considerable amount of money. Maud, when properly trained, will make an acceptable typewriter, and may in time be trusted with minor tasks requiring no exercise of judgement. As she matures, she shall run the household, thus precluding the need for a housekeeper. I would have preferred an amanuensis with a more agreeable appearance, but such is life.

27th March, London
Memorable day. After seven years of searching, I have found the best clue yet to *The Book of Alice Pyett!*

How strange is Fate, that my search should have led me back to the Reading Room at the British Museum where it began – and that the trail points to Marsham Hall in Norfolk, of all places. I gather that old Butler-Parry is an affable fool who lives for his guns and his fishing-rods. So much the better. I wrote to him today, and pray for a speedy response.

As I was leaving the Reading Room, Jacobs sidled up and enquired about my 'quest for the delectable Alice'. Yes, mock all you like, you beady-eyed little Hebrew; I shall soon wipe the sneer off your greasy Levantine snout.

N.B.: No dreams for days. Piccadilly helped.

30th March
Still no word from Butler-Parry, but I remain convinced that his archives contain *The Book*. If – when! – it is found, it will be essential to keep the discovery quiet from Jacobs and my 'friends' in Academia. I must be free to publish as I see fit: first the monograph detailing my search, then my translation and exegesis.

31st March
I had to speak sharply to Ivy, for she'd dusted my desk carelessly. She was sullen, thrusting out that mouth of hers.

On leaving, she paused with her rough red hand on the door.

Her black hair betrays her Gypsy blood. According to local tradition, Gypsies settled at Wakenhyrst after it was abandoned during the Black Death. The girl has the boldness of her race, and no doubt its dishonesty. I shall have to keep an eye on her.

2nd April

Agreeable visit from old Grayson after dinner. He brought his volume of Charcot studies.

I gather that today's medical men rather deride the Frenchman's work, but our good doctor remains loyal, having in his youth witnessed some of the great man's demonstrations. Grayson gave a lively account of watching the Frenchman perform ovarian compressions on a comely young patient with hysteria. Apparently she was clad only in her shift and the amphitheatre was strongly lit, the better for the gentlemen of the audience to observe her convulsions.

The photographs in Grayson's volume are remarkable. Via hypnosis, Charcot could make his female hysterics do whatever he wanted. One woman ate charcoal, believing it to be chocolate. Another crawled on all fours, barking like a dog. I should have liked to have seen that.

We talked late into the night and I rang for brandy. Ivy brought it, scarcely concealing her pique at being kept from her bed. After she'd gone I quipped that she would make a promising subject for a psychological study à la Charcot. Grayson chuckled. 'Psychological study! If you please to call it that!' A vulgar remark, but I couldn't entirely suppress my mirth.

It's that mouth of hers. It puts me in mind of the groom's trick of taming a mare by twisting her lip in a rope.

3rd April
Dream came twice. Confound old Grayson and his photographs.

5th April
Dream most troublesome. Chloral and Dover's Powders no help.

Excerpt from Grayson's book on physiology: 'Woman is an animal that micturates once a day, defecates once a week, menstruates once a month and parturates once a year. Her inclination to copulate depends upon her rank, the lady being never so inclined, the female of the labouring classes always.' How true. They do everything they can to inflame our baser instincts. Take Ivy. An illiterate born in a pigsty, she exists solely to satisfy her bodily appetites. No imagination, no curiosity. Magnificent shape.

16th April: Easter Sunday
Deo gratias, a solution has been found! Ivy in my study, twice after morning service. In certain respects she resembles her namesake of the plant kingdom, *Hedera helix*: surprisingly strong, and entwines with vigour.

Dinner with Maud proved something of a trial. Those hands.

17th April

Cum Ivy, stans. Bene. Is this a sin? I think not. God wishes me to work, and for that I must be healthy. To keep my health, I need to vent. *Ergo,* I must have Ivy.

18th April

Three weeks since I wrote to Butler-Parry and still no reply.

Cum Hedera super terram: a much-needed distraction. Without my leave she loosened her hair, so I punished her by making her braid it tight, then I twisted it round my wrist. *In delicto* I yanked harder. She bared her teeth like an alley cat.

Later

I've discovered another parallel with her namesake, the plant *Hedera:* a strong and delectable power of suction.

19th April

At last a note from Butler-P.'s steward explaining his master's silence! He's on a fishing trip in Norway, thus I may not expect a reply until the middle of *July!* Frustrating, but also a huge relief. I'd been imagining all sorts of reasons for his silence, mostly involving that snake Jacobs. I *must* be patient. *The Book will* be found.

Cum Hedera in nocte. Bene.

27th July

Surely Butler-Parry is back from Norway? Why still no reply?

I *must* be patient. The past three months have passed agreeably enough. My monograph is proceeding well, and with daily connection my health is fully restored. No more dreams.

28th July
Cum illa bis, sed non bene; illa habet mensam.

10th August
At last a reply from Butler-Parry! I write in high excitement at the railway station. I'll miss my little *Hedera*, but it's a relief to escape Wake's End. All those females fouling the air with their yeasty stink.

13th August
Momentous day: PYETT IS FOUND!
I write this at Marsham Hall with the precious parchment before me on the desk. Pyett will prove a coy mistress, very hard to read, but already she is yielding riches. It will take months to lay bare all her secrets. I can scarcely wait.

This will make my name. Everything for which I have toiled shall be mine: the respect and envy of my peers, the admiration of the public. What renders my discovery even sweeter is that I've made it at the perfect time, when my clerical and household problems are cheaply resolved and my health restored. A blessed, blessed day.

10th September
Returned in triumph to Wake's End. I thought I was fatigued,

but having resorted to my little *Hedera* I feel invigorated and refreshed.

Tomorrow is Friday. On Monday I shall go up to London and buy the new edition of the lexicon of Middle English. I know it's irrational, but when I begin my translation I must have a pristine lexicon to hand, not that much-thumbed copy from my 'Varsity days.

Of course I could have had the new volume sent here; but what if Jacobs or one of his ilk chanced to learn of my order? Why risk tipping him off that I've found Pyett, when I can go to London myself and collect the volume *sub rosa*? (And if that means I can make a celebratory detour to Piccadilly, so much the better.)

The stage is set for my great labour to begin. *Deo volente*, nothing can stop me now.

Maud closed the notebook and replaced it in Father's desk. The house was silent, the servants not yet about. She went to stand at the window.

A misty, overcast dawn. This part of the grounds was still sunk in shadow. To her left, dank willows overhung the Lode. She followed it to the dark corner where the stream met the black wall of the yew hedge. She pictured the Lode flowing beyond it into Harrow Dyke, then into the River Lark, then the Ouse, and on to the sea.

Put not your faith in men, she thought. That out there is all you can trust: that hedge and that wet grass. Those dripping trees.

As if it were happening to someone else, she observed the pieces of her past – Maman, Father, herself – rearranging to make a different pattern.

She saw her childhood peel off and float away like a piece of waterweed in the Lode.

Saturday remained overcast, and that night there was a storm. It was still raining in the morning, but by Sunday evening the rain had stopped and Wake's End was blanketed in fog. Despite this, Father took his weekly tribute of flowers to Maman's grave as usual, having forgotten to do so before morning service.

On Monday he didn't come down to breakfast, as he'd caught a chill in the fog. His trip to London was therefore postponed. A few days later, Maud learned from reading his notebook that he hadn't cancelled London because of a chill.

It was because he'd found the Doom.

Thirteen

From the Private Notebook of Edmund Stearne
16th September
Why did this have to happen now? It's too vexing. Almost as if some malicious will were out to spoil my success before it's even begun.

Today was tedious as only damp Sundays can be, and the most tedious part was having dinner with Maud. I told her to order it for five and escaped soon after, citing the flowers for Dorothy as my excuse. The rain had stopped but the churchyard was shrouded in fog. Despite it, and being reluctant to return home, I decided to make a circuit around the church. I wish to God I hadn't. Then I would never have found it.

A murky afternoon. The birds had settled to roost and the yew trees were utterly still. That's what I dislike about fog: one moment there's nothing, the next there's something – and never any warning. As I took the path that skirted the tower, I diverted myself by reflecting that in Pyett's time this graveyard wouldn't have been nearly so quiet.

It would have been raucous with pedlars and livestock, perhaps even a cockfight; and of course no headstones, only the churchyard cross. Its mutilated stump still stands to the left of the south porch opposite the family vault.

But I'm prevaricating. In the fog, the north end of the churchyard was even less appealing than usual, and in one corner the workmen had flung their refuse. Amid a tangle of brambles and wet grass, I made out a dreary pile of whitewashed planks. It was the cladding which had been torn from the chancel arch to make way for the plasterers; presumably the workmen had left it here to await burning.

I hesitated, for the path would only take me nearer the refuse. But that wasn't the whole reason for my reluctance to go on. I didn't like the *feel* of the place. Beyond the churchyard wall the dead reeds in North Fen stood as pale as bone. Behind me I heard rustling, and glimpsed some creature slipping into the fog; I think it was a stoat. Its movements were furtive, and left a disagreeable impression.

That was when I saw it. An eye in the grass, peering at me. For an instant my heart misgave me and I had the strangest sensation of *guilt*; as if I'd been caught committing some crime, and the eye had seen me do it. On looking closer, I perceived that in fact the eye was crudely painted on one of the whitewashed planks. It was round, with a black pupil and yellow-brown iris tinged with red. It stared at me with a knowing leer that I found indescribably repulsive.

What happened next I can't clearly recall or understand. I know that I caught a strong marshy whiff from the fen, and in my fancy – though at the time it seemed as real as the ground beneath my feet – I perceived greenish water with something long trailing in it; whether hair or weeds, I couldn't tell. The next moment the image was gone, for a magpie lit on to the planks and startled me with its ugly chatter.

Shooing away the bird, I admonished myself aloud for my foolishness: 'Edmund, if you can be startled by a bird and a piece of wood, you are in greater need of rest than you had supposed!' However, I was uncomfortably aware that my sole reason for speaking aloud was to make light of my alarm – and that in this I only half succeeded.

Then it occurred to me that the painted eye might be of some antiquity. My historian's curiosity aroused, I forced my way through the brambles towards it. Stooping over the plank, I caught a sharp smell of wet lime. I drew out my handkerchief and dabbed at the wood, for some reason choosing a spot adjacent to, but not quite touching, the eye. My handkerchief came away soiled with lime; and there on the plank I perceived that I'd uncovered part of the head to which the eye belonged. The head was a swampy green and covered in spikes or perhaps scales, those at the top being outlined in red, as if lit from behind by flames.

I knew then, and I know now, that what I have found is of very great age. In fact, I would stake my reputation on its being mediæval.

A cursory glance revealed that other planks in the pile also bore patches of green, yellow or black pigment, where the rain had rinsed off the whitewash. From this I surmised that the painting must be of considerable size, extending across several planks.

What an astonishing turn of events. In our ignorance, we on the parish council had decreed that the chancel's unsightly cladding must be torn down. How wrong we were. To judge from what I found this evening, those very planks comprise some sort of mediæval panel painting.

Presumably some time after it was created, the work fell foul of the iconoclasts of the Reformation, who whitewashed it into oblivion. And there it has remained, undisturbed for four centuries. Had it not been for last night's storm, the sexton would have made a bonfire of the whole thing, and no one would have been any the wiser.

A remarkable discovery indeed, and one in which as an historian I ought to be keenly interested. Why, then, as I stooped over the thing in the grass, was I so very reluctant to examine it further? Why was I tempted instead to turn over the plank that bore the offending eye, so that it might not be found by others? In short, why did I want to hide it, in the hope that it would be consigned to the fire?

It was an ignoble impulse, and of course I didn't turn over the plank. Much as I dislike the thing – and I do quite unaccountably detest it – the thought that so important a discovery might be permanently lost was abhorrent to me. Indeed, perceiving that water from a yew tree was dripping on to the very plank which bore the eye, I grasped it by one end and shifted it out of harm's way.

But that was as much as I would do. Not for an instant was I tempted to summon the sexton and show him what I'd found. Nor did I have the slightest desire to claim the discovery as my own, or associate myself with it in any way. Indeed I half-hoped that it might *not* be found. At any rate, I turned my back on the wretched pile and headed home.

Later

It's now nearly midnight, and despite a glass of brandy and water I remain out of sorts. The fog hasn't lifted. I can see nothing beyond the window.

It seems an ironic twist of Fate that I should be the one to chance upon that thing. And it hasn't escaped me that it was I who argued most strongly for the chancel's restoration, and contributed half the funds. I brought about the very work that led to the painting's discovery. So in a sense, I have caused it to be found.

Of course, one must remember that it has *not* yet been found. If old Farrow or one of the workmen happens to notice it tomorrow, then well and good. If not, I shall say no more about it. It has nothing to do with me. I shall leave it to God to decide.

But I do rather wish that I hadn't touched it.

17th September

What a disagreeable fuss. Old Farrow did notice the eye, and he duly summoned the rector and Miss B. They're all of a twitter, and would be calling the thing a miracle if they weren't afraid of being thought unacceptably High.

Of course they sent for me, and I duly feigned amazement. I told them that despite the painting's undoubted historical importance, I was far too busy to attend to it myself and I advised them to contact the Society of Antiquaries in London. And O malign Fate, whom should the Society send to make an inspection, but that oily little Hebrew Jacobs.

How he revelled in it, rubbing his hands in glee at my 'misfortune' at having missed making the discovery myself. Well, let him gloat. He's busy arranging to have the planks conveyed to London for restoration. The sooner the better, and may they never return.

I'm writing this in some discomfort, as I've scratched my hand. It happened in the churchyard when I was pushing through the brambles, or perhaps when I was moving the plank. It's not serious, merely an unpleasant reminder. But it almost feels as if I've been bitten.

Which is perfectly ridiculous, and plainly the result of a constitution strained by overwork. Nothing a brisk walk, a hearty dinner and a little calomel and laudanum won't overcome.

20th September
Such a brouhaha over that wretched painting – and all engendered by Jacobs, who is thoroughly enjoying what he vulgarly calls 'the limelight'. No doubt he is responsible for the advent of that man from the local newspaper in Ely, as well as people from *The Times*, the *Telegraph* and the rest; they've descended on the village like crows on a carcase. I have instructed the servants to admit no one save close acquaintances, but this has prompted a ridiculous rumour that I'm sulking because I wasn't the one to discover the painting. Well, so be it. The devil take the lot of them.

The scratch on my hand remains irksome. If it doesn't improve soon, I shall send for Grayson.

24th September

Much better. My hand is improving and the fuss over the painting has subsided; or rather, it has re-located to London, where restoration is expected to take many months.

At last peace has returned, and I may begin work on Pyett. One bonus of this whole affair is that it has thrown Jacobs *et al.* completely off her scent. I was therefore able to order my new *Lexicon of Middle English* via Hibble, rather than travelling up to London myself. I received it this morning, and plan to start work tomorrow. Translation first, that shouldn't take long. Then the real prize: the exegesis.

28th September

Something annoying has happened – and on my birthday, too.

Maud gave me a present which she made herself. She observed me closely while I unwrapped it. It's a watch-chain, woven from a braid of Dorothy's hair. I was so repelled I could hardly keep my countenance. What *possessed* the girl to do this? And how? She must have cut off a lock in secret and kept it all this time; and now to have created this – when she knows how strongly I dislike mourning tokens, let alone women's hair.

Is she merely thoughtless, or does she deliberately seek to goad me? I can't believe it's the latter; she is devoid of imagination and incapable of such subtlety. No, I fear she has been too much in company with Miss B., and has fallen victim to the old maid's nauseating sentimentality. Yes, that must be it. Maud has either forgotten my dislike of mourning tokens, or else her feminine inconsistency has led her to assume that I would make an exception in the case of my own wife.

Still, it's of no consequence, as I shan't wear the offending article. Indeed it would be wrong to do so, as it would only encourage the girl's morbid fancies. However, I confess that I am unsettled; and as I have been sleeping badly, I shall yet again postpone the translation. Tomorrow is Michaelmas. I shall start in the morning without fail.

As I recall, our old nurse used to warn us never to eat blackberries after Michaelmas, for by then the Devil will have spat on them. Odd how one's memory retains such boyhood nonsense, when so much else has been consigned to oblivion.

Fourteen

'THERE'S a piece in *The Times* about our painting,' Maud told Father as she poured his morning tea.

'I wasn't aware that it belonged to us,' he said drily.

'I mean the parish, Father.'

'Then you ought to say so. Inaccuracy in speech fosters inaccurate thought.'

Handing him his cup, she attended to her own. 'According to the article, the painting shows the Last Judgement and dates from the fifteenth century. The same time as Alice Pyett.'

Without responding, he helped himself to devilled kidneys from the sideboard.

'Apparently when fully restored, it may be the finest of its kind in England. Were there many paintings of the Last Judgement in the Middle Ages, Father?'

'I think you know that I don't care to discuss my work at the table, Maud. Since you're so interested in ecclesiastical art, I suggest you consult a volume in the library and leave me to enjoy my newspaper in peace.'

'Yes, Father.'

'And in future have the goodness not to touch *The Times* until I've finished with it. You know my dislike of man-handled newsprint.'

She smiled. 'Sorry, Father.'

He hated it when she mentioned the painting. That was why she did. He hated being reminded of Maman too. That was why she'd made the watch-chain. He said he'd lost it, but she knew he was lying. She'd caught the stink of burning hair coming from his study.

It was three months since she'd first read his notebook. For weeks she had raged at him in silent fury. You killed Maman and you didn't care. You were *relieved*. Nothing matters to you but yourself. You don't care about anything or anyone except your own precious needs. She had raged at herself too: for being so gullible. Those humiliating fantasies of ministering to his every wish.

At meals she would watch him with her fists in her lap. I know what you are, she told him in her head.

She had spells of breathlessness and her eczema grew worse, but she no longer wore the detested lace gloves. If the sight of her scabs disgusted him, well and good. She took a perverse pleasure in seeing him wince.

She punished Ivy too. Now and then when she was in the library she would ring for the girl and tell her to fetch a volume from a top shelf. She would observe the slow flush that crept up Ivy's neck. Then she would snap her fingers as if she'd just remembered her mistake. 'But of course, you can't read. That will be all, Ivy. I'll fetch it myself.'

In the library she found Moore and Blackthorne's *Mediæval History* and looked up wall paintings.

At a time when few men knew their letters, the common people relied on their parish church for the truths of the Gospel, which were depicted on its walls in brilliant colours. The most prominent painting was usually that of the Last Judgement, with the triumphant Christ presiding over Heaven and Hell. This would be above the chancel arch, so that worshippers had it always before them; and as its message had to be understood by the dullest peasant, painters devoted less attention to the Saved in Heaven than to the torments of the Damned. Also known as a Doomsday or a Doom, surviving paintings of the Last Judgement may be seen at...

Maud closed the book and gazed out of the French windows. Frost spangled Chatterpie's perch, but the magpie had already been and gone. In the orchard Clem raised his cap. Maud responded with a smile. She'd seen less of him over the winter, although on one treasured occasion he had shyly admired her skill at typing. She'd offered to type a letter to his cousin in Bury and he'd said he would think on it, but to her disappointment he hadn't mentioned it again.

Father came in with more pages for her. He asked if he had any engagements and she told him they were due at the Rectory for tea. He frowned. 'Heaven preserve me from idle old maids.'

When he'd gone, Maud set to work. As she typed, she wondered why he had taken such a strong dislike to what people were now calling the Wakenhyrst Doom. Occasionally over the winter she'd checked his notebook, but he'd written nothing since the day she'd given him the watch-chain, so she was no closer to an answer.

From The Book of Alice Pyett,
transl. & exegesis by E.A.M. Stearne
Here begins a treatise which by the mercy of Jesus shall relate the life of this sinful wretch Alice Pyett, who was blessed with the gift of sacred tears.

Twenty-two years after she had her first crying, the Lord commanded her to have her revelations written in a book, so that His goodness might be known to all men. Accordingly this creature found a priest, who set a pair of spectacles on his nose and wrote what she told him in the year of our Lord fifteen thirteen.

When this creature was fourteen years old, she was given in marriage to a worshipful burgess of Bury St Edmunds, who was then aged forty-one. For some months thereafter this creature enjoyed her sinful life, for her husband let her go about in a fine kyrtle and gown, fashionably slashed and underlaid in many colours.

Then as nature would have it, this creature was got with child, and in succeeding years she was brought to bed of seventeen children. During that time she began to long for chastity. So she said to her husband, I may not deny you my body, but I no longer wish to lie with you. But her husband insisted that she should continue to pay the debt of matrimony, and he used her as he had before. And this creature obeyed with much sorrow, and she would rather have licked the ooze in the gutter. And she began to hate the joys of this world.

'Father,' Maud asked innocently as they were having tea at the Rectory. 'What's "the debt of matrimony"?'

The rector spluttered into his teacup. Miss Broadstairs turned puce.

Father regarded Maud coolly. 'My dear, you're not an historian. I'd rather you simply transcribe what I give you without trying to understand the medieval idiom.'

'Yes, Father.'

'Another scone, Dr Stearne?' Miss Broadstairs said brightly.

'Thank you, no; superlative as they are.'

Watching Miss Broadstairs fidget with the teaspoons, Maud wondered how the rector's daughter had come by the knowledge of what men did to women in the bedroom. Perhaps she too had once watched a pair of dogs disporting themselves in the mud.

The Book of Alice Pyett had begun with pages of rambling prayers, and for weeks Maud had typed Father's drafts without taking in a word. But it was different now that Alice had embarked on the story of her life.

At first Maud had been puzzled that Father should see fit to set prose of such frankness before his fourteen-year-old daughter. Then she had realised that he didn't expect her to understand it. To him she was merely an extension of the typewriter.

As she typed, she found herself thinking about Maman.

Like Alice, Maman had been married young: in her case, at sixteen. Like Alice, Maman had never been allowed to *do* anything; she'd always had things done *to* her. She had been 'given in marriage' and 'permitted' fine clothes – although only if Father approved of them.

And he hadn't stopped there. Recently, Maud had been startled to learn from Miss Broadstairs that her mother's name had not in fact been Dorothy, as she'd always believed. Maman had been christened Dorothée. Father had re-named her on their marriage. Like a pet.

Maman's family had made its fortune in tortoiseshell, and Father had been happy to take her money, while expunging all trace of her origins from her habits and manners. But he'd approved of the continental custom by which on her marriage she had ceased to sign her own name, and had thereafter written: Epse. Edmund Stearne, meaning Epouse (wife) Edmund Stearne.

It was Father who had decreed what Maman ate, read, did and thought. If he'd ever given her a choice in anything, he'd been the one who decided what she could choose *from*.

Like Alice, she had continued to pay the debt of matrimony. Maud wondered if it had been as distasteful to Maman as it had been to Alice. And whether Father had cared.

As Maud sat in the Rectory drawing-room, she watched Miss Broadstairs anxiously watching Father for signs of boredom. He left early, assuring his crestfallen hostess that Maud would remain behind to keep her company. The rector left with him.

Smiling away her disappointment, Miss Broadstairs gently enquired whether Maud's eczema was any better. Maud said it was not, and Miss Broadstairs patted her shoulder. 'Not to worry, dear. Appearances aren't everything.'

Maud looked at her with sudden hatred. *I'm not like you*, she wanted to snarl. *You may be content with sorting dirty jumble and riding your bicycle for an hour on a Saturday afternoon but don't ever try to make common cause with me.*

All at once, her defiance crumbled. This is my future, she thought bleakly, as she stared at Miss Broadstairs' hunched shoulders and self-effacing smile. I will be an ugly old maid whose only purpose in life is to keep house for Father.

On the wall behind Miss Broadstairs hung the pair of engravings which Maud had known since childhood. Last year *Woman's Mission: the Helpmeet of Man* had fed her fantasies of mattering to Father. Now the picture that horrified her was *The Comfort of Old Age*: a woman devotedly holding a spoon to the lips of a feeble old gentleman in a Bath chair.

That will be me, thought Maud. Richard and Felix will get married and leave, but no one will marry me because I am plain. I will be the maiden aunt who stays at home and does nothing until she dies.

To prove that she wasn't Miss Broadstairs, Maud began secretly reading Father's newspaper instead of simply skimming it for mention of the Doom.

She read about Class Warfare and the Suffragist Movement and Liberty dresses, which seemed to involve not wearing stays. Most of it she didn't understand, but she longed to bob her hair and become a New Woman – whatever that meant.

Miss Broadstairs always declared that science wasn't for girls, so Maud took to reading her grandfather's books, as she used to do before Maman died. Maud especially enjoyed one by a gentleman named Darwin, as it was all about Nature. It made the startling assertion that the animate world had created itself, without the need for God.

The week before Christmas, Maud happened upon something even more intriguing. She was in Ely with Father, and in Hibble's she found a booklet called *Plain Words for Ladies and Girls by Dr Anthony Buchanan, A Physician.* While Father was elsewhere, she slipped her find among the books he'd selected and told the assistant to wrap them up. The lad obeyed without question; and as it was Maud's task to unwrap the purchases when they got home, she easily extracted her prize and took it unnoticed to her room.

Dr Buchanan proved disappointingly vague on what he termed 'connection', but he was a revelation when it came to the curse. 'The menses,' he wrote briskly, 'result from the monthly maturation and discharge of the unfertilised egg. The widespread fallacy that a female is impure at such times is without foundation. Provided she washes the genital parts and uses napkins, there is no uncleanliness and she need feel no shame.'

Thoughtfully, Maud removed one glove and scratched the back of her hand. *There is no uncleanliness.* They had lied to her. They had taught her to feel ashamed for no reason.

Still scratching, she turned to the chapter on babies. Her liking for Dr Buchanan curdled. According to him, a pregnant woman's bodily health was 'almost wholly under the influence of her mind. She must not give way to fretful emotions, especially to false alarm at the fancied danger of her condition. It is important to convince her that her terrors are groundless: that pregnancy is not a state of infirmity or danger, and that the few instances she may have known of miscarriage or death were owing to the improper conduct of the women themselves.'

A God-fearing man, Dr Buchanan also inveighed against married women taking measures to prevent conception. 'No right-thinking gentleman should allow his wife to adopt such wicked practices.'

Maud thought of the Dead Hand and Biddy Thrussel's herbal tonic. Maman had been devout. She would have known that what she was doing was a sin, but she'd done it anyway. She must have been desperate. *Not* every *night, eh?*

There was a tightness in Maud's chest which made it hard to breathe. She went on scratching until she drew blood.

Next morning her eczema was worse again. She found her grandfather's etymological dictionary and looked up 'eczema'.

'From the Greek, *ekzein*: to boil over.' Like lava.

Fifteen

AT Christmas the dykes froze. Maud heard the swish and crackle of skates along the Lode. Three weeks after New Year, she lost her faith.

It happened quite suddenly. She simply woke up and it was gone. As she lay in bed it occurred to her that between religion and superstition there was no difference, since both were based on unreason. To kill a man to redeem the sins of others was as irrational as tapping a hole in one's eggshell to stop a witch using it as a boat.

The relief was immense. She felt as if a stone had been lifted off her shoulders. The thorny walls that had bedevilled her childhood were no more. They'd been swept away like a riverbank in a flood. Jubal was right. It was all moonshine.

The best of it was that she no longer had to worry about Maman down in that horrible vault. The vault was just a hole in the ground with bones in it. Maman wasn't there. She wasn't anywhere.

It was Sunday, so Maud went to church as usual with Father. She sang and knelt at the proper times, but she didn't pray. Instead she looked around her at the headless stumps of saints smashed in the Reformation by people who'd happily worshipped them a few years before. She gazed at the ceiling with its interlocking beams and large wooden angels; at the little grinning devils by their feet.

She thought, this church was built in the years after the Black Death had killed a third of the people. It was built out of fear. It's a bribe to God: *Please don't do it again.*

'*All things bright and beautiful,*' she sang, '*the Lord God made them all.*' Presumably, the Lord God had also made the malaria which had killed nine of the blacksmith's children in Wakenhyrst, prompting his desperate wife to smother the last one in its cradle, 'to get it over with.'

Maud thought of Maman waiting in the south porch eleven times to be churched. Father and Mr Broadstairs favoured the old-fashioned ways which decreed that a woman was unclean after confinement, and must be cleansed before she could resume her place in the congregation. For some reason Leviticus stipulated that the period of uncleanliness was twice as long if the baby was a girl. Having a girl made you twice as dirty.

'*The rich man in his castle,*' sang Maud, '*the poor man in his cot.*'

Moonshine. All moonshine.

During the sermon she continued to reflect on 'all things bright and beautiful'. The Lord God *didn't* make them all. The herons and warblers in the fen, the starlings and willows and purple marsh-grass: it existed because of Mr Darwin's process of evolution. Maud found this reassuring. Nature was all there was. And Nature was enough.

She became aware that Father was also gazing about him. He appeared unsettled. She wondered if he was thinking about the Wakenhyrst Doom.

The Society of Antiquaries had completed the restoration and the Doom had been exhibited to the Fellows at the Ordinary Meeting in London. Yesterday Lady Clevedon had called at Wake's End in high excitement. 'No thank you, Maud, I'll only stay a moment. Ah, good morning, Dr Stearne, I bring *splendid* news! You're aware that last night Lord Clevedon was Guest of Honour for the unveiling at Burlington House? I fancy you declined your own invitation?'

'My work...' murmured Father.

'Quite so. *Well*, the Society has *finally* agreed that since we funded the greater part of the restoration – including of course your own very handsome contribution...'

Father inclined his head.

'... it's only right that our Doom should return to St Guthlaf's!'

'Oh, that's excellent news,' cried Father. To Maud's astonishment, he seemed genuinely pleased.

She asked Lady Clevedon if the Doom was to be hung in its old place above the chancel arch.

'Oh no, dear, I gather that parts of it are a trifle indelicate – naked sinners and so forth, it wouldn't do at all. We're having it hung in the chamber at the foot of the tower. There it can be seen on request, but the rector will hold the key, so it won't distract the villagers at worship. I think that most proper, don't you, Dr Stearne?'

'Quite so, Lady Clevedon. When may we look forward to the painting's arrival?'

'In a fortnight. I've asked Miss Broadstairs to arrange a small private view on the fifteenth of February: the Parish Council, local "notables", sherry, that sort of thing. I hope we may count on you and dear Maud to attend?'

'We'd be delighted.'

After Lady Clevedon had gone, Maud said, 'And shall we really attend, Father? I should so like to see the Doom.'

'Of course we shall,' he said with every appearance of surprise. 'Didn't you hear me tell Lady Clevedon?'

'I thought you might change your mind.'

'Why?'

'Well, because... Sometimes it seems as if you don't – like the Doom.'

'What an extraordinary idea. How could I form a view when I've never set eyes on it?'

He was looking down at her with an incredulous smile and she felt very stupid and young. She also realised that she'd come alarmingly close to betraying the fact that she'd read his notebook.

The sermon came to an end. Sensing Maud's eyes on him, Father turned his head. Did she imagine a glint of amusement in his light-blue glance?

She had no idea whether he'd genuinely lost his antipathy for the Doom, or whether this was a pretence. *You're no match for me*, his eyes seemed to say. *Don't attempt to fathom what's in my mind.*

As they were leaving St Guthlaf's, Miss Broadstairs inter-cepted them. 'I hope you don't object, Dr Stearne, but I wonder if I might have a quiet word with Maud?'

'By all means,' said Father, not bothering to conceal his relief that she wasn't after him.

'Maud, I have something important to ask you,' said the rector's daughter when they were alone in the vestry. 'And I know that you will answer with perfect honesty, as you always do.'

'Yes, Miss Broadstairs,' mumbled Maud. She wondered how soon she could escape.

'I couldn't help noticing that you weren't praying. Are you feeling quite well?'

'Quite well, thank you.'

'Forgive me but I don't believe that you're being entirely frank.'

Maud didn't reply.

Miss Broadstairs sighed. 'Why won't you confide in me?'

'There's nothing to confide. Please, I must go, Father is most particular about meals—'

'You know I do notice things,' said Miss Broadstairs in a hard voice that made Maud blink. 'You think I'm just a foolish old maid. But I've lived longer than you and I know rather more than you suppose.'

'I don't doubt it,' said Maud.

'Oh, I think you do. I think you've decided that you've outgrown my father's sermons. That's it, isn't it?'

Maud tried to edge around her, but Miss Broadstairs

caught her arm in a painful grip. 'Girls your age, they always know better. Don't give me that sullen stare. Tell me why you didn't pray!'

'Very well,' Maud said stonily. 'It's because I don't believe in God.'

Miss Broadstairs let go of her. She gave a scornful laugh. 'I know what's happened. You've been reading some *book* and it's led you astray. Something by Mr *Darwin*, perhaps? And now you believe that instead of God's great design, the world simply *happened*, entirely by chance.'

'That's not what Darwin said,' muttered Maud.

'Ah, and *you* understand it so much *better* than I, as you're so much *cleverer*!' Her horsey features had gone rigid. There was a blob of spittle at the corner of her mouth.

'It has nothing to do with Darwin,' retorted Maud. 'I worked it out for myself. When Maman died you told me that Father let the baby live instead of her because a baby is born in sin and if it isn't baptised it can't go to Heaven. A *baby*? How can it be born in sin, it's never done anything!'

Miss Broadstairs flinched.

'Hasn't it ever struck you as horrible,' Maud went on, 'that the symbol of our religion is an instrument of torture? "He suffered on the cross that we might live..." *Why?* How can torturing a man do any good? How can blood wash away sin? Because God says so? Well, it doesn't! My mother's blood didn't wash away my father's sin!' Her voice cracked. She was back in the hot June dawn, staring at the scarlet stain on the divan and breathing the sickly-sweet smell of Maman's blood.

Miss Broadstairs was making gobbling noises in her throat. Maud turned and fled the vestry.

She didn't get far. The path was icy and she slipped and would have fallen if Clem hadn't grabbed her elbow. 'Steady, Miss.'

'Thank you,' she panted.

Through her thick winter coat she felt the strength of his hands. She forgot all about God and Miss Broadstairs, she was conscious only of Clem. Her eyes were level with his collar. Above his muffler she saw the brown skin of his throat, and a patch of golden hairs on his jaw that his razor had missed. She saw his mouth. She breathed the warmth of unwashed flesh, and her own flesh responded with a tight hot throbbing between her legs.

'Shall I walk you home, Miss—'

'No I'm fine,' she croaked. 'Thank you, Walker.'

Somehow, she found her way back to Wake's End and up to her room. Her face in the looking-glass was bright-eyed and almost pretty, a different girl from the one who'd trudged to church with Father. This Maud had brutally despatched Miss Broadstairs and had stood chest to chest with Clem. This Maud had wanted to kiss his throat and clamp her mouth to his.

She repressed a spurt of jittery laughter. This is impossible. You're only fourteen.

But the new Maud, the one who wanted to touch and be touched by a handsome young man, replied calmly: Yes, but that's the same age as Alice Pyett when she was wed.

Maud pictured Miss Broadstairs' horror if she ever found out. And Lady Clevedon's, and Father's.

'Your daughter's in love with the under-gardener,' she said aloud. 'How do you like that, Father?'

Sixteen

THE 29th of January was St Agnes' Eve, an auspicious
night for love charms. All the female servants
believed in them and Maud had grown up knowing how
to read the name of one's future husband in a curl of apple
peel, and how to count the years till the wedding by the
number of times a cuckoo called.

Last Midsummer's Eve, Ivy had plucked an ivy leaf from
outside Father's study and tucked it in her bodice. '*Ivy,
ivy, I pluck thee*,' she'd chanted with her sly smile. '*In my
bosom I lay thee*.' According to the charm, the first man
she encountered would be her husband. She later admitted
with a grin that she had indeed met a man, but she wasn't
saying who.

Midnight approached and Maud waited, wrapped in her
coverlet. The fire had gone out and her room was glacial.
Outside, the fen lay frozen beneath a thin crescent moon.

Moonshine, she thought wryly. If Jubal had known what
she was doing he would have spat his contempt in a stream
of tobacco juice – and he'd be right. Maud knew very well

that all this was nonsense, but she still wanted to do it. No doubt Father would attribute such inconsistency to the fact that she was female.

On the bed lay the penny knife she'd bribed Daisy to buy in Wakenhyrst. She picked it up, enjoying its weight in her hand.

The clock downstairs chimed midnight. Tightening her grip on the knife, Maud jabbed its tip with all her strength into the bedpost. *'Tis not this post alone I stick,'* she whispered, *'But Clem's heart I wish to prick. Whether he sleep or whether he wake, I'd have him come to me and speak.'*

Her voice didn't sound like her, and the words of the old charm – or was it the knife? – gave her a heady feeling of power.

She did not for one moment believe that this would have any real effect, but for the first time in her life she understood how wisewomen felt. And witches.

'Miss Broadstairs thinks you must be ill,' Father told Maud at dinner the following week. 'You don't look ill.'

'I'm not. I'm perfectly well,' replied Maud, taking a second cutlet from the dish Ivy was holding.

'She says in her note that I oughtn't to let you type my work. She says it's giving you "odd ideas". Can that be true?'

'Of course not. I never pay any attention to what I type.'

'Well, in future you'd better keep what ideas you have to yourself. You appear to have upset her.'

'I'm sorry for that, Father. Is she up and about yet?'

'In a day or so, I gather. We'll say no more about it.'

'Yes, Father.'

It was nearly a week since the 'quiet word' in the vestry, after which Miss Broadstairs had suffered a nervous attack and taken to her bed. As Maud helped herself to potatoes, she was struck by the fact that she felt neither guilt nor remorse at having caused the rector's daughter to fall ill.

It's her own fault, Maud decided as she spooned mustard on her plate. She got in my way.

From The Book of Alice Pyett,
transl. & exegesis by E.A.M. Stearne

After bearing her fourteenth child in great bodily pain, this creature tried to hang herself, for she longed to be out of this sinful world. Her husband's manservant cut the rope, so she ran to the river and threw herself in; but her gown kept her afloat and she could not drown. She fled to the house of her sister, who put her to bed and went to fetch this creature's husband. While this creature was alone, she tried to stab herself with a blade, but her husband and sister returned and took it from her. After that she was locked in a chamber and tied up day and night...

The front door slammed. Maud stopped typing and went out into the passage.

To her astonishment, both pairs of study doors stood

open and the room was empty. How extraordinary. Father never left his desk exposed to prying eyes.

Having made sure there was no one about, Maud swiftly checked the drawer where he kept his notebook. It was gone. It had been gone since the day of Lady Clevedon's visit. Maud suspected that Father had taken it to his bedroom, but so far she hadn't dared look.

Glancing up, she was startled to see him through the window. He was in the garden, in the corner where the yew hedge met the Lode. It was freezing, the lawn was white with frost; but he stood hatless and coatless, staring down at the Lode.

What was he *doing*? Surely there was nothing to see but dead reeds poking through ice.

And he'd left his desk in disarray. His pen lay where he'd flung it, ink spattered across the page. Had something in Pyett upset him?

Keeping an eye on him in case he turned round, Maud scanned the paragraph he'd just written.

Then this creature was very ill and people said she would die, so her husband sent for a priest, that she might confess her sins. But this creature had a thing on her conscience that she had never revealed in all her life. And now not even to her confessor would she reveal it, even though she knew that for this sin she would be damned, and would suffer the torments of hell for eternity.

Seventeen

From the Private Notebook of Edmund Stearne
9th February 1912

I admit it, that passage in Pyett was a shock. But the shock has worn off and I'm thoroughly ashamed of myself. How melodramatic to have rushed from the house – and in the middle of winter! I'm lucky I didn't catch a chill.

What did I *imagine* I was doing out there? I really can't say. All I know is that as I stood staring at the Lode, I experienced the strangest sensations of guilt and fear – especially fear – even though I had no idea of what I was afraid. Then an image came to me of something submerged: I think it was hair – or perhaps weeds. I had a powerful conviction that there was something under the ice. Something alive, fighting to get out. I didn't know what it was, I only knew that I was frightened and intensely desirous that the thing should remain trapped, so that it couldn't reach me.

The cold brought me to my senses. The whole experience can't have lasted more than ten seconds – and yet it remains with me still.

What tricks the mind plays! Until I read that paragraph in Pyett about her 'unconfessed sin', I had never imagined her as being capable of any kind of sin, let alone sin of such gravity that it would weigh on her conscience for years. It is *this* that shook me. That's why I experienced such an intense reaction today. I've become so engrossed in my translation that in some unaccountable way I seem to have associated her sin with myself. That's why I felt guilty and ashamed – when in fact the guilt is hers.

I must guard against becoming excessively involved with my work, it can't be healthy. And it doesn't help that I've been sleeping poorly for the past week. That can't be for lack of connection, that side of things is quite satisfactory.

Perhaps it's all the fuss about the Doom. Miss B. and the rector talk of little else. They're preparing what they're now calling 'the west gallery', i.e. the room in the tower, for the thing's arrival. All this hardly conduces to peace.

Cum Ivy, stans. Sed non bene.

Later
It occurs to me that the image of something submerged which came to me this afternoon at the Lode was the same that I had in the churchyard when I saw the eye in the grass – that is, when I found the Doom. An odd coincidence. Although perhaps not so coincidental. In both instances I was near water. No doubt that is what caused it.

12th February
This morning I found it devilishly hard to concentrate in church. I have been worshipping in St Guthlaf's since I was

old enough to hold a hymn book, and I know every inch of its appointments. Why then should it have taken me until today to notice quite how much of a flavour of the *fen* it has about it?

Of course I've long been familiar with those toads on the chest near our pew, but I don't think I've ever noticed that the green man at the base of the font is peering from a clump of bulrushes; or that so many of the grotesques on the corbels are carrying eel glaves.

I suppose such features are hardly surprising, given that the stonemasons who built this church would have been local men. At that time the fen stretched from here to the Wash. Naturally they incorporated it into their carvings. It's simply odd that I've never noticed until now.

But it wasn't only that. I kept catching whiffs of the fen itself: a swampy rottenness that seemed to come and go, making it doubly distracting. Marsh gas in the middle of winter? How can that be?

No one else seemed to perceive it. Certainly not Maud, who sang as loudly and unmusically as ever. Though I daresay that's to be expected. Her organism is less finely tuned than mine, her perceptions not nearly as keen.

13th February
Awful dream, awful. It cast a pall over the whole day. I write this after dinner, and am still not fully recovered.

I dreamed that it was summer and I was standing at the edge of the Mere – which in itself is remarkable as I haven't been near it since I was a boy. In the dream I was horribly reluctant to look into the water, and yet at the same time

I felt a strong compulsion to do precisely that. I tried to pull back, but I *could not*. Some unseen will was battling my own, forcing me closer to the edge. As I approached, I became aware that something was rising from the deep. I could not – I *would not* – lean over to see what it was; but I knew, with the perception one has in dreams and which doesn't require sight, that the thing was rising inexorably towards me. Nearer and nearer it came. I tried to scream, but what came out was a wheezing cry. Dread squeezed my chest. If the thing broke the surface...

I woke. It was morning, and some bird was pecking at the window. As I lay panting and shuddering, I saw writing printed on the ceiling in angry black letters: WAKE.

With a cry I awoke – this time, for real. The bird was still pecking at the window. Tumbling out of bed, I flung aside the curtains and raised the blind – and that wretched magpie of Maud's flew off with its clattering cry.

Insupportable. I shall speak to her about this.

14th February

The whole parish is in a state of high excitement, for tomorrow the Doom will be unveiled. It arrived yesterday, the ghastly Jacobs having allowed ample time. He took it upon himself to accompany it from London, so of course he'll be attending its unveiling – which rather casts a damper on the whole affair. I gather that all went well in transit, and it is now safely installed in the chamber at the foot of the tower. No one has yet been allowed to see it except the rector and Miss B. It remains shrouded, and the door to the tower is locked. A sensible idea, I think.

This morning, even though there was nothing to see, the congregation was distracted, people whispering and craning their necks at the locked door. There has been so much interest among the lower orders that Broadstairs has arranged a second, public 'viewing', to be held the day after our more select gathering. Concerning the latter, Miss B. has been making herself a nuisance. Her housemaid being indisposed, she has asked if she may 'borrow' Ivy to help serve the refreshments. Why must the wretched female trouble me with such trivia?

The moment the service ended, she trotted up and offered to vouchsafe me an advance 'peep' at the painting. I declined, saying that I didn't wish to spoil the suspense of her soirée (nor do I want to be beholden to her!).

I wish now that I'd taken up her offer. It would have been a relief to have seen the thing in private, and got it over with. Why this apprehension? I ought to find the painting of particular interest, not least because Pyett herself must have seen this scared work many times.

15th February

In the previous entry, instead of writing 'sacred', I wrote 'scared'. An odd mistake to have made. I think I shall ask old Grayson for a nerve tonic.

I write this at five o'clock in the morning, having slept poorly. I didn't imagine that smell in church the other day, it was there again yesterday, even though all the windows were shut. Moreover the weather was windless: no breeze to waft a miasma from the fen. And oddly enough, I couldn't smell the fen at all when I went out into the churchyard.

So why could I smell it inside the church?

Doubtless the stink is coming from below. I shall speak to Farrow about the drains.

Later

It took ages for the sky to lighten, but at last dawn has broken. A black frost, and strangely still. An important day for the parish – or so some would have us believe. Tonight I shall behold our Doom.

Eighteen

'I CAN'T say that I care for that hat,' said Father as they walked home under the stars.

'Don't you, Father? It's only my old one with a new ribbon. Are you feeling any better?'

'I told you, it was only a momentary indisposition. I can't be the first man with whom Miss Broadstairs' "refreshments" have disagreed.'

Maud turned her head to hide a smile. It was a cold, clear night and the stars were astonishingly bright. She was in an excellent mood.

She had thoroughly enjoyed the unveiling of the Doom. The room at the foot of St Guthlaf's tower had lent a fitting air of medieval discomfort to Miss Broadstairs' soirée. Its thick stone walls had glinted forbiddingly in the glare of the gas-jets, and the ambience of a dungeon had persisted despite the warmth from two paraffin heaters and the press of bodies.

The Doom itself was far larger than Maud had expected, a giant wooden semi-circle that occupied the whole of the west wall. It was covered in dustsheets until the rector called for silence and Lady Clevedon pulled the cord to a smattering of applause.

There followed a startled silence. Someone gasped. Someone else cleared their throat.

Dr Jacobs, being the most familiar with the painting, took it upon himself to speak. 'Isn't it *splendid*? Rustic – *naïf*, one might almost say – yet with undeniable moral force.'

'Quite so,' murmured Dr Grayson, ogling a large naked female whose rosy flesh was painted in unflinching detail, with brownish nipples and a slit between her legs.

'Marvellous colours,' Lady Clevedon said stoutly.

'Wonderful,' echoed Miss Broadstairs. 'But – why does Satan have that second face on his, er, lower parts?'

There was more coughing, and the rector pretended not to have heard.

'It's a metaphor, dear lady,' said Dr Jacobs. 'For the, um, baser appetites.'

'Ah,' said Miss Broadstairs.

Dr Jacobs turned to Father. 'What do you think, Stearne? Fascinating, eh?'

'Indeed,' said Father.

Maud had watched him closely when Lady Clevedon pulled the cord. Unlike everyone else in the room, he'd ignored the naked sinners in Hell. His eyes had gone straight to Satan. But it wasn't the Devil's strangely green face that had held his gaze, nor the repulsive second head that jutted from between Satan's legs. It was the scroll which the Devil gripped in one scaly fist, with its motto in emphatic black Gothic lettering: *This sinner is mine, because of his sin.*

Christ sat on a rainbow at the top of the Doom, presiding over the Day of Judgement. In the background the newly resurrected dead were climbing out of their graves: some still shrouded from head to foot like bolsters, others emerging pinkly naked. Angels led the Saved to a bland green Heaven, while devils dragged the Damned into Hell.

In the foreground a giant, winged St Michael stared serenely skywards as he weighed a terrified little soul in a pair of scales. Satan, also a giant, confronted the saint with a grin; he clearly intended to claim the soul for his own. In keeping with tradition, the Prince of Darkness had horns, a tail and a pair of large bat-like wings. But his hook-nosed features and scrawny limbs were a swampy green, and in his ragged knee-breeches and sleeveless jerkin he looked for all the world as if he'd just come in from the fen.

Behind him, between the Jaws of Hell, hordes of lesser demons were gleefully torturing the Damned. Here the painter had outdone himself and fitted each torment to its sin with sadistic attention to detail. One devil had disembowelled a paunchy glutton and was stuffing his entrails down his throat. Another had speared the tongue of a naked female gossip and was swinging her screaming over his shoulder.

'Vivid, ain't it?' chuckled Lord Clevedon at Maud's elbow.

'I think it's hideous,' she said.

'Ha ha, very good!' Having done his duty by her, he shuffled off to raid Ivy's tray of savouries.

'Not to your taste, Miss Stearne?' said Dr Jacobs with his mouth full.

'On the contrary, I like it. It's so remarkably frank. After all,' she added, catching Miss Broadstairs' eye, 'this is what the Bible says. Isn't it?'

This is what your faith means, she told Miss Broadstairs silently. You can dress it up with cherubs if you wish, but the man who painted this picture was rather more honest. He knew that it all boils down to a threat to keep people in line. That sketchy promise of Heaven if you do what you're told – and the certainty of endless torture if you don't. *Take that, peasants. Now back to the fields and don't even think about improving your lot.*

'Dr Stearne, are you unwell?' Lady Clevedon said shrilly.

'He's gone as white as a sheet,' exclaimed Dr Jacobs.

'Ivy, bring water!' cried Dr Grayson.

Father's face was the colour of bone, and he was staring fixedly at the Doom. But now it wasn't Satan's motto that held his attention. It was something in the bottom right-hand corner that Maud couldn't see.

'Maud, don't just stand there!' snapped Miss Broadstairs. 'Help your father!'

'I'm fine,' mumbled Father – and vomited on to the flags.

His breath still smelled as he held the gate open for Maud. He must be mortified, she thought with glee.

Oh, it had been a splendid evening, so much to savour! Lady Clevedon gamely pretending that her skirts hadn't been splashed. Ivy on her knees, mopping up.

Father retired early, but when Maud went upstairs an hour later, she saw a light beneath his door. She guessed he was confiding his thoughts to his notebook. At least she hoped so, although she would have to wait another day or so to find out. He had no reason to go out tomorrow, and she made it a rule never to venture into his dressing-room – where he'd taken to keeping the notebook – unless she was certain that he was out of the house.

Far from minding this delay, she rather enjoyed it. It heightened the anticipation; like reading one of those serialised stories in Cook's *Family Chat*. And just as if she were reading a serial, she made a point of never skipping ahead to Father's last entry. She always picked up from where she'd left off.

This sinner is mine, because of his sin.

What sin could Father possibly have committed that would make him react like that?

It couldn't be what he'd done to Maman. He considered condemning her for the sake of Baby Rose as no more than his Christian duty, and in no way a sin. Nor did he regard what he regularly did with Ivy as anything but the satisfaction of a lawful appetite.

Suddenly, Maud remembered what Jubal Rede had told her the first time they'd met: 'He oughter know about sin.' Jubal had been talking about Father. What had he meant?

Crossing to her window, Maud raised the blind. The frost-spangled fen lay coldly beautiful beneath the rising moon. The Lode gleamed like eelskin. The spindly shadows of the naked willows reached towards the house with bony hands.

Whatever sin Father committed, she promised the fen, I will find out.

She felt alive in all her senses and eager for the hunt.

Nineteen

From the Private Notebook of Edmund Stearne
15th February

Why is this happening? Over the years I've seen countless depictions of the Day of Judgement. I'm a mediæval historian for Heaven's sake! So why at this evening's unveiling should the Doom have made me ill?

Perhaps Grayson is right, and it wasn't the Doom; merely an unsavoury savoury (his little joke) and the fumes from those wretched paraffin heaters.

There's something else too. As I beheld the Doom, I experienced the same waking dream that I did on first reading of Pyett's sin. The floating hair. And I did distinctly smell meadowsweet. In the middle of winter? I suppose it could have been scent worn by one of the ladies – but what about the hair?

I suppose the Doom *is* rather out of the ordinary, possessing as it does such a pronounced *local* flavour. 'A whiff of the fen', as someone remarked. Its demons attack their victims with the hooked prongs of eel glaves, and the tiny black imps weighing down the scales have the bulbous eyes of toads. What struck me most forcibly is that the Jaws of Hell, which in other Dooms are those of a fiery dragon or a Leviathan, are here depicted as a monstrous eel.

That in itself probably explains why I felt unwell, conjuring as it does unpleasant memories from my boyhood. Nurse Thrushie locking me in the corner cupboard when I misbehaved. Her endless tales of 'bad sperrits'. Ferishes, Jack-o'-Lanterns, Black Shuck; all ready to lure you to a miry death if you ventured into the fen. And as I recall, they didn't only inhabit the fen. Why, there was even supposed to be an 'evil haunt' in church.

Yes that must be it, childhood terrors exacerbated by paraffin fumes. I only wish the women hadn't made such a to-do. Miss B. clucking around me like a hen, Lady Clevedon pretending not to be vexed about her flounces. Maud unfilial and aloof. Only Ivy was any use, although let's not forget that she has her own motives for helping. The other night when she thought I was asleep, she stole over to the chaise longue and stretched out naked. I saw how she gazed about her with that proprietorial air; how she caressed the velvet chaise, while probing with her tongue the fleshy mound on her upper lip. She became more aroused than she ever is with me. I know what she wants. The little chit fancies herself as mistress of Wake's End. Good luck to her!

To remind her who's Master, I took her from behind, *coitus more ferarum.* I made her bite the pillow. *Bene.*

Women are all the same. Devious, hypocritical, corrupt. They never admit what it is they really want.

Later

I feel much cleaner, having rung for Ivy and vented copiously. Venting has cleared my mind, and I now perceive what I didn't before. I haven't yet mentioned the worst thing about the Doom: that devil in the corner. *He* is what made me ill. Did I deliberately avoid referring to him, or have I only just realised that he is the root of my unease?

I can see him now. He squats obscenely in a clump of reeds, splaying his hind limbs to expose his parts. His scaly head is lit from behind by the ruddy flames of Hell, but he is in every particular a creature of the swamp. His hide is greenish-black, his claws are webbed, and his features resemble those of a toad. He has just snared a naked sinner with his eel glave, and yet he is leering not at his victim, but at me.

It's the same eye that I saw in the churchyard on the night I found the Doom. It's the eye in the grass. And it's looking at *me*.

17th February

'The eye in the grass' indeed! What nonsense. There's nothing like a spot of toothache to restore one's sense of reality. It seems I've been grinding my jaws in my sleep and have split a molar; the dentist extracted it this morning. I found the pain a welcome distraction. Henceforth I shall heed old Grayson: plain food, brisk exercise, regular connection. That's the ticket.

The door to the tower remains locked, which is helping a good deal. At first I was still disagreeably aware of the Doom behind it, and strange as it sounds, I felt *watched*. But now I scarcely think of it at all.

18th February

I had to speak to Maud about that wretched magpie. While I was at my desk, the creature lit on to the chimneystack, and its infernal clamour echoed so loudly that I could have sworn it was in the room; I was so startled I spilled ink on my work.

Maud had the temerity to assert that it wasn't her bird but some other magpie, or even a crow. I told her I would not tolerate the creature near the house, and forbade her to feed it. The girl is even plainer when she sulks.

I described the bird's clamour as 'infernal', which puts me in mind of what Thrushie used to say: that if you see a seventh magpie, you'll see the Devil by and by. Doggerel, yet perhaps with a kernel of truth. Magpies steal and are generally vicious. I won't have it near the house.

The scar on my hand is troubling me. It has become red and inflamed. I have an idea that I've been scratching it in my sleep.

Later

I keep thinking about eyes. That devil in the corner of the Doom. One eye is open, the other half-closed in a lecherous wink.

I fancy I now know why I was so affected by the eye in the grass. *Cave, cave, deus videt.* Beware, beware, God sees all. The stars were extraordinarily bright on the night they unveiled the Doom. They put me in mind of what our governess used to say: that stars are holes through which God watches what we do. 'If you're naughty,' she told us, 'God will see. He will throw you into a burning pit where the Devil lives.'

'Which star is the hole that God looks through?' Lily wanted to know.

'All of them,' said Miss Carter.

'What, all at the same time?' Lily said sceptically.

'All at the same time,' replied our governess.

My sister badgered her with more questions but I'd heard enough. Ever since then, the night sky has held no beauty for me. I can't quite rid myself of the belief that above me are millions of eyes.

19th February

Until now, I've never noticed how many devils inhabit our church – I mean, its architecture and appointments – nor have I perceived how many of them evoke 'a whiff of the fen'.

They crouch at the base of the font and cling to the capitals, they positively throng the ceiling. This last came as an unpleasant surprise, for I'd always believed that those little creatures grinning from the corbels were merely grotesques. But during Morning Service it occurred to me that they might be devils.

I've just consulted Herbert's *Ecclesiastical Glories of England*. I wish I hadn't. 'St Guthlaf's, Wakenhyrst, Suffolk: Gothic arcades that would grace a cathedral are flanked by a spacious nave beneath a superlative hammerbeam roof. Its interlinked beams are supported by arched braces from which float large horizontal wooden angels with outstretched wings, the hems of their gowns brushing corbels crammed with leering demons.' So there we have it. Our church is full of devils. There are angels, but not as many.

28th February
Maud lacks a woman's solicitous instincts to a deplorable
degree. As my hand was still troubling me, I was forced to
ask her twice to bring iodine, and then she made no offer
to assist. I had to *order* her to bathe and bandage the lesion,
or she would have left me to do it myself.

She is sulking again because I scolded her about that bird.
She still feeds it, though she denies it to my face. I told her I
would not tolerate guile. To mark my point, I made her copy
the whole of Leviticus twice.

15th March
Slept badly. Another black frost. I could distinctly hear the
ice on the Mere: much unearthly grinding and cracking.

My hand remains troublesome. II Corinthians 12:7: 'There
was given to me a thorn in the flesh, the messenger of Satan
to buffet me.' I exaggerate, but it really is rather trying.

17th March
During Morning Service I found myself musing on the
common belief that when statues of saints and the like
were destroyed in the Reformation, this left our churches
unprotected from the forces of evil.

An old wheelwright in Blythburgh once assured me
that this explained his church's famous black mark. He
said that when 'they' (i.e. the Puritan iconoclasts) painted
over St Christopher, they unwittingly let in the Devil in
the form of a great black dog. The infernal hound raised a
lightning storm and struck two people dead before exiting
through the door, leaving behind the well-known scorch

mark. It made not a jot of difference to the old fellow when I pointed out that since St Christopher had been whitewashed a good sixteen years before the great storm of 1577, the Devil had certainly taken his time in arriving.

Yesterday I consulted our parish records. It is as I supposed: the Doom and its supporting 'candlebeam' were indeed limed over during the Reformation. The records are amusing in their Puritan scorn for graven images, describing the Doom as 'good onlie to rost a shoulder of mutton, but evill in church'. So where does all this take me? The Doom is a *sacred* painting, I mustn't forget that. Even if I believed the nonsense of the common people, its return to St Guthlaf's in its naked state would surely *protect*, rather than harm.

Why then do I have such a powerful feeling that this painting has nothing sacred about it? That on the contrary it possesses a quality of the infernal?

I think it must be the primitive vigour of the imagery. The man who painted that Doom believed in Hell as completely as he believed in his own existence. Such conviction is almost enough to make me believe in Hell myself.

Twenty

21st March

At last the thaw has set in. Icicles dripping from the eaves, water gurgling and trickling in the gutters. I slept badly. I kept fancying I could still hear the ice on the Mere.

22nd March

I begin to understand why Pyett's was the age of wonders and demons. I begin to grasp how swiftly unreason, like an unclean flood, seeps into the deepest crevices of the mind.

After evensong I remained so long in prayer that when I came to myself, everyone had gone. The church was in darkness except for a candle on the altar and I surmised that the rector, not wishing to disturb me, had quietly departed, telling the sexton to leave me a light.

'Hulloa?' I called, in case old Farrow was still about. I received no answer. Clearly the sexton had also gone home. As I rose to do the same, I heard a noise in a distant part of the church. It wasn't the sound of the latch in the porch, it was nothing so familiar. It was the click of claws on stone.

I shrugged it off as the quirk of an ancient building – but then it came again. It wasn't a rat, it sounded larger than that; perhaps a stoat? Although there was something almost furtive about it, suggesting a greater intelligence than such creatures possess. I also had the disagreeable impression that whatever it was had emerged from the room in the tower which holds the Doom.

The next moment I knew this to be impossible, for that room remains locked. I considered crossing the nave to make sure; but I've never liked being alone in St Guthlaf's at night – too many shadows – so instead I left by the shortest route, taking the candle from the altar and extinguishing it only at the last moment. I did not look back.

Having left via the vestry, I emerged into the north end of the churchyard. For some reason I remembered that by tradition, this is the area reserved for suicides, stillborns and evil spirits: 'the Devil's part,' as Thrushie used to call it.

The darkness was almost palpable, for the moon had not yet risen and the sky was murky and overcast. A thin mist lay low upon the ground. The headstones jutted through it like teeth. With one hand on the wall of the church, I groped my way along the path. It occurred to me that I was going 'widdershins' instead of clockwise, thus earning myself untold bad luck (were I a believer in such things). How Thrushie would have scolded me! And how I wished I didn't keep recalling her and her nonsense!

As my eyes adjusted to the murk, I saw with relief that I had reached the south end of the churchyard. I made out the dark bulk of the family monument, and the lych-gate beyond. A flicker of movement caught my eye at the corner of my vision and I turned. Nothing there. And yet there had been *something*, for *something* had caught my eye.

The night was very still. My breath sounded unpleasantly loud and somewhat uneven. Around me I made out the hunched shapes of yew trees. I've never liked them. I read somewhere that this churchyard stands a yard higher than its surroundings because of all the bodies buried here since Saxon times. For a thousand years these yews have fed on human flesh.

All this passed through my mind as I stood listening in the graveyard. The church loomed, deep black against the charcoal sky. It seemed not a place of sanctuary, but the menacing relic of a savage and haunted past.

Then, a few yards to my left, I glimpsed a dark shape slipping behind a headstone. It ran fast and very low to the ground, and it was larger than a stoat, though not large enough to be human. I felt for my clasp-knife, but didn't take it from my pocket.

From nowhere a wind blew up, wafting a dank smell of rotting vegetation. In the fen beyond the churchyard wall, I heard the brittle rustle of dead reeds. The wind stirred the mist, and I realised that what I'd glimpsed was no creature. My eye had been deceived by shifting ribbons of vapour.

As abruptly as it had arisen, the wind died. The reeds went still. The silence throbbed in my ears. The inhuman silence of the fen.

Again I glimpsed movement. This time I saw it more clearly, if only for an instant: something slipping over the churchyard wall. A moment later I heard a soft splash as the creature entered Harrow Dyke. An otter, then. I found that I'd had been clutching the knife in my pocket. Relinquishing my grip, I withdrew my hand and wiped my palm on my overcoat.

I reached the house without further incident, and found to my disgust that the smell of decay had worked its way into my clothes. I had Ivy draw a hot bath, and felt immediately better. However, on leaving the bathroom, I chanced to peer through the round window at the end of the passage – and I distinctly saw something swimming across the Lode. It was just above where the Lode meets Harrow Dyke, and it was definitely *not* floating débris, for it was moving upstream. Towards the house.

It *must* have been an otter.

Although I did not think that otters had such long fur.

23rd March

There must be something wrong with the drains, for that swampy smell has infiltrated parts of the house, particularly my study. It is giving me a headache.

This afternoon Ivy was late drawing the blinds. I had to ring for her twice, and then I had to *tell* her to tend the fire. She ought to have noticed without being told. I had returned to my desk and the girl was kneeling at the grate when that wretched magpie clattered on to the roof. The noise echoed so loudly down the chimneybreast that I nearly repeated my accident with the inkwell.

I gave orders that tomorrow Ivy must have the bird destroyed. Still on her knees, she twisted round and grinned.

'You seem out of sorts, sir. Shall I fetch you some tea, sir?' I rose from my desk and told her sharply to stay where she was. On her knees.

24th March
Much better. The drains have righted themselves and that fenny stink is gone. Also my hand is much improved, thanks to Ivy and her aunt Biddy Thrussel's medicinal vinegar. Moreover I can at last work in peace, now that the magpie is destroyed.

Slightly unfortunate circumstances, but that can't be helped. I'd returned from Ely with Maud, and on entering the library she chanced to see the carcase hanging in the shrubbery. Apparently Ivy had caught the bird in a snare and wrung its neck, but having been called away, she'd neglected to cut it down.

Maud uttered a cry and ran to the window. She stood there staring while I rang and gave orders for the carcase to be removed. She soon recovered her composure, however, and by evening she'd forgotten the whole affair. By nature she is phlegmatic and insensitive. She lacks the capacity for strong emotion.

Later
Ivy is surprisingly sensible about the Doom. 'Ugh!' she told me with a shudder. 'They knew what they was doing when they whited it over.'

Yea, from the mouth of an illiterate rustic comes truth. That painting is neither sacred nor infernal. It is merely an unsightly daub. I will think no more about it.

Twenty-one

'*I*'M sorry about your bird, Miss.'

'Thank you, Walker.'

'Is there ought I can do?'

'No, thank you.'

'Very good, Miss.'

'Um... Walker?'

'Miss?'

'Actually there is something. His perch. Could you take it away?'

'At once, Miss.'

'Thank you.'

She was proud that she comported herself so calmly. After all, nothing could bring Chatterpie back. It was only rational to carry on. So when Ivy flaunted an iridescent tailfeather in her hat, Maud's response was measured and calm. 'Don't you know it's bad luck to kill a magpie?'

'I dun't believe in bad luck, Miss.'

'That doesn't matter. It believes in you.'

Seeing Ivy's eyes widen gave Maud a momentary satisfaction, even though she knew that what she'd said was meaningless. Chatterpie was dead. She had to accept that. There was nothing to be done.

Sleet battered the windows like shot, and every so often she glanced up from her typing and received a fresh jolt on seeing no perch in the laurel bush. Clem had done what she'd asked the same day, but now she wished he hadn't. It was too soon. It felt as if Chatterpie had never existed.

She would have liked to have marked the magpie's death in some way: to have cut off her hair in mourning and thrown it in his grave. Only Chatterpie didn't have a grave. Ivy had flung him on the bonfire.

From *The Book of Alice Pyett,*
transl. & exegesis by E.A.M. Stearne
Despite the burden on her conscience, this creature could not bring herself to confess her secret sin. And her dread of Hell became so great that she—

A magpie thudded on to the chimney stack, and Maud pressed the wrong key. She put her hands in her lap. Father liked his drafts to be perfect. She would have to begin again.

While the magpie clattered about on the chimney, she discarded the spoiled page and loaded a clean one in her typewriter. The magpie glided down to the lawn and shook out its wet feathers, then paraded before her at a swift waddling run, as if seeking her attention. It wasn't, of course. It had no special gleam in its eye and no grey scar on its leg. It wasn't Chatterpie. Chatterpie was dead.

Maud's hands began to shake. There was an ache behind her eyes. Very deliberately, she rose and left the library, took her coat and hat and let herself out of the front door; quietly, so as not to alert Father. Sleet stung her face. The pain in her chest made her gasp.

The coach-house was deserted. It was nearly noon and the servants had gone for their dinner. Maud ducked into the harness-room and hid behind the feed bin. She heard Blossom and Bluebell munching their feed. Her breath came in heaving gasps. She felt as if her head was about to explode.

Footsteps on the gravel, then Father's voice: 'Ah, Walker. Have you seen Miss Maud?'

Maud clapped her hands across her mouth.

'Yes, sir,' said Clem, startlingly close.

'Well, where is she?'

'I think I seen her heading for church, sir.'

'Good Heavens, at this time of day?'

'Yes, sir.'

An exasperated sigh. 'Very well. Go on with your work.'

'Yes, sir.'

Still with her hands over her mouth, Maud listened to Father walk away.

'Master's gone back indoors, Miss,' Clem said quietly.

She wanted to thank him but she was crying too hard. He touched her shoulder. 'There, now.'

'It was m-my *fault*,' she panted between jerky wrenching sobs.

'No, no—'

'Yes it *was*! I f-fed him, I made him come to his p-perch. If he hadn't tapped on the window—'

'He'd of been on the roof, or the gables. Thass what chatterpies do.' He stood beside her, patting her shoulder as if she were a horse.

After a while her sobs eased.

'I'd give thee my kerchief,' he said. 'Only it's not dainty enough.'

Maud sniffed. No one had ever applied that word to her. Wiping her eyes with her fingers, she pinched the bridge of her nose to hold back the tears. 'I don't even have a body to mourn,' she said savagely. 'She flung him on the bonfire as if he was rubbish.'

'Ah now that's where you're wrong, Miss.'

She peered at him. 'What do you mean?'

He grinned his shy grin. 'I pulled en out the fire, din't I? He'm up the hayloft in a scrap of sacking. A mite singed, mind. But the frost's keeping en fresh.'

'Oh Clem, *thank* you! That's the best present I've ever had!'

'What, a half-burned chatterpie?'

She gave a spluttery laugh.

He had one elbow on the feed bin. She saw the snaky veins on the back of his hand and his knobbly wristbone. She touched it with her fingertip. He flinched, but didn't pull away.

She realised that she'd called him by his first name.

'Clem,' she said again for the joy of saying it aloud. 'Thank you, Clem.'

From *The Book of Alice Pyett,*
transl. & exegesis by E.A.M. Stearne
Despite the burden on her conscience, this creature could not bring herself to confess her secret sin, and her dread of Hell became so great that for weeks she was amazingly tormented by spirits. Devils pawed her and hauled her about, scorching her with flames. She beheld the torments of Hell, where the souls of the damned are eternally fried in fire as if they are fish in hot oil, while others are endlessly drowned and brought back to life in freezing meres, only to be drowned and drowned again...

'Father, shall you need me after tea?' said Maud, handing him the latest page of Pyett.

He glanced up from his desk. 'Really, my dear, I can't quite say. Had you something you particularly wished to do?'

She wanted to take Chatterpie's body to the Mere, but she realised that she'd made a mistake in seeking permission. Father never told her if he needed her until the last minute. Even if he said he didn't, he frequently changed his mind and interrupted her just when she'd settled down with a book. Sometimes she wondered if he did it on purpose;

but on the whole she thought not. She wasn't important enough for that.

'There's nothing particular I wanted to do,' she lied. 'I'll be in the library if you need me.'

Soon afterwards he brought in another page for her to type. 'I should like this before luncheon if you can manage it.'

'Yes, Father.'

He glanced out of the French windows, and she saw him notice the absence of Chatterpie's perch. For a moment his light-blue eyes met hers. Neither of them mentioned the bird.

When Father had gone, Maud sat with her hands in her lap. The last few pages in his notebook had included sketches of the devils in St Guthlaf's, and also one of Chatterpie. Maud had seen it the day after the magpie was killed.

I hate you, she told Father silently. You killed Maman and now you've killed Chatterpie. You have forfeited my love. From now on there can be only hate.

It was the first time she'd admitted this to herself and she felt no guilt; merely satisfaction and a sense of strength.

As it turned out, Maud was able to visit the Mere after all, because Father developed eye-strain and went upstairs to rest; or to have connection with Ivy, Maud didn't care which.

It was a raw March afternoon with no hint of spring in the air. The sleet had turned to freezing mizzle, and a bitter east wind shivered the surface of the Mere. Clem had done a good job of wrapping the carcase. Only Chatterpie's sharp black beak poked out of the sacking, reminding Maud of the day when she'd rescued him and wrapped him in her pinafore.

Chatterpie had been dead for two days and was beginning to smell, but that was good. It was part of Maud's penance. Cutting off a lock of her hair, she tucked it inside the shroud and bound it in place with a black satin ribbon criss-crossed around the pathetically small corpse. Then she tied the bundle to a brick she'd brought from the kitchen garden. She couldn't have said precisely why she did all this, except that it was important to offer part of herself to the fen: to ensure that Chatterpie would be at peace.

Geese rose from the Mere in a clatter of wings, and when she raised her head to watch, she saw Jubal on the far side. He was standing fishing on his punt with Nellie behind him. He looked just the same as when she'd last been in the fen, before Maman died. Maud nodded at him and he nodded back, but went on fishing. She was grateful for that.

Telling Chatterpie farewell, she leaned over and dropped him in. He was gone in seconds. She didn't cry. She was long past that.

The wind rattled the reeds. Maud remembered the starlings shape-shifting like a giant hand. She told herself that the fen would endure and so would she. But Chatterpie was still dead.

'May Father be punished for what he did,' she prayed to the fen. 'May his secret sin – whatever it is – eat away at him like acid. May he continue to see devils in church. And may his fear of the Doom grow and grow like weeds—'

She broke off. She stared down into the dark brown water which was Chatterpie's grave. An idea had come to her: a gift from the fen.

She knew the precise date when she would put it into effect. It would mean waiting a couple of months, but that was all right. She knew how to wait.

Easter came and went, and at the end of May, Maud turned fifteen. Still she bided her time. On the 9th of June it would be three years since Maman had died.

The week before the anniversary, Maud went in search of Clem. She found him in the glass-house, scalding flowerpots. 'There's something I want you to do for me,' she said.

His cheeks darkened with the deep, slow flush she'd come to love. 'Anything, Miss.'

In common with most villagers, he was intensely superstitious, but he was pragmatic enough not to let it get in his way. Like Cole, he wasn't afraid to venture into the fen, as long as he had a sprig of rowan in his cap and said the right charm.

'It's the season for eel-babbing, isn't it?' said Maud.

He grinned. 'Fancy thee knowing that.'

'Bring me one, Clem. I want you to bring me an eel.'

Twenty-two

From The Book of Alice Pyett,
transl. & exegesis by E.A.M. Stearne
After this creature had been tormented by evil spirits
for several months, there came a blessed day when the
air above her opened as bright as lightning and she saw
many white things flying like specks in a sunbeam. Then
Jesus came in the likeness of a most beauteous man, and
he sat upon her bedside and said, Daughter, recover and
be at peace.

After that the devils ceased to torment this creature,
and she grew as calm in her wits as she was before, and
was delivered from her sickness.

From the Private Notebook of Edmund Stearne
6th June 1912
I take comfort from Pyett's recovery, as it mirrors my own.
I'm ashamed at the extent to which I've allowed that

painting to unsettle me. I think bad air from the fen had a lot to do with it.

Fortunately, summer has brought no more disturbances – be they from ill-executed daubs or importunate birds. My work is proceeding apace, and the household seems tolerably well run; I must give Maud some credit for that. I feel fully restored and have scarcely thought about the Doom.

9th June

This morning, Ivy found an eel in my washbasin – *or so she says*. She *says* that as she knows my dislike of the creatures, she made haste to remove it. A likely story. The chit either put it there herself, or else it never existed and she concocted the whole thing to alarm me and make herself appear indispensable.

When I confronted her she became indignant, insisting that she'd found a large black eel coiled in my washbasin. 'Stone dead it wor,' she assured me. She swore to it on the Bible. I scolded her severely for that, but she still wouldn't confess. I had to threaten to dock her wages, and even then she admitted her guilt so grudgingly that one would have thought her confession were the falsehood, not the prank itself.

But it must have been her. None of the other servants would dare perpetrate such a trick. I shall have to watch Ivy. She is (in vulgar parlance) 'getting above herself'.

Strange how the mind works. I find the notion of an eel in my washbasin so revolting that I had Daisy scrub it out with lye.

When I was a boy I once saw Cook making eel pie.

After the creatures had been cut up, the parts continued to move. 'Nowt so strong as an eel,' Cook said. In Pyett's time they believed that eels arose spontaneously from the ooze in the fen. Perhaps therein lies my dislike of the creatures. They inhabit the slime, and will eat any dead, rotting thing that sinks into it.

10th June

I had that dream again. As before, I was standing beside the Mere, and although I haven't been near the place in thirty years, it felt extraordinarily *real*. I smelled meadowsweet and I was conscious of reeds brushing my naked calves. I heard the high thin screams of swifts.

As before, I was terrified of something that was rising from the deep. I couldn't move, I could only watch it come closer. Nearer and nearer it rose, until it was floating just beneath the surface. Its face was obscured by a clotted mass of hair that shifted and swayed in a manner I found indescribably horrific. I tried to flee but my legs wouldn't move. I knew that in another moment the hair would part and the thing would see me with its dead white eyes and my heart would burst...

With a cry I awoke. In my confusion I fancied I heard a dreadful wet snuffling somewhere nearby, and I saw waterlight on the ceiling, a shifting green glimmer inter-twined with the trailing shadows of weeds. What can have happened? I wondered. Has the Lode invaded the grounds during the night and crept up to the very walls of the house, bringing with it some denizen of the fen? Is it there now, crouching like an incubus on my windowsill? Glaring at me?

Then I came fully awake – and of course there was no waterlight on the ceiling and no web-footed demon crouching on the sill. It was simply greenish sunlight filtering through the leaves that stirred and trembled around my windows.

To my consternation I perceived that the window opposite my bed was partially open, its blind half-raised and its curtains flapping. Drifting in from the fen came the most revolting marshy stench.

How could this have happened? Since I became Master of Wake's End it has been my fixed rule that all windows giving on to the fen *must* remain *shut*. Any servant who disobeys me is dismissed forthwith. They all know this. Who then could have raised the sash?

Later
Whoever it was, they must have done it while I slept. I find that thought peculiarly disturbing.

11th June
I really ought to refrain from brandy after dinner. There's no need to invent a furtive 'someone' stealing into my room; the riddle of the window has been more prosaically solved. Yesterday while cleaning the room, one of the maids doubtless raised the sash for a moment to shake out a duster – as they are permitted to do – and then neglected to lower it. When I retired, I failed to notice this because the blinds and curtains had already been drawn; and as the night was still, there was no breeze to alert me.

At morning prayers, I drew attention to this error and reminded the servants of my orders. I reminded them too that my rule is a simple matter of hygiene. All manner of unwholesome things emanate from the fen. By that I mean miasmas, mosquitoes, and bad air. They must be kept *out*.

12th June

This household is becoming more and more lax. First there was that deplorable affair of the window. Then on Monday the pie-crust at luncheon was scorched. And on three separate occasions Maud has handed me pages containing errors.

I've also had to speak to her about excessive familiarity with the servants, having twice seen her talking to Walker in the orchard. I warned her that she will cause trouble for the lad by distracting him from his work. She was chastened and promised it wouldn't happen again.

13th June

I've been feeling strangely oppressed and anxious. The house is pervaded by a dank, marshy smell, like that which troubled me last year. I had the drains thoroughly checked then, and have no wish to incur further expense by repeating the exercise.

For some reason the smell is most pronounced in my study and my bedroom. There's no accounting for it as we've had no rain for weeks; and yet the strange thing is that the curtains feel slightly damp to the touch. When I pointed this out to Daisy she had the impertinence to query whether it was indeed so. Well, I surely didn't imagine it! I've ordered fires lit in all the grates and the rooms thoroughly aired.

This has occasioned much grumbling behind my back, as the maids complain about lugging coal in this hot weather. Why do they think I pay them, if not to work?

It's all most vexing and I've been unable to do anything useful on Pyett. I re-write sections I've already translated, while neglecting my exegesis, which remains little more than a few scribbled ideas.

This morning when I sat down in my study with a book, I was disturbed by a furtive scrabbling at the windowpane. It wasn't the tapping of a bird; this sounded more like claws. On raising the sash, I thought I glimpsed something scuttling off into the ivy. I've ordered young Walker to cut back the plant around the windows, and set rat traps. If that fails, Cole shall summon Abe Thrussel with his ferret.

14th June
I know now that Ivy has been causing this business with the window. This evening on retiring I found the same sash raised, although I'd made a point of ensuring that it was securely shut before I went down to dinner. That's when it came to me. As with that affair of the eel, Ivy has been seeking to unsettle me by playing tricks with the window, thereby hoping to enhance her usefulness and importance.

I taxed her about it and of course she denied everything, but I know she's lying. Any more of this nonsense and she shall go.

Later
Odd how a memory can pop into one's head, even though one hasn't thought of it in decades.

This evening I'd scarcely put out my candle and composed myself for sleep when I recalled an incident from my boyhood. Nurse Thrushie grabbing my hand and spreading my fingers to display what she maintained was webbing; although like so much of what she told me, this was a malicious fabrication. 'See that?' she hissed. ''Tis the bad blood showing through. I know you, Master Eddie. I know what you did.'

The memory is so vivid that I can feel her cold rough hand squeezing mine. And yet it happened when I was a boy.

Did that dream about the Mere somehow cause me to remember this? It hardly matters. I *know* what brought it to the surface. I've been sleeping in a badly aired room that smells of rotting weeds. I shall have words with Daisy in the morning.

15th June
It isn't Ivy who has been opening my bedroom window, it can't be. It happened again last night, when she wasn't in the house: she was in Wakenhyrst for her mother's latest confinement and only returns tomorrow.

How then do I account for the fact that this morning I woke to find the window once again half-open? That marshy smell was even stronger than before, and one corner of the curtain was hanging out. When I pulled it in, it was wet.

How did this happen? It didn't rain last night, and no matter how heavy the dew, it could not have rendered that curtain soaking wet.

Later

Re-reading Pyett has brought me to my senses. In her time, fear of Satan was at its peak; her Book teems with demons and evil spirits. It is this which has unsettled me. Why, every time I sit down to my work, I am forcibly reminded of that wretched Doom – and of the devil in the corner.

Do be sensible, Edmund. Nightmares and monsters are all very well for women and children, but not for historians! And while you're about it, you might also remember your Shakespeare: ''tis the eye of childhood that fears a painted devil.'

16th June

Quite unaccountably, another memory has surfaced from my boyhood. It seeped into my mind this afternoon as I was working.

At the time, Daisy was outside scrubbing the front steps. She must have accidentally overturned the pail, for I heard a clatter and the sound of water. Suddenly I was a boy again, watching water dripping on to the scullery flags as they carried her in from the Mere.

She was brought in horribly changed. Her mouth and eyes were netted with weeds and her hair was tinged with green. Her body was bluish-grey and obscenely swollen. In places her flesh hung in shreds, like india-rubber, and there was a tattered hole where her belly had been, for the eels had eaten her from the inside.

It's too much. I can't write any more.

I know what you did.

Twenty-three

17th June

But *is* it a memory? Or is it only what I *think* I remember? Is it perhaps what I merely overheard the servants say? After all, I was only twelve years old at the time, I wouldn't have been *allowed* to witness such horror as that.

No, it's far more likely that I heard the servants gossiping, and that over the years my brain has transmuted their tittle-tattle into the *semblance* of a memory. It is this which came to me so disturbingly in my study when Daisy knocked over her pail. It is this which last night deprived me of my rest.

Later

Something else occurs to me too. *What did the servants actually see?* We all know how the lower orders exaggerate. Why, they may even have made up the whole thing! There may be *no foundation whatsoever* to my so-called 'memory'. Of course the death itself occurred, that is established fact; but in all probability she was brought in from the fen essentially intact. Nothing remotely like that dreadful mutilated corpse.

19th June

It's no use. For the past two days I've been deceiving myself. That memory is real. It comes to me at odd times of the day and night, and the details are such that no servant would be capable of imagining – or indeed could possibly have known. That yellow ribbon still tangled in her long fair hair. The scratch on her thigh which happened as she climbed naked into the boat.

So now I know. The vision is real. Which means the rest of it is real too: the grey shreds of india-rubber flesh, the slimy green weeds befouling her face. The eels.

But why should all this return to me now? What's the *use* of my brain resurrecting the past, when all it can do is horrify? It is this which I find most disturbing: the fact that the vision has the power to come and go at will, despite all my efforts to keep it out.

'At will', that's an odd phrase to have used. But it is how it feels. As if some malevolent will were acting against me: forcing me to remember, for some occult reason of its own.

From The Book of Alice Pyett,
transl. & exegesis by E.A.M. Stearne

This creature's first crying came about in this wise.

A week after Our Lord Jesus first sat on her bed and delivered her from her sickness, he came to her again, this time at night as she lay beside her husband. And Jesus said: Daughter, you must give up eating meat and eat instead of my flesh and blood. For I take you, Alice, for my wedded wife. And I must be intimate with you and lie in bed with you, and you shall lick my wounds and suck my blood.

And this creature gladly did as she was bidden, and Jesus so ravished her spirit with sweetness that she heard a rushing sound as of bellows, and a blackbird sang loudly in her right ear.

The next morning was Trinity Sunday, and as usual this creature went to church with her husband. But when she beheld the blessed rood, she felt such a fever of love for Our Lord that she burst into violent sobs. To the consternation of those around her she fell down and wept as if her heart would break, roaring and writhing and making remarkable faces. She cried all day and she did not stop until evening. And this was her first crying.

After that she could not behold a crucifix or even think of Christ's Passion without bursting into uncontrollable tears and sobbing for hours on end. Her husband scolded her. But Jesus said: Be not afraid, Daughter, for your crying is a special gift that God has given you because he loves you above all others, and praises your devotion.

20th June
I was more correct than I knew when I noted that Pyett's recovery from her illness mirrors my own. The parallels are striking. Indeed they are more than merely parallels,

for they provide a key to my sufferings – and enormous comfort.

Pyett once committed a grievous sin, which for many years she concealed even from herself; and when that memory finally returned to her awareness, it proved so painful that it gave her hellish visions of demons and the tortures of the damned. So too has it been with me.

BUT – and this is the point – Pyett's *awareness* of her sin *proved her special virtue.* She *knew* she had sinned, and Jesus blessed her for that; it is *why* he bestowed the gift of sacred tears. This has been my epiphany. One can only be saved *if one is aware of one's sin. Therefore* it follows that if one *is* aware of one's sin, *one is saved.*

So it is with me. Like Pyett, I have been reminded of my sin. Therefore like Pyett, I too am saved.

Twenty-four

From *The Book of Alice Pyett,*
transl. & exegesis by E.A.M. Stearne

This creature's cryings now came every day and lasted five or six hours, so that she turned the colour of lead. People spat on her and said she must be drunk, or that she could leave off weeping if she wanted and only wept to be thought godly. Many wished her at sea in a bottomless boat.

This creature's husband said: What is wrong with you, woman? You must be quiet as other wives are, and card wool and spin. And the priest said: Christ's own mother did not cry as much as you. Get out of my church, for you are annoying people.

In time, some said that this creature must be troubled by evil spirits. But others said that she had the Holy Ghost in her, and they listened to her speak of the Gospel, and begged her to pray for them at their dying.

For this she was taken before a great cleric in a furred hood, who said: Woman, you must not speak of God to the people. Then this creature said: But my lord, I think the

Gospel gives me leave to speak of God. And the cleric said: Ah now we know she has a devil in her! For Saint Paul himself has written that no woman may preach – so that if a woman should try, it follows that she must be possessed by a devil.

Then the cleric ordered this creature to stop speaking of God, or else she would be burned as a heretic and a Lollard. And the cleric showed her a cartful of thorns which had been laid ready to burn her.

'Father, do you think Pyett may simply have been mad?'

'Whatever do you mean, Maud?'

'Well, she had seventeen children, so perhaps it was some sort of hysterical illness. Or maybe she was deranged by the memory of her sin – whatever it was.'

He looked at her. 'I'm afraid, Maud, that being female, you lack the imagination to understand a visionary like Pyett. May I trouble you for the marmalade?'

'Oh I'm sorry, Father, here it is. But if women lack imagination, then why did God choose Pyett to be a mystic?'

He sighed. 'Precisely *because* she lacked imagination. She was merely a vessel into which He poured His grace. For the same reason, women were believed to be more prone to demonic possession, being weaker and therefore more prone to sin.'

'Oh I see. But then—'

'Maud, if you can't curb your curiosity, go and read my translation of Pyett's Preface, wherein she states that God's purpose in choosing her was "to comfort other sinners by revealing His unspeakable mercy". Now kindly allow me to finish my breakfast in peace.'

'Yes, Father.' She helped herself to another slice of toast.

When he saw that she wasn't leaving, he shook out his *Times* with a frown. She smiled to herself. Her hopes of unsettling him with the eel had come to nothing, and he hadn't written anything in his notebook after declaring himself saved two days ago; but she was not downhearted. That eel had got Ivy into serious trouble. And thanks to the notebook, Maud had learned a little more about Father's sin.

She'd been startled to discover that it had involved a drowning, particularly as he had only been twelve years old at the time. That was the same age as Maud's brother Richard, an obnoxious lump who spouted schoolboy slang on the rare occasions he came home and tormented the servants with practical 'jokes'. She couldn't imagine Richard committing a mortal sin. And yet apparently, Father had.

It made sense of the fact that on the death of his father, he'd taken the unusual step of sacking the entire staff. He hadn't wanted anyone in his household to remind him of his boyhood.

But what had he *done*? Surely he hadn't drowned whoever it was himself? Could 'connection' have had anything to do with it? But how would that lead to a drowning? And was connection even feasible for a boy of twelve?

Thoughtfully, she dabbed quince jelly on a morsel of toast.

It would take time, but she would find out what Father

had done. Then she would devise some way to punish him. She would not rest until Chatterpie was avenged.

A rabbit sped across the road and Blossom shied, making Maud clutch the dog-cart with one hand and Clem's sleeve with the other.

'Coom oop, yer old divil!' Clem told the mare. He cleared his throat. 'Beg pardon, Miss.'

She beamed at him. 'Oh that's all right.'

Shortly after breakfast, Father had told her to go to Ely and collect a parcel of books from Hibble's. He'd been so absorbed in his work that he'd merely grunted when she'd told him that as Jessop was busy cleaning out the feed bins, Walker would drive her instead.

A whole morning with Clem, she thought blissfully as they clopped along in the dappled sunlight of Prickwillow Lane. This is the best day of my life. I don't ever want it to end.

Everything was perfect. The weather was fine but not oppressively hot. High-flung clouds drifted in a sky of tender blue, and as they crossed the bridge over Harrow Dyke, Maud spotted the cobalt flash of a kingfisher.

The labourers in the fields were too busy cutting hay to notice a boy and a girl in a dog-cart. Maud rationed her glances at Clem's face, but she found that she could feast her eyes on his hands without even turning her head.

Halfway to Ely, he said he was warm and asked if he might take off his jacket. When he rolled up his shirtsleeves, the sight of his brown forearms made Maud feel faint.

She hadn't touched him since the harness-room, or called him Clem to his face; but earlier as he was helping her into the dog-cart, she'd guessed from his grave expression that things had changed for him too.

She wondered if he thought about her at night, as she did about him. She would lie for hours, imagining putting her hands on his shoulders and pushing back his hair from his forehead. In her most daring fantasies she never went further than undoing the top button of his shirt and kissing the base of his throat; but she thought of that endlessly. She told herself that this had nothing to do with dogs copulating in the mud, or what Father did to Ivy. This was different because it was love.

The willows were left behind and Ely cathedral rose into view above the fields.

'I want to ask you something,' said Maud, keeping her eyes on the dusty white road. 'When I first met you, you said your name was Clem, but I've noticed that all the other servants call you Walker.' She shot him a glance. 'Why is that?'

Taking off his cap, he wiped his brow on his wrist. The sight of the damp hair on his neck made her dizzy. 'Only Mam called me Clem, Miss,' he said quietly.

'Oh. Then did you mind when I did?'

'No no, I likes it.'

She sucked in her lips. 'Do you still miss her?'

He was silent for so long that she thought he hadn't heard. At last he touched his breastbone. 'It's patched up in here. But it'll nivver be the same.'

'But that's *exactly* how I feel about Maman!' she cried.

'Dear Clem,' she added under her breath. This time she was sure he hadn't heard, because she hadn't meant him to. She'd just wanted to say it out loud.

They reached Ely in time for luncheon. Maud had been worrying about this, but Clem solved it for her by dropping her at the White Hart where she always lunched with Father, and taking himself off with a promise to collect her from Hibble's at three. Lunching together would have been impossible. But as Maud ate her venison pie in the inn's private dining-room, she cursed her lack of initiative. Couldn't she have managed a picnic on the way home?

To console herself, she gobbled her raspberry fool, then made a detour to the haberdashers', where she treated herself to one of the new long corsets. It was a slightly alarming sheath of india-rubber and clock-spring steel that reached almost to her knees. The girl in the shop said it was very effective at subduing the hips. Maud was too embarrassed to try it on and made her disguise it by wrapping it up twice.

She reached Hibble's at a quarter to three, with just enough time to select two promising novels for herself and have them included in Father's parcel. Clem was waiting outside. He'd shared an apple with the mare. Maud smelled it on his breath when he helped her into the dog-cart.

Mysteriously, the morning's carefree mood had turned to constraint. As they headed home, Clem sat in silence. Maud glanced at her gloved hands in her lap. She thought of the eczema beneath the Nottingham lace. I am hideous, she thought. He can't possibly like me.

He was taking the other route back, through Wakenhyrst and over the Common. As they left the village, they came upon a boy relieving himself behind a hedge. Maud pretended not to notice, but the boy sniggered at Clem, who repressed a grin.

For the first time it occurred to Maud that he too was a village boy. Village boys were coarse and foul-mouthed. They lived for killing things and chasing girls. What if Clem was the same?

Halfway across the Common, he yawned. 'Beg pardon, Miss.'

She blushed. 'You seem tired. Have you been eel-babbing again?'

He grinned. 'Fancy thee knowing that, Miss.'

She felt a bit better. 'Why do you always go at night?'

'Why, becorze that's when they bites, Miss. You needs a warm dark night when the moon rises late and there's a bit of a wind from the south or south-west.'

She glanced at him in surprise. It was the most he'd ever said in one go. 'But aren't you afraid to be in the fen at night, what with the ferishes and the hobby-lanterns?'

'I don't take no notice, Miss, long as I've my bit of rowan. 'Sides, old Jubal keeps an eye out for me.'

'Is Jubal a friend of yours?'

'Sort of a cousin, Miss.'

'But how extraordinary! I've been friends with Jubal since I was little! But that's a secret, so promise you won't tell.'

'You, friends with old Jubal?' He whistled. 'An't you the rum un, Miss Maud!'

She basked in the compliment. 'Do eels taste nice?'

'Proper good eating. Now dun't tell me you an't nivver ate a eel?'

She giggled. 'Heavens no, Father won't allow them in the house!' Even talking about eels gave her a visceral thrill of transgression. And how appalled Father would be to see her chatting familiarly with the under-gardener, and calling him Clem.

'Clem,' she said suddenly. 'Will you take me eel-babbing?'

He snorted. 'Not likely, Miss!'

'Oh, *please*.'

'No!'

'Oh *Clem*, I do think you're most fearfully mean!' But she was laughing, and so was he.

Hibble had muddled the order and Father was vexed.

'But this volume is *Anglo-Saxon*!' he exclaimed. 'Really, Maud, I don't expect Hibble to know these things, but surely you're aware that I've no interest whatsoever in the *eighth* century?'

'It wasn't Mr Hibble who made up the parcel,' said Maud. 'It was his assistant. Ought I to send it back?'

With a frown Father flicked through the offending volume. 'No, we'll leave it for now. It may not be completely useless. But I shan't pay for it, and I shall dictate a stiff note.'

'Yes, Father.' She bit back a smile. Her two novels and the new corset were safely hidden in her room, and the bookseller's error had proved a godsend, as it had made Father forget his displeasure at seeing her in the dog-cart with Clem.

She was in such high spirits that she astonished Nurse by taking Felix for a walk in the grounds.

Because Maud never cooed over her brother, the four-year-old regarded her with awe. Sometimes when she set off for a walk she caught him staring after her wistfully.

Now he walked obediently at her side with his small damp hand in hers. To her surprise he seemed fascinated by the waterweed in the Lode. He gazed in rapt silence, breathing through his mouth.

An emerald dragonfly darted past. Felix laughed and pointed a chubby finger.

The insect disappeared among the reeds. Felix turned his golden head and peered after it. It came back and hovered before him. He pointed again and cast Maud a questioning glance.

'It's a dragonfly,' she told him.

He clapped his hands and crowed with delight: 'Agon*fly*!'

Maud repressed a twinge of guilt. Poor little scrap. None of this was his fault.

After depositing him back in the nursery, she dressed hurriedly for dinner. She had begun to hatch another plan and she was impatient for bedtime.

This plan was shockingly risky, but for that very reason she knew that she *had* to do it. And it had to be tonight: a warm, still night with a southerly breeze and a waning crescent moon that wouldn't rise until long after midnight.

It was also the 24th of June. That was the Feast of St John, although Maud preferred the old name, Midsummer's Night. A powerful night for love charms, and a propitious one to venture on to the fen and go eel-babbing with Clem.

Twenty-five

*T*HE night was so dark that if it hadn't been for Clem's fair hair, Maud would have lost him.

The villagers always went babbing in North Fen on the other side of the church, but Clem was one of the few who ventured into Guthlaf's Fen. Being part of the household, he was allowed to use the foot-bridge, which was where Maud lay in wait for him behind an elder tree. Her plan was to follow him till he reached his babbing spot, and only then declare herself. He would be horrified, but by then it would be too late.

At first he took the path along the Lode, as if he was making for the Mere, but halfway there he turned left and headed along Slape Dyke, into the heart of the fen. Maud was relieved. Being out here at night was alarming enough without going near the place where an unknown woman had drowned thirty years before.

The fen was much quieter at Midsummer than it was in the spring. Maud was glad that she'd decided to go barefoot. The frogs and owls had fallen silent, and the breeze scarcely stirred the sedge. The silence was broken only by the song of a marsh warbler and the occasional whirr of a duck's wings.

As it was a warm night, she'd left her coat at home and wore only a light lawn blouse and her gored skirt that she'd shortened to ankle length. The new corset remained in its wrappings in her room.

Darkness gave her a sense of ease and freedom she'd never known before. She was no longer Maud, the plain, clumsy fifteen-year-old whom nobody liked. She was a creature of the fen, slipping gracefully through the reeds with her long hair flowing free.

A moorhen flew up with a clatter of wings and she nearly cried out. Briefly, Clem turned. By now her eyes had adjusted to the gloom, and she saw the pail he carried and his canvas bag. His eel glave was balanced over one shoulder.

He hadn't gone far when he stopped at a clump of trees and set down his things. Maud crept closer and crouched behind a willow. She watched him take off his jacket and hang it on a branch, then roll up his shirtsleeves and amble downstream. She heard water hit the dyke. She stifled a jittery giggle. Clem came back buttoning his trousers.

Suddenly, Maud was terrified. What was she *doing*, crouching in the dark, watching an under-gardener urinate in the dyke?

A nocturnal jaunt on Midsummer's Night had seemed a marvellous idea when she was getting ready in her room. What a thrill to unpin her braids and brush her hair till it hung glossy and thick past her waist! 'Oh, Father, if only you knew,' she'd told her reflection in the looking-glass. The face that stared back had been wide-eyed and eager.

Yes, it had seemed the height of daring. Now it was merely embarrassing. Pranks were for pretty girls, not for her. What if Clem was annoyed that she'd spoiled his babbing? What if he didn't like her as much as she liked him? She ought to slink off home before he found out she was here. But she was too scared and she didn't know the way.

Clem knelt on the bank, hunched over something he'd taken from his bag. Mustering her courage, Maud emerged from the willows and cleared her throat.

With a cry he sprang to his feet. 'Who's there!' he hissed. 'Jubal? That you?'

'Clem it's me,' whispered Maud.

'*Miss Maud?*' He sounded horrified.

'D-don't fret thyseln,' she stammered, unthinkingly lapsing into village talk. 'I told thee I wanted to go babbing—'

'Oh no, Miss Maud, this'll nivver do! What if Master finds out?'

'He won't.'

'He might—'

'He won't! I won't tell and neither will you!'

He scratched his head. 'I spose thass so. Old Jubal's down by the Mere. 'Sides, he'd nivver tell.'

'Well then. Sit down and learn me how to bab.'

He was silent. Then he snorted a laugh. 'Give me a reglar turnup you done, an no mistake.'

'I'm sorry.'

He was shaking his head. 'The night's as dark as black hogs an she follows me into the fen! There nivver was a one like you, Miss Maud, thass the truth.'

Her heart leapt. 'Don't call me Miss Maud,' she chided happily. 'Tonight I'm simply Maud.'

The best place for babbing is a stretch of water about four foot deep and as close to the bank as you can find. Eels want a sandy or gravelly bottom with willows on the bank, as they like to clean themselves among the roots that grow in bunches like chimney-sweep brushes.

To make your bab, you take your can of big fat earthworms that you dug up before and that you set to soak in a mess of cowpiss and muck-juice. Then, using a piece of wire that you've filed sharp for a needle, you thread your worms on a yard or so of worsted – it needs to be red, to keep away witches – and you tie the two ends together, coiling your worms into a clump the size of your fist and weighting it with a scrap of lead. And that's your bab.

Next you tie your bab to a piece of strong cord five foot long, and you tie that to a hazel stick about the same length. Now you're ready to go babbing.

You sit yourself down on the bank and dangle your bab in the water, just letting it touch the bottom now and then – but *gently*, so you'll feel when an eel bites. And soon enough it'll bite, and snag its teeth in the wool. That's when you've got to give your stick a good strong swing, to land your eel in the pail you've set ready on the bank.

'Thass the tricky bit,' said Clem, deftly executing this manoeuvre yet again. 'You need just the right swing to land your eel – for as soon as he's out the water he'll get hisself loose of that bab, and if he an't in your pail he'll be back in the dyke quick as a lamplighter. Now you try,' he said when he had five fat black eels squirming in his pail.

Nervously, Maud grasped the hazel stick. 'How will I know if he's biting?'

'You'll feel it. No, hold it in both hands. So.'

'I wish you'd let me prepare my own bab.'

He snorted. 'An get your hands all mucky?'

'Can I do it next time?'

'No. T'aint no manner o' use you arstin.'

'Nothing's happening.'

'Do you have a bit of patience!'

She smiled to hear the smile in his voice.

They sat shoulder to shoulder on the bank, Clem with one hand on the hazel stick, his fingers close but not touching hers. Normally that would have sent Maud into paroxysms of embarrassment over her eczema, but not here in the dark. Clem had washed his hands downstream, so as not to offend her with the stink of cow-dung, but she could still smell it on him. She loved it because it was part of him.

'How many eels do you catch in a night?' she said, scowling with concentration.

'Ten, twenty. Depends how long till the moon's up. When I gets no more bites, I come away home. But if it's warm, then instead of going back up-village I sleeps out here an goes straight to work in the morning.'

'Sleeping in the fen. That must be wonderful.'

'Proper damp it can be, an midges summat awful.'

Something rustled in the reeds. Maud gave a start. 'Did you hear that?'

'Only a hedgepig. Lift it a bit, you're on the bottom.'

'Sorry.' She loved that they'd swapped rôles, and he was the one giving orders.

The breeze had dropped, and a faint white band of mist lay along the dyke.

'I din't rekkinize you with your hair down,' Clem said quietly. 'Thought you was a witch.'

Maud's face grew hot. 'I hate having long hair,' she said abruptly. 'I asked Father if I could have it bobbed. You should've seen his face. "My dear Maud, bobbed hair is unbecoming to a pretty woman; on you it would be hideous."'

Clem made a movement of protest. 'Nivver hidjus! But I don't hold with you cutting it, it's rare pretty.'

Pretty. He said it was pretty.

'Your hair's nice too,' she said shakily. 'It's golden. As if it's made of the sun.'

He'd left off his neck-kerchief and undone the top button of his shirt, and in the gloom she made out the dark column of his throat and the line at the base where the sunburn ended and the paler skin began. Tears pricked her eyes. She fought the urge to press her face to his chest.

In the distance, something shrieked. 'What's *that*?' she whispered.

Clem chuckled. 'Stoat on a coney. We're not the only ones out hunting.'

The mist was rising. Soon it would be above their heads. Maud loved it, she felt as if she was floating. 'What sound do eels make?' she said dreamily.

'They don't. 'Cept on warm wet nights when they're on

the move. If you sits quiet by the dyke, you can hear em in the reeds. Hundreds of em with their heads just above the water, making little soft sucking noises.'

'What does that sound like?'

Bending close to her ear, he made soft rapid smacking noises with his lips. His breath tickled her skin, and she shivered deliciously. 'Now you try.'

She tried, then broke off with a giggle. She saw the glint of his teeth, very close. She stopped smiling. Suddenly their lips were touching, brushing, pressing against each other. Maud had never felt anything so wonderful as his mouth. Dropping the hazel stick, she put her arms around his neck. She felt his arms about her waist, holding her against his chest. She was making little high mewing noises as if she was crying – only she wasn't, she was the happiest she'd ever been. She wasn't embarrassed or awkward, she had never felt so confident or so sure.

Clem's arms tightened about her so that she couldn't breathe, and for a moment she was frightened.

But only for a moment.

Twenty-six

From the Private Notebook of Edmund Stearne
25th July 1912

This morning I had an idea which frightened me.

I was in church, musing on something Miss Broadstairs had put into my mind. She has recently conceived an interest in matters Anglo-Saxon, particularly in 'our own dear St Guthlaf'. As I was making my way into the porch she babbled something about a 'patronal feast' which she is planning for his 'saint's day', complete with 'wake pudding' and other folkloric delights.

That reminded me of the volume which Hibble sent in error last month. It's a translation of *The Life of St Guthlaf*; I think I read it years ago at Cambridge, but haven't since. A few weeks ago when I found it in my parcel of books I glanced through it and was disagreeably struck by certain parallels that suggested themselves. However, I put the volume aside and gave it no further thought until this morning, when I was reminded of it by the wretched Miss B. I couldn't concentrate on the service. My thoughts kept returning to *The Life of St Guthlaf*. I kept remembering that St Guthlaf had been plagued by demons.

Involuntarily my gaze drifted upwards to the grotesques on the corbels, and I was startled to notice something I never have before. They all possess rather similar physiognomies, with repulsive toad-like mouths and bulging eyes. What struck me even more forcibly was that it is the very same physiognomy as the devil in the Doom.

Of course, I soon realised *why* this should be. It's because the men who carved these grotesques and the man who painted the Doom were all local artisans, and since they doubtless shared the unoriginal turn of mind common to men in that station of life, they naturally imitated each other's work.

It's obvious when one thinks about it, and I'm annoyed that I should have allowed such a trifling coincidence to unsettle me. My nerves must be a touch disordered. I shall ask old Grayson for a tonic.

26th July

I wish I knew *why* the Doom alarms me so. I haven't set eyes on it since it was unveiled, but I can't seem to forget it. I keep telling myself that *it is only a picture. It can't do me any harm.*

I also wish I hadn't conceived that ridiculous notion about the carvings on the corbels. Try as I might to concentrate on my prayers, my thoughts keep returning to them. The more I force myself not to look at them, the more I feel compelled to do so. The worst of it is that I can't rid myself of the impression that, like the devil in the Doom, they are all looking at me.

27th July

This morning Ivy gave me some rather unpleasant news. I confess I was shaken, although I quickly surmised that the little chit might be lying, and her news merely a clumsy ruse to achieve her ends.

Even if it does turn out to be true, it is most definitely *not*, as she seems to imagine, a reason for me to make her mistress of Wake's End! There are other ways of dealing with such annoyances.

1st August

I've been foolish. I should have left well alone. For days I've been plagued with nagging doubts: do those grotesques really share the same features as the devil in the Doom, or am I imagining it? This afternoon I could bear it no longer, so I obtained the key from the rector and went to find out.

I hadn't been in the room in the tower since the night the Doom was unveiled, and to my relief, the feeling of the place was completely different. Instead of flickering gas-jets and leaping shadows, I was greeted with cheerful yellow sunlight streaming through the window. Moreover, in the same way that bright light betrays every flaw in a woman's complexion, so the sun revealed the Doom for what it really is: a rustic daub amateurishly painted on rough wooden planks.

Having no wish to prolong the encounter, I stayed only a moment. It was long enough, however, for the sky to cloud over and the light to change. In an instant the brightness dimmed to a peculiar, unhealthy grey, very lowering to the spirits.

The devil in the corner does indeed share the same loathsome physiognomy as his fellows on the ceiling. As I left the room, he leered at me and I almost fancied that he winked, actually winked. *I know what you did*, he seemed to say.

Which simply shows that old G.'s nerve tonic hasn't yet taken effect. Perhaps a dose of laudanum will help it along.

The thing to remember is that now I know the worst. I know that the devil in the corner looks the same as those on the ceiling. Therefore I can stop thinking about that wretched painting. I never have to look at it again.

2nd August

Miss B.'s 'patronal feast' has been and gone, *Deo gratias*. She insisted on holding it in the nave and even strewed rushes on the floor to evoke an 'Anglo-Saxon feel'. I was struck by the disagreeably musty smell that the rushes produced. It felt as if the fen had found its way in.

Maud was sulky and her eyelids were swollen and pink; whether from a head-cold or from weeping over some girlish drama, I neither know nor care. Although I hope it isn't a cold, as I shouldn't like Felix to fall ill. The boy is a pretty, biddable child, if a thought too plump and not as bright as I would have wished. Sometimes I wonder at the fact that neither of my sons possesses half Maud's intelligence. It's such a waste.

4th August

Miss B.'s rushes have been swept from the nave, but the mustiness persists. Of course the weather has been fearfully damp, so the smell must be due to a leak somewhere; although when I raised this with Farrow he denied it indignantly.

'But my hassock feels damp,' I insisted, pointing to the offending article in my pew. 'How do you account for that?' He shook his jowls and insisted that there was no damp in his church, &c &c. The man's a fool. Does he think I imagined it?

10th August
An odd thing happened this afternoon.

I was taking my usual stroll in the grounds and had reached the lawn outside my study, near where the yew hedge meets the Lode. I was observing the effect of cloud-shadow on the church tower in the distance when I distinctly heard a faint splash behind me. On turning, I saw nothing – except that the reeds on the other side of the Lode were stirring, as from the passing of some creature of the fen. Normally I would have dismissed this as an effect of the wind – only there was no wind. And I distinctly felt *watched*.

That's not such an uncommon feeling when one is outside, so I shrugged it off and strolled to the kitchen garden for a word with Cole. The old fellow is growing very bent, and complains frequently of his 'rheumatics'. He gave me to understand that he wouldn't object to being put out to pasture, as he has a daughter in Bury who is willing to take him in. He thinks highly of young Walker, and believes the lad quite capable of assuming the rôle of head gardener.

It's not such a bad idea. I like Walker. He's quiet and respectful, with an agreeable demeanour. It strikes me that he might be able to help me in that other matter.

16th August
I'm still conscious of that staring from the fen. I can't shake off the feeling that something has been *let loose* – and that it's out there now, biding its time. Waiting to come in.

What do I mean by 'something'? I haven't the least idea. Nor do I know where 'it' has been released *from*; or why 'it' should wish to enter the house. It's merely one of those unpleasantly vague feelings that one has sometimes and which can be so difficult to dislodge, precisely *because* they are so vague. It's rather like the experience of worrying about something when one is half-awake: no matter how often one reasons away one's disquiet, it always seeps back.

25th August
Has Ivy been lying about her news, or is she telling the truth? She has definitely put on more flesh. If by some ill chance she is indeed gravid, it would be the most confounded nuisance. No, I must face facts, it would be worse than that. The servants would learn of it, then the whole parish. I can't have a scandal. I won't have it. *I won't have it.*

But there is no need for concern. If the worst turns out to be true, then she must apply to her aunt Biddy Thrussel and they must take measures to get rid of it. Should that fail, I shall put into effect the idea I had after my talk with Cole. Yes. One way or another, there is no need for concern.

5th September

Still very conscious of that staring from the fen. It's strongest when I return from church. It makes me almost dread walking home.

Tonight after evensong I decided that enough was enough, so I told Maud that I wished to take a turn about the grounds alone, then marched through the orchard to the Lode. What a ridiculous sight I must have presented, standing on the bank with my hands on my hips, defying – what, precisely? The shadowy willows and the reeds tossing in the wind?

On turning to go inside, I was struck by the contorted forms of the apple trees. They looked for all the world as if they'd been playing some trick behind my back, and had only just fallen still.

Unaccountably, I also experienced a profound reluctance to pass near the well. I used to feel the same thing when I was a boy. I used to avoid peering into it, for I dreaded seeing my reflection in the water. For the same reason, I used to go to great lengths to avoid catching sight of myself in looking-glasses, particularly at night. Although that wasn't quite for the same reason. In the case of looking-glasses, I had the usual childish fear that I might glimpse some monster behind me.

In the case of the well, what I dreaded was something reaching up from that filthy black water and dragging me down.

Twenty-seven

13th September

The nights are beginning to draw in. Pyett is yielding more riches than I ever dared hope, and each day I'm impatient to reach my desk – although annoyingly, ideas for my exegesis remain elusive. I daresay I am too distracted to marshal my thoughts. It is vexing that I should be afflicted with this – what shall I call it? Oppression? Malaise?

For days I've told myself that it's simply the onset of autumn. I have suffered similar attacks in the past, but this year it's different. I no longer feel watched when I'm in the grounds or walking to and from church; now I feel it when I'm *inside* the house. I'm plagued by the irrational conviction that there is something outside, peering in at me through the windows. It's particularly strong in my study. When I'm at my desk I can't refrain from glancing to my left, at the carriage-drive; or over my shoulder at the lawn and the Lode beyond. I rarely feel it in the other rooms except in my bedroom, where it's strongest of all. I have the oddest feeling that I need to keep an eye on one particular window, the left-hand of the pair that overlooks the fen. There's never anything to be seen, only dreary willows overhanging the Lode and in the distance the reedy blur of the Mere. Yet I feel compelled to keep watch.

Though it shames me to confess, I probably glance out of that window a dozen times a day. It's the first thing I do when I wake and the last before I retire. I keep myself in check when I'm with Ivy, otherwise Heaven knows how she'd use it against me; but I allow myself more latitude with Steers. The other evening as he was helping me dress I found myself inventing pretexts to keep him with me. I mustn't do that again. I can't let the servants suspect anything amiss.

Brandy helps, as does old G's tonic. I daresay he's right and I've been over-doing my work on Pyett. This is nothing that a few days' rest won't set right.

But that's just it, I'm not sleeping well. I keep waking and lighting my candle to check the window – although I've no idea what it is that I think I might see. It's the waiting I don't like. This dreadful sense of anticipation focused on that window. This fear of what will happen next.

16th September

This unrelenting rain is playing havoc with my nerves. For days the house has echoed with trickling, dripping and gurgling. Draperies feel damp, my books are soft to the touch. Everything smells of mould. The windows admit a dim green subaqueous glimmer that sets my teeth on edge.

I insist on fires in every room, although it's not nearly cold enough to warrant them; and yet nothing dispels this infernal damp. Small wonder that I'm sleeping badly. I shall double my usual dose of laudanum until the weather improves.

Later
Woken by a high thin cry on the fen. It sounded like something hunting. No otter or stoat makes such a sound. The only birds that scream like that are swifts, but they've long since flown south. Besides, whatever made that cry was hunting at night.

17th September
I can't rid myself of the feeling that it's coming closer. But what do I mean by 'it'?

Again I was woken in the night, although whether by that cry or something else I couldn't tell. Half-asleep, I lay watching the curtains blowing in the breeze. Then I started awake, for the window was open. It *couldn't* be, I'd checked it ten times before retiring. And yet I heard the rustle of plush curtains, and despite the darkness I saw how they billowed. Then as I fumbled to light my candle, the rustling abruptly ceased. In the flare of my match I saw the curtains hanging motionless. They'd stopped moving so very suddenly, as if hands had grasped them and yanked them still.

Once my candle was lit, I cast about but found nothing out of place. I felt the night breeze on my face, and turning, I saw the curtains stir a little, sucking faintly in and out – almost *mockingly*, in a manner I found rather hard to bear. Getting out of bed, I crossed to the window with my candle. I opened the curtains and raised the blind. And of course there was nothing there. No malevolent web-footed creature peering in.

With a shrug I drew down the sash and made to draw the blind – and that was when I saw something lying on the sill. My first horrified thought was that it was a lock of hair, for it was long and thin and glistened in the candlelight. Intending to fling it out into the garden, I picked it up – and nearly shouted in disgust. It was a strand of waterweed: slimy and soft, like drowned skin. In my revulsion, I had let the thing fall, but now, with a grimace, I picked it off the sill between finger and thumb and flung it into the darkness. My fingers smelled of rotting vegetation. When I wiped them on my nightshirt, they left a greenish-black smear.

I wish I hadn't touched that thing. But I couldn't leave it on the sill. I could not have endured that.

18th September

Edmund, Edmund, this foolishness must stop! 'Drowned skin', indeed! Someone has been playing tricks on you – and that someone shall be punished.

This evening I returned from my bath to a distinct awareness of something amiss in my room. One glance established that my limmell stone wasn't hanging in its place on the bedpost, but had been laid on the rug in front of the window.

After the initial jolt, I was merely irked. Who would have played such a prank? Certainly none of the servants; and Maud wouldn't have dared, not after that episode when she was a child. Who else is left? Answer: Ivy.

I've decided not to have it out with her. I shall pretend it never happened. If she thinks she can unsettle me by such ploys and thereby become mistress of Wake's End, she is sadly mistaken.

First she said she was gravid. Then, when she saw that that wouldn't work, she told me she'd got rid of it by means of the wisewoman's potion. I suspect she was lying about the whole thing, for her belly never mounded. She concocted this farrago in order to threaten me with scandal and thereby coerce me into marriage.

Whether I am right, or whether she did indeed succeed in ridding herself of a genuine inconvenience, I intend to ensure that I can never again be exposed to such a threat. I shall see to it that the chit is married off. Then, were she ever to fall pregnant, there could be no breath of scandal.

19th September

The awful thing is that I'm not entirely convinced that what just happened was a dream.

I was woken in the middle of the night. This time it wasn't a cry from the fen. It was the certain knowledge that there was something in the house.

I lay on my back in the darkness, striving to calm my racing heart. For an age I lay listening. I heard rain gurgling in the gutters and pattering against the windowpanes. The room smelled musty, with an odd, sulphurous tang that reminded me of marsh gas.

At last the noise came again. It was outside in the passage: the click of claws. My door wasn't locked, and I knew that its old-fashioned iron latch would prove no obstacle. I longed to grasp my limmell stone for protection but I couldn't move, my body would not obey my brain. I could only lie rigid, listening to the thing coming closer. It moved awkwardly, lurching and brushing against the wall, very low to the ground. Nearer and nearer it came, with a stealthy yet unhurried purpose that I found indescribably horrifying.

Suddenly, the noises stopped. It was outside my door. In the stillness I heard the drip, drip of water. The sound wasn't coming from the gutters, it was inside, in the passage.

Something touched my door: a soft, furtive pressure that made it creak. Then I heard a single harsh breath, violently expelled.

I don't know what happened next. I only know that I woke long after my usual hour in a sweaty tangle of bedclothes.

I *must* stop the laudanum for the next few days. I can't endure another dream like that. I've also arranged for sturdy locks to be fitted on the doors. That ought to help.

24th September
What happened the other night was no dream. I know that now. It comes out of the fen at night and it has found its way in.

This evening shortly after I'd retired to bed, I heard a noise downstairs. This time I wasn't alarmed, I was outraged. This is *my* house, I wanted to shout. In the name of Christ, be gone!

With my lamp in one hand and my crucifix and limmell stone in the other, I went out into the passage and strode to the top of the stairs. I halted. Something was on the bottom step. I didn't *see* it so much as perceive it with the perception one has in a dream, when one is aware of something without the aid of sight. But I did perceive it, and I knew that I was fully awake. I smelled the oil in my lamp and the sulphurous odour of marsh gas. I felt a chill draught around my naked ankles. I saw the shadowy form at the foot of the stairs begin to crawl towards me. Two eyes stared up at me. They blinked out. My knees buckled. My lamplight rocked wildly. By the time I'd steadied myself on the banister, the thing was gone.

I can't write any more. I shall take whatever I need to put me to sleep and pray God that I have no more dreams.

25th September

How differently things appear in the morning after a hot bath and an excellent breakfast! I have enjoyed a highly productive day and achieved a very great deal. There's nothing like analysing the situation and taking control to improve one's spirits. I feel completely restored.

To put the matter plainly, the question before me is this: Am I to be a target in my own house? Answer: No, a thousand times no. There is no *need* to endure this outrage, it *must* and it *shall* be brought to an end *forthwith*. I have the power and the means to make whatever changes I desire to my own property, and today I took the first step. I have always disliked the fen. It is unsightly, unpleasant and unhygienic, nothing more than a source of damp and disease.

Why should I cower in my bedroom because some water rat has taken to frequenting the house by night, no doubt seeking scraps left lying about by negligent servants? Well, the creature shall frequent my house *no more*. I've had Walker set traps in every room, and he is outside now, doing the same in the grounds.

But that's only the start. I need a more lasting solution, and this morning I embarked on precisely that. Directly after breakfast I called on Lord Clevedon, from whom I obtained the name of the engineer who recently drained one of his pastures. Providentially, the fellow was still in the neighbourhood and I interviewed him this very afternoon. His name is Davies and I found him greatly to my liking: pragmatic, plain-spoken, and with thirty years' experience of managing marshlands. He assured me that my plan is eminently feasible and I retained him on the spot. I've paid him a premium to implement my orders as a matter of urgency, and tomorrow he begins his survey, with a view to drawing up plans to drain the fen.

Twenty-eight

'BUT Father, you can't drain the fen!'

'Kindly moderate your tone, Maud, I won't have you screeching like a fish-wife. Nor will I have you telling me what I can and cannot do. When I last inspected the title deeds, the fen was mine. I rather think I may do with it as I please.'

'I'm sorry, Father.' Maud set the teapot on the tray and clasped her hands in her lap.

She had learned of his plans by reading his notebook the previous night, while he was taking his bath. All through dinner she'd been forced to pretend that she didn't know. She'd hardly slept. The day had passed in a daze. Father had only mentioned his plans now over tea: casually, as she handed him his cup.

'Please, *please* don't do this,' she said.

He stared at her. 'Why should I change my mind?'

Because I love the fen! she wanted to shout. Because it's the only place where I've ever felt happy and free. But he would look at her with those glacial blue eyes and ignore her objections as over-emotional and female.

She tried another tack. 'This house was built on the fen. Without the fen its whole character would be ruined—'

'I hadn't appreciated that you were interested in aesthetics,' he said drily.

'It would also cause great hardship in the village. They depend on the fen for waterfowl and fish—'

'Nonsense, they prefer North Fen as you well know.'

'Not Jubal. The fen is his home!'

'Then he must find another. Jubal Rede is a drunken wastrel who's never done an honest day's work in his life. He should be thankful I've tolerated him as long as I have.'

Maud watched him stir his tea. He gave his spoon a little shake, then laid it noiselessly in his saucer. 'What about the Mere?' she said quietly. 'Do you intend to drain that too?'

His lips tightened. 'I gather that will be harder, but by no means impossible.'

Yes, that's what you really want, she thought savagely. The Mere reminds you of your sin. You want it to disappear. Then you can pretend that what you did never happened.

This is my fault, thought Maud as she stood in her bedroom gazing out at the fen. I started it by putting that eel in his washbasin. Stupid, *stupid*. Everything you do goes wrong.

Rain beat against the panes, and below her on the path Clem ran to the back door with his jacket over his head. It was three months since Midsummer's Night and he'd hardly said two words to her – apart from the next day

when she'd found him in the glass-house. He'd pretended
he hadn't seen her and slipped away. When she'd tracked
him down he'd gone scarlet and stammered an apology.

'*Sorry?*' she'd cried. 'What have you got to be *sorry* for?'
It had taken her days to realise that he was frightened of
losing his place and wanted nothing more to do with her.

And now he was going to marry Ivy. Well of course he
was. What man could resist those dimples and that figure?

He and Ivy were keeping it secret from the other servants
for now, but Ivy had made sure that Maud knew. She had
found Maud in the library and 'let slip' her news.

Somehow Maud had maintained her composure. Ivy had
caught that lip of hers between her teeth and looked at her.
'You'll never get him now,' she'd said in a low voice.

Maud didn't reply.

With her hands on her hips Ivy glanced about her and
tossed her head. 'All these books. Where'd they get you, eh?
You can wait till Doomsday in the arternoon, you'll never
get Clem.'

'And you don't even want him,' said Maud, her heart
fluttering in her chest. 'You don't want Father either. What
you want is this house.' It gave her a sick satisfaction to see
Ivy's eyes widen.

'But Wake's End doesn't want you,' Maud went on. 'Do
you have any idea how old it is? It was a priory in Saxon
times. Then in Tudor times one of my ancestors rebuilt
it. But you don't know what I'm talking about – because
you're nothing. You come from the gutter. That's where
you'll end up.'

'You can't get rid of me,' muttered Ivy.

'Go about your work,' Maud said shakily.

She managed to keep her countenance until the house-maid had gone. Then she fled to her room.

Ivy was going to marry Clem.

'Well what did you expect?' Maud snarled at herself in the looking-glass. 'What man *wouldn't* choose her over you?'

In an agony of self-loathing she pictured Clem smiling down at the housemaid as he murmured the love charm: 'Ivy, ivy, I pluck thee. In my bosom I lay thee.' Then he would kiss her. And afterwards he would sheepishly confess that one summer's night, Miss Maud had followed him into the fen and he'd lost his head and given her a kiss. How they would laugh about that together! Poor ugly Miss Maud, whimpering and mewing with gratitude in his arms.

How could she have deluded herself into believing that he cared for her? Such things didn't occur except in books. *Pride and Prejudice, Jane Eyre…* They were merely stories. Stories written by plain single women consoling themselves by inventing handsome heroes who fell in love with plain single women – because in real life that didn't happen.

'*Stupid!*' cried Maud, clawing the scaly skin on the back of her hand.

She had prayed to the fen to punish Father, but instead it was the fen that was being punished. The truth was, the fen had no power. It was simply a beautiful reedy wilderness, and soon it would no longer exist.

She ripped a patch of skin off her forearm. Good, let it bleed. She dug in her fingernails. The pain was like snow settling in her mind, turning her thoughts white.

From *The Book of Alice Pyett,*
transl. & exegesis by E.A.M. Stearne

After this creature had been threatened with burning, she
spoke no more of the Gospel. And she began to fear that
what people said was true, and that she had been deceived
by an evil spirit, so that all her visions and cryings came not
from God, but from the Devil.

At that time there were many disturbances in the parish.
Cattle were afflicted by the murrain, and people fell ill with
the ague, and were much affrighted by the thing that cries
in the night. It was said that these disturbances were the
work of an evil spirit, and that some person in the parish
must be possessed. And many said that this creature was
the one who was possessed.

Even her eldest son said so. He related how one day
she had told him sharply to desist from lechery, and how
the next day he had fallen ill with the pox, so that his face
became full of pustules. And he said this was proof that
this creature had an evil spirit in her and had caused him
to fall ill.

To drive the Devil out of her, the people put hot irons
to her head and made her stand in the river in winter, and
other things that caused her much suffering. But still the
troubles in the parish went on. Then this creature cried to
our Lord: 'Lord, show me that you are truly God, and not
some evil spirit who has led me astray all these years. Show
me that these visions and cryings are not the Devil's gift.'

Then Jesus came to her and said: 'Daughter, be not

afraid, for these gifts are not the Devil's but my own. And know that those people who work against you also work against me. For your tears are to the angels as spiced and honeyed wine, and your sufferings have earned you most high reward in heaven.'

From the Private Notebook of Edmund Stearne
1st October
By George, the old saying is true: God does indeed move in mysterious ways. Pyett prayed for grace and it was granted to her. I also prayed for grace, but it has taken me a while to perceive that it has been granted to me too.

Last month I was in turmoil. First I mistakenly thought I was saved, because I'd remembered my sin; but my turmoil continued – the nightmares, the staring from the fen, the waterweed – and now I know why. Pyett has helped me see that *the turmoil came from God.* It was His way of telling me that I must atone for my sin.

But *how* must I to atone? I'm not a Catholic, I can't make confession; nor would God wish me to. No, the answer is subtler and more suited to my sin. It was *God* who put into my mind the idea of draining the fen. That is why I felt such peace the moment I decided to do it. That is why I've been at peace ever since.

Draining the fen will cost a great deal of money and it will take up my time and therefore hinder my work. I've had to instruct my attorney to resolve the uncertainty over the boundary with North Fen, and Davies tells me that I may not expect to see the land drained before next summer. *But none of this matters!* My decision to drain the fen has been made: *that* is the point. *All these obstacles are merely part of my penance.*

'I'm sorry,' Maud told the fen. 'I'm sorry I couldn't save you. Or Chatterpie. Or Maman.'

It was a dead, windless day and the Mere was the colour of lead. The sky was as grey as tears. Maud had stopped crying. She knelt in the reeds at the water's edge, hugging herself and rocking back and forth. She felt exhausted and fragile, as if she was made of glass.

By next summer, all trace of the fen would be gone. No more frogs and otters and owls. No more geese flying overhead in great beating phalanxes of wings. No more shimmering reedbeds and emerald dragonflies. No more vast, wavering visitations of starlings.

Father was at peace because he was doing penance for his sin. And how very convenient, she thought, that his penance should require no confession. No one need ever know what he had done.

The water was shockingly cold when she plunged in her hands. She watched the blood lift from her fingers and float away. She rinsed her bloodstained handkerchief. Her courses had started unexpectedly as she was heading for the Mere. A blood sacrifice, she thought wryly. A ritual farewell to the fen.

Something nudged her in the back and she turned to

see Nellie wagging her tail. Jubal stood a few paces off, scowling at Maud. He wore his usual wrappings of grimy sacking, but he'd tied a grubby square of canvas about his shoulders to keep out the cold.

'You've heard about the fen,' said Maud.

He nodded. 'You mun't let en do it.'

'I can't stop him, Jubal. He thinks it's God's will.'

Jubal spat a stream of tobacco juice at the reeds. 'Well, I got summat to tell you thass nought to do with God.'

Slowly, she rose to her feet. 'It's about what happened when he was a boy. That's it, isn't it?'

His small black eyes narrowed. 'If I tell, you'll stop en draining the fen.'

'Jubal I can't—'

'He'll not want folks knowing. He'll keep it hid no matter what.'

She licked her lips. 'I think I know – at least, I suspect – that a woman drowned here a long time ago. That's true, isn't it?'

He hesitated. 'There wor a drownding, thass true enough. But it wun't no woman.'

'Who was it? What did Father have to do with it? Do you know what happened?'

He squinted up at the sky. 'Oh, I know all right,' he muttered. 'I wor there.'

Twenty-nine

*F*ATHER had had a sister who died when she was little. That was what Maman told Maud one Sunday when she'd asked about the name on the family tomb. It was the only time Maud had heard Lily mentioned and she'd soon forgotten her. She had enough dead brothers and sisters of her own.

According to Jubal, Miss Lily had been two years younger than her brother, although you'd never have known it. Proper little tartar, she was. Once when Master Eddie hid her beetle collection she chased him round the orchard with a warming-pan till he promised to give it back.

Master Eddie took after his mother. He loved drawing and listening to stories. Miss Lily was the image of her father, old Master Algernon. She always wanted to find out how things worked, and all about wild creatures and their ways. Master Algernon used to take them into the fen for what he called 'nature rambles', and it was always Miss Lily demanding to know the name of every flower and animal and bird. That sort of thing bored Master Eddie. He only cared for fairytales.

That's how it happened. It was the summer when Master Eddie turned twelve; Miss Lily would have been ten. It was July, and hot as hell, the smell of meadowsweet as thick as treacle, the swifts screaming overhead. The air was fairly crackling with that breathless feeling you get when it's coming on to storm.

The nature ramble was over and Master Algernon had gone back to the big house, leaving Master Eddie and Miss Lily playing in the fen. He often let them do that and they never come to no harm. Now he just told them not to stray and to be sure and be home for tea. That was the last time he saw his daughter alive.

What he didn't know was that Master Eddie had taken a fancy to acting out some old tale from up the Sheres about a soldier named Percy-something who rescues a princess from a dragon. At first Miss Lily had no liking for it, but Master Eddie kept on at her so in the end she said yes, *provided* he gave her his shut-knife with the tortoiseshell handle.

By this time they'd fetched up at the Mere. That's where Jubal saw them. They didn't see him, though, he made sure of that. He was only a lad himself and he'd been set to singling beets in the fields, but instead he'd run off to the fen to go after pike. He didn't want Master Eddie telling on him or he'd get the strap. That's why he stayed hid.

At first Master Eddie was scared of the Mere. 'Stay where I can see you,' he told his sister.

She laughed at him. 'Oh Eddie you're such a coward! Ferishes don't exist!'

He scowled at her, but soon cheered up when he found an old rotten rowboat stuck in the reeds. 'Pretend the Mere is the sea,' he told his sister. 'Pretend this boat is the rock they chain her to. In you get and I'll tie you up.'

'You first,' she retorted. 'You're heavier than me, I want to be sure it doesn't leak.' She was no fool, was Miss Lily.

Master Eddie made a fuss, but there was no budging her, so in he climbed and checked the boat for leaks. He said it was fine. That was his first mistake.

He started badgering his sister to take off her clothes like the princess in the story. Miss Lily grumbled about midges, but now she was getting keen on the game too, so she told Master Eddie to turn his back and she started unbuttoning her frock. Jubal didn't look either. He liked Miss Lily. She would have taken on something awful if she'd caught him peeping.

Next thing he knew she was sitting in the boat with her hair hanging loose around her. Rare pretty it looked, yellow as a guinea and all crinkly from her plaits.

After that she laid herself down in the boat and Master Eddie tied her wrists to the oar-locks with her hair ribbons, so that she'd be like the princess in the story who was chained to the rock. From where Jubal hid in the reeds, all he could see were her little pink fingers poking up. He could hear her, though, complaining about the scratch she'd got on her leg as she'd climbed in. 'And if I get splinters it'll be *your fault*,' she warned Master Eddie. 'And make sure you tie the boat to that stump *before* you push it clear of the reeds.'

'Don't be so bossy!' he snapped. 'Now be quiet, you're supposed to be terrified.'

He wanted to pretend that the oar was his spear and use it to fight the dragon, but the oar was too heavy, so off he ran to look for a stick. That's what killed her. Either he hadn't tied the knot aright, or else the rope was rotten through, but the next thing anyone knew, the boat was drifting out towards the middle of the Mere and Miss Lily was in a rage and shouting for help.

Jubal made to go after her, but Master Eddie came running, so he ducked down again.

'Edmund you *idiot*!' Miss Lily was yelling. 'I *told* you to tie it to the *stump*!'

'I jolly well *did*!' panted Master Eddie. He was doing his damnedest to reach the boat with the oar, but he only succeeded in pushing it further out. And by now the wind was coming up and it was getting on to rain.

Master Eddie threw down the oar and stood with his hands on his hips. It was no use wading after her, she was too far out and the Mere was too deep. Besides, he couldn't swim. None of them could.

'Run and *fetch* someone!' ordered Miss Lily.

'I *can't*!' yelled Master Eddie. 'They'll see you with no clothes on and I'll get thrashed!'

'Don't be such a *muff*, Eddie, that can't be helped! Run and fetch someone *right now*, I'm getting cold!'

All Jubal could see of her was her little clenched fists. But now and then the boat would rock as she twisted up and tried to bite through the ribbon round her wrists; and then he would see the top of her golden head.

All this time Master Eddie had been standing wringing his hands at the water's edge. Jubal made to leap to his feet and run for help, but just then Master Eddie spun round with a cry. White as a sheet he were, as if he'd seen Black Shuck himself, so Jubal panicked and ducked down again. And now Master Eddie was off like a hare up the path to the big house, and Jubal was proper relieved, for he knew it wouldn't be long before the men came and rescued Miss Lily.

He dursn't shout out to her but he waited in the reeds while the sky turned black and the rain came lashing down and the boat drifted into the middle of the Mere. He grew frightened. If they found him here they'd ask what he was doing skulking in the reeds and Miss Lily out there with no clothes on. He'd be in the worst trouble in all his life. So he panicked and ran along home as fast as he could. Besides, it wouldn't be long before Master Eddie came back and brought help.

At that time Jubal was still living up-village. That night he got the strap for going fishing instead of singling beets and next day they set him to stone-picking in the corner field. It was only around owl's light that he was able to make his way to the fen.

What was his shock when he saw three men dredging the Lode with glaves.

He asked what they was about, and they told him that Miss Lily had missed her way among the dykes and never come home. 'We been out all night dragging the ditches,' they said.

At that Jubal sweated cold. 'What about Master Eddie,' he said, careful not to reveal what he knew. 'Don't he know nothing about where she is?'

'That's just it,' said the men. 'Seems they was playing at hide-and-seek and Miss Lily ran and hid, and Master Eddie couldn't find her. Proper state he were in when he fetched up at the big house.'

Jubal was in a proper state too. He thought about telling the men to go and look in the Mere – but then they'd ask how he knew, and what could he say? So instead he made shift to run away.

He ran all the way to the Mere, and there he found no sign of Miss Lily or the boat. He searched the reeds all around, but it was no use.

He told himself that Master Eddie was bound to lead them to the Mere. But Master Eddie never did. Master Eddie kept as quiet as the grave.

Why didn't Master Eddie say nothing about it? Many a bitter hour Jubal have wondered about that. He can only think that at first Master Eddie panicked, fearing that Miss Lily would tell on him about the tying up and making her take off her clothes, and he couldn't have borne the thrashing and the shame. And maybe there did come a time when he wanted to speak, but by then it was too late.

It was three days before they found her. Morning and night Jubal went and searched the Mere, and on the third day just after dawn he sees two men in a punt, pulling at something with boat-hooks: something grey that rolls over when they touch it. He sees a slick of fair hair floating on the surface. But that's all he sees, for he takes to his heels and runs as fast as he can lay feet to ground. And all his days he have remembered that grey thing rolling, and that fair hair floating in the water.

Later, he heard it newsed about that they found her clothes on the bank, and they reckoned she'd gone in for a bathe. They never found no trace of the boat. It must have sunk and been swallowed up by the mud. Jubal guessed that she must have bitten through those ribbons that tied her to the oar-locks; but if any trace of ribbons was found round her wrists, no one ever said. Or maybe the ribbons were gone. Maybe the eels ate them, as they ate her away from the inside.

Miss Lily have been dead this thirty year and more, but all his life Jubal have blamed himself. He should have spoken out when there was still time and she could have been saved.

The summer after she died he was set to work as boot-boy up at the big house. But Miss Lily lay uppermost in his mind, so after a twelvemonth he ran away to the fen. He's been here ever since.

Most people dursn't go into the fen by night, for fear of ferishes and whatnot; but Jubal knows that's moonshine. He knows there are worse things that haunt the fen. And in summer, at owl's light, when the smell of meadowsweet is choking thick and the swifts are screaming in the sky, those screams get inside his head and it's Miss Lily screaming for help. Then Jubal makes sure to have a thick plug of bacca always about him and a flask of good strong poppyhead tea, the stronger the better.

But it's never strong enough to stop the screaming in his head.

Thirty

From The Book of Alice Pyett,
transl. & exegesis by E.A.M. Stearne

This creature was greatly comforted to learn that her visions came not from the Devil, but from God. However, as the parish continued to be plagued by sickness and by the thing that cries in the night, many people still believed that she was possessed.

So at Martinmas this creature again spoke to God in her head, and God said: Did I not assure you that these disturbances are in no wise your fault? Know that I have caused a carter of your parish to be possessed by an evil spirit, for I wish to chastise the people, as I sometimes burn their houses with lightning in order to frighten them, so that they might fear me.

Then this creature told her husband, and he, wishing to save her from the people's false blame, paid twelvepence for a new candlebeam in Wakenhyrst Church, and threepence to the priest for certain prayers to be said over the carter who was possessed. And after that the evil spirit plagued the parish no more.

The next year this creature felt a great longing to go on pilgrimage for her soul's health. Her husband gave her permission to go, so she went on pilgrimage to North Marston, then to York, Canterbury, Santiago and Rome. And she was gone many years.

During all that time her cryings continued, so that her fellow pilgrims scorned and avoided her. But this creature welcomed her sufferings, knowing that they proved Jesus' special love for her; and if any day came when she was not scorned or insulted, she would be very gloomy in her thoughts.

And now that old age has come upon this creature, she has paid a friar to write down her tribulations in this her book. And she hopes that when people read it they will be encouraged not to resent their troubles, but to thank God meekly for them, knowing that their patience will be rewarded in Heaven. And everything in this book is true. And people should believe the words of this creature, for they are the words of God.

'Wakenhyrst?' exclaimed Maud. 'But I thought Pyett lived in Bury.'

'She did,' Father said irritably. 'Until her husband bought the mill off Prickwillow Road.'

'So – they would have worshipped in St Guthlaf's?'

'Well of course.'

She thought about that. '"Candlebeam", isn't that an old Suffolk word? I think I read somewhere that it means the panel on which the crucifix is mounted.'

'What if it does?'

'Well then perhaps the new candlebeam to which Pyett refers, that her husband paid for – perhaps that's our very own Doom.'

A muscle twitched beneath his eye. 'Jumping to conclusions is the mark of an undisciplined mind, Maud.'

'Yes, Father. Although the timing does fit. Doesn't it?'

But he was already heading back to his study.

A hit, Maud thought, a palpable hit. It gave her a grim satisfaction to mention the Doom whenever she could, and watch her father flinch. Any opportunity to disturb his God-given peace.

Loading a sheet of paper in her typewriter, she began to type.

All these years he had acted as if he was God. Quoting the Bible, setting the rules at Wake's End. And he had left his own sister to drown.

It was nearly three months since Jubal had told her. Now when she looked at Father, she saw a different man from the one she had grown up fearing and loving. Others might excuse what he had done as the tragic blunder of a terrified boy. Not Maud. 'Master Eddie' had been twelve years old: only three years younger than she was. If she had been in the same position with Richard or Felix, she wouldn't have run off and abandoned them merely to avoid a thrashing.

And he'd had plenty of time to remedy his mistake. According to Jubal, while the men had been searching for

Lily, the cook had fed Master Eddie jam tarts in the kitchen. Then his nurse had put him to bed, and next morning he'd had his breakfast and sat down to lessons with his governess. At any time he could have told them where to find Lily, but he'd chosen not to. He had never owned up. And now he thought he could atone for his sin simply by draining the fen.

'And people should believe the words of this creature,' typed Maud. 'For they are the words of God.'

Christmas was two days away. At morning prayers Father had been reading St Matthew's Nativity. He read beautifully and he looked a pillar of rectitude: handsome and immaculately groomed, utterly in control. For years he had concealed his sin, and he meant to go on concealing it. That was what Maud couldn't forgive. She was angry with him for disappointing her. She had always looked up to him, even after she'd learned to hate him; but now she couldn't look up to him any more. Because he was a coward.

And now she had this burden of knowledge. She didn't know what to do with it. Three times since Jubal had told her he had sought her out again, wanting to know if she'd confronted the Master and got him to stop draining the fen. Jubal thought it would be easy. He thought that if they so much as threatened Father with exposure, the fen would be saved.

Poor innocent, unworldly Jubal. He didn't realise that that would never work for the simple reason that no one would believe him. It would be his word against Father's; and who would credit a penniless drunk whose wits had been addled by years of poppyhead tea against the word of a gentleman landowner and a respected historian?

But there must be *something* she could do.

Once or twice she considered telling Clem: humbling her pride and seeking his help. But what if he suspected this was a pretext to get near him? What if he told Ivy and they laughed at her? Besides, what could Clem actually do?

At other times Maud saw herself as a lone heroine like Joan of Arc, battling to save the fen. She would *never* give up until she'd found the way – and until she'd exposed Father for what he truly was.

Then her lofty visions would come crashing down, and she would see herself as *she* really was: a fifteen-year-old girl whom no one would believe.

And then too, a voice at the back of her mind would warn her to take care. If Father could do such a thing when he was a boy, what might he be capable of now?

He might even be dangerous.

That struck her as ludicrous. But once it had taken root, she couldn't get it out of her head.

From the Private Notebook of Edmund Stearne
23rd December, 1912

What Maud said this afternoon about the Doom reminded me of a passage in *The Life of St Guthlaf*. I've just looked it up, and it's even worse than I thought. It has given me the most appalling idea.

The translation isn't of the best, but the Anglo-Saxon is there on the facing page, and there's no escaping the meaning. '*Flaxan mid deofol gefulde.*'

The timing fits. And if I'm right – *if* – then it explains why I've always felt such a violent antipathy towards the Doom. *Because it isn't merely a painting. It is far more than that.*

Later

If I am right. That's the question. I think I shall find the answer in Pyett. The parish records will probably help too. Pyett is downstairs. For the parish records I must wait until old Farrow arrives at the church. He'll be early, as today is Christmas Eve. I've only a few hours to wait. I must pray for patience.

Dear God, I hope I'm wrong.

Thirty-one

*O*N Christmas Eve, Father came downstairs looking unwell. He didn't read the Bible at morning prayers and took nothing for breakfast but a cup of tea. Then he told Maud that he would be out all day, and left the house.

As soon as he'd gone and the servants were busy elsewhere, she went to his dressing-room and took his notebook from its hiding place under his shirts.

From the final entry she learned that some phrase in *The Life of St Guthlaf* had given him 'the most appalling idea'. Whatever it was, it had something to do with the Doom, and she surmised that he'd gone to consult the parish records, to determine whether it was true. Beyond that she was none the wiser, as the phrase which had alarmed him was in Anglo-Saxon: *flaxan mid deofol gefulde*.

She searched the house, but couldn't find *The Life of St Guthlaf*; she guessed that Father had taken it with him to the church. She couldn't find a dictionary of Anglo-Saxon either, so she was unable to work out what the phrase meant.

Father returned shortly before noon and asked her with

distant courtesy to vacate the library. He was in there for nearly three hours; then he went back to St Guthlaf's. Maud was unable to ascertain which books he'd consulted, as he'd left no volumes out of place.

Just before tea-time, she heard his footsteps on the gravel. She ran to the window. His face was grey but rigidly composed, and he walked with one shoulder higher than the other. Listening at the door, Maud heard him tell Ivy that he wanted neither tea nor dinner and would be in his study, not to be disturbed.

Christmas at Wake's End had scarcely been celebrated since Maman's death, and this Christmas Eve was no exception; even the servants' festivities in the back offices were muted. Richard was in Scotland staying with a schoolfriend, and as Maud had no desire to join Felix and Nurse in the nursery, she dined alone.

Daisy put a few sprigs of holly on the picture frames in the dining-room, then left Maud to her solitary meal. She'd ordered things that she liked but that wouldn't inconvenience Cook: a roast pheasant with bread sauce and carrots; damson pudding and custard, and ginger beer.

When she'd finished, she raised the blinds and stared into the dark. It hadn't snowed that winter, and in the orchard the leafless trees shivered in a sleety rain. She thought of Chatterpie swinging on the well-bucket. She remembered Clem's brown throat, and the sunlight gilding the hairs on his forearms. Abruptly she turned from the window and went upstairs.

At half past eleven she came downstairs again, put on her outdoor things, and waited with the rest of the household in the breakfast-room until Father emerged from his study. Then they all trudged off through the sleet for Midnight Mass.

St Guthlaf's was at its busiest, and Mr Broadstairs was perplexed and displeased when Father abruptly insisted on moving to a different pew.

'But Father,' whispered Maud. 'We've always had this pew!'

'Not any more,' he muttered, shouldering past an astonished Miss Broadstairs and ignoring the startled glances of the congregation.

He took a pew on the other side of the aisle, near the door to the tower which housed the Doom. During the service he remained impassive, although at times he stared fixedly at the door to the tower, or leafed through his Bible as if searching for something.

Maud rather enjoyed the curious glances of the congregation. Whatever the 'appalling idea' Father had had last night, he richly deserved to be shaken out of his God-given peace.

She was also conscious of a faint unease. She was beginning to wonder where all this might lead.

On Boxing Day the weather turned colder and the Lode was filmed with ice. Father pressed on with his plans to drain the fen, dictating letters to his attorney and to Davies the engineer, which Maud typed.

He also continued working on Pyett. Maud was now

losing interest, as Alice's account of her pilgrimage consisted of rambling exhortations to God. Father's translations arrived in disjointed fragments, sometimes breaking off mid-sentence. This was at odds with his extreme composure, which Maud was starting to find unsettling.

Two days after Boxing Day he drove himself to the Rectory, returning a few hours later, vexed and irritable. The following afternoon Maud came downstairs to find Clem and a score of villagers stripping the ivy from the house. Father had given orders for every scrap to be removed, and for all shrubs within twenty feet of the house to be grubbed up. He was paying them handsomely to get the job done in a single day.

Maud couldn't ask him why he was doing this because he had driven to Wakenhyrst. When he came back he went straight to his study. From then on he had all his meals brought to him there.

That night Maud sensed the old house shivering without its shaggy coat of ivy. She too felt exposed and unprotected. Next morning, instead of the soft green light that she'd loved, she woke to a strange flat glare. She thought of all the wild creatures who had made the ivy their home. When she was little she had believed that not even Father could get rid of them. She had been wrong.

Cole could offer no explanation for Father's orders, but he told Maud that a few days before, the Master had asked him all manner of odd questions about plants. He'd also given orders that one plant in the flowerbed by the library French windows should be spared. Its name meant nothing to Maud. It was Solomon's Seal.

Two days before New Year's Eve, Daisy complained that she'd found salt all over the house.

'*Salt?*' said Maud. 'What on earth do you mean?'

The old housemaid compressed her lips. 'What I said, Miss Maud. Little piles of salt all over the place. Doorways, fireplaces, sills. He wun't let me sweep it up, neither. And I found oil round the breakfast-room winders. Yes, Miss, salad oil. That's what I smelled.'

That afternoon, Maud was typing at her desk when she was startled by the crash of breaking glass. Putting her head into the passage, she met the equally startled glance of Cook at the other end. At the same moment they both noticed that the glass dome which housed Maud's old friends the stuffed bats was missing from the side-table.

The study doors opened and Father appeared. He frowned at Maud. 'What do you want?' he snapped.

'I – heard a noise,' she faltered.

'Go back to your work,' he said. Behind him the study was hazed with smoke, and she caught an acrid odour like scorched fur.

The following morning Maud heard Daisy telling Cook that Father had indeed smashed the glass dome and burned the stuffed bats.

'Made a proper mess of his grate,' grumbled Daisy. 'Took me an hour to get it clean. It's not right!'

'You mean *he's* not right,' muttered Cook.

Daisy smothered a laugh.

Quietly, Maud returned to the library and sat at her desk.

First the ivy, now the bats. Both her childhood guardians gone in a matter of days.

He's not right, Cook had said.

Maud sat very still. What Cook had said had given her an idea. For the first time since Father had decided to drain the fen, she knew how to stop him.

She would need the help of someone in authority. That meant either Dr Grayson or Mr Broadstairs.

The rector would be difficult, because since Maud's confrontation in the vestry with Miss Broadstairs a slight coolness had arisen between the two households. Maud decided to tackle the doctor and sound him out indirectly. Only if he proved unwilling to help would she swallow her pride and apply to the rector.

As it turned out, Father made things easy for her by announcing that he needed certain books in Ely and would be gone for two nights, returning on New Year's Day. It was a crisp, frosty morning and he insisted on driving himself in the dog-cart, rather than taking the covered carriage. He left after breakfast, bundled up in his Astrakhan coat and a carriage cloak.

The moment he'd gone, the whole household breathed more freely. The servants were jubilant because without him they could see in the New Year properly. Maud was relieved because she could summon Dr Grayson unobserved, and put her plan into effect.

She also checked Father's notebook. She was shocked to find that there were no new entries. He hadn't written a word since the 23rd of December, when he'd mentioned his 'appalling idea'. The last line was the one she'd read a week ago: 'Dear God, I hope I'm wrong.' The only change was that beneath it Father had ruled two straight black horizontal lines.

The rest of the page – indeed the rest of the notebook – was blank. The inference was clear. Her access to his inner thoughts was at an end. He intended to write no more.

He had finished with his notebook.

Thirty-two

JT was a joke among the female servants that Dr Grayson liked to get so close that you could count the bristles in his nostrils. When Maud was little, he used to take her on his lap and cup her buttocks in his palms.

Since Maman's death she had avoided him. If they did meet, an image would come to her of Maman lying on the divan with the doctor standing between her legs, his large freckled hands stained scarlet to the wrists. Maud knew she'd never actually witnessed this, but she saw it in her mind.

When Dr Grayson sat down beside her on the drawing-room sofa, she tried to forget this by concentrating on his smell of unwashed tweed and stale cigars.

'Now then, my dear. What seems to be the trouble?' His smile was a trifle forced. It was New Year's Eve and the sky was heavy with snow.

'I'm afraid I've brought you here on a pretext,' she said in a rush. 'You see, I'm not the one who is indisposed.'

His bushy eyebrows rose. 'Indeed?'

MICHELLE PAVER

She launched into her prepared account of Father's odd behaviour: the sudden abandonment of the family pew, the burning of the stuffed bats, the oil and the salt.

The doctor's smile congealed. 'And where is Dr Stearne now?'

'In Ely, buying books. He's not expected back till tomorrow.'

'*Books*,' said the doctor, pinching his nostrils between finger and thumb. 'Well, now. Buying *books* is hardly cause for concern. Is it, my dear?'

'No, of course not.'

'Nor is destroying an ornament one dislikes. Or deciding to worship in a different pew.'

'What about scattering salt all over one's house?'

Again his eyebrows rose. 'Surely you know better than to listen to servants' tittle-tattle. Now if that's all, my dear, I ought to be on my way.'

Maud was on the point of telling him about Father's fear of the Doom; but it occurred to her that he might tell Father, and then Father would know that she'd been reading his notebook. 'Surely what I've told you is enough?' she insisted.

'Enough for what?' said the doctor with a hint of irritation. 'What do you wish me to *do*?'

I wish you to declare him unhinged, she wanted to cry. I wish you to do whatever doctors do with people who act like this! Do anything, as long as you stop him draining the fen!

But she could see that it was hopeless.

'I gather you're excessively fond of reading,' said the

238

doctor. Putting one heavy paw on her shoulder, he gave her a little shake. 'Fewer books, my dear. That's the ticket. We don't want you depleting your nerve power.'

'I am not the one who is unwell,' she said stiffly.

'You must allow me to be the judge of that. I shall do you a kindness and say no more about this nonsense—'

'It isn't nonsense!'

'It most assuredly is. Why, nothing in what you've said about your father strikes me as irrational in the least. You, on the other hand, appear erratic and disturbed. Considerably disturbed. At best what you've told me is disloyal and unfilial; at worst it verges on hysteria – perhaps even neurasthenia.'

'I am not hysterical!' retorted Maud. 'I've simply told you what he's done!'

The doctor did not reply. From his breast pocket he drew a notebook and scribbled a line, then tore off the sheet and handed it to her. His square face had gone stiff. His eyes were glassy. 'Take this,' he said without looking at her. 'For the rest, I think we can trust to a milk diet and a twenty-minute walk every morning to set you right.'

Maud took the paper in silence.

'See that you follow my instructions to the letter,' he added, rising ponderously to his feet. 'Otherwise I fear we shall have to arrange a rest cure in a sanatorium. I take it you're aware of what that would entail?'

Sullenly, she shook her head.

'Eight weeks' total seclusion and bedrest. No sitting up, no using the hands in any way, no stimuli of any kind. And most certainly *no books*.'

New Year's Eve is not a Christian festival. That was why it was never observed at Wake's End.

Or rather, Father never observed it. The servants did. They knew that New Year's Eve is of the utmost importance because what happens then determines what will happen in the forthcoming year. They also knew that you must be especially careful around midnight, because whatever you're doing at that time is what you'll be doing for the next twelve months. This is why you have to keep all the fires blazing, and you mustn't break anything, or lend money, or cry. You mustn't wear black, as black betokens mourning. Nor must you fall asleep before the turn of the year, because sleep is akin to death.

It's also vital not to take anything out of the house on New Year's Eve; that includes rubbish, ashes from the grate, and even potato peelings. You have to wait until you've let out the Old Year by opening the back door, and then let in the New by opening the front. Only in this way can you be assured of a good year. Only in this way can you know that the luck of the house has been retained.

Maud knew all this as well as any housemaid, and although she was sure it was nonsense, she saw no harm in observing the rules. Thus while the servants grew merry on kitchel cakes and spiced elderberry wine, she tried to ensure a good year for herself by doing her favourite things.

It was too dark to go for a walk in the fen, but she ordered her supper on a tray in the library, which was her favourite room, and she had her favourite foods: venison pie and apple cheesecake with ginger beer. Then she settled down by the fire and read her favourite bits in *Robinson Crusoe*.

The servants were particularly nice to her because she was giving them no trouble. Daisy even brought her a glass of sherry when she rang for one. It made Maud pleasantly giddy, and she thought how wonderful it would be to live like this always: alone at Wake's End (except for a servant or two). She might even buy a dog.

On the chimney-piece the hands of the carriage clock inched towards midnight, and she drank a toast to Chatterpie and Maman.

Suddenly, her spirits plummeted. Her appeal to Dr Grayson had failed. She was appalled at the risk she had run. What if he told Father? What if she was sent away on a rest cure? It wasn't the thought of eight weeks without books that she found unbearable. It was what she might find when she returned: the fen gone and the house surrounded by a bleak wilderness of mud.

It was nearly midnight. From St Guthlaf's came a muffled peal as the bell-ringers began to toll the death of the Old Year. A burst of laughter at the end of the passage; then Maud heard Ivy running to the front door, ready to let in the New Year.

The clock on the chimney-piece began to chime. As the last stroke of midnight died away, the bells of St Guthlaf's broke into joyous peals – which grew suddenly louder as Ivy flung open the front door.

'*You!*' exclaimed the housemaid in a startled voice.

Throwing down her book, Maud ran out into the passage – and came face to face with Father.

'But – you were staying in Ely,' she faltered.

'Happy New Year!' he cried, tossing his hat to a gaping Ivy. At the other end of the passage the servants stared with open mouths. Father's face was flushed with cold and he was *grinning*.

Maud stammered an apology about letting the servants make merry, but he brushed that aside. 'I rather think that I too would like a glass of the traditional elderberry wine,' he chuckled, throwing his coat on the ground and striding to the library fire, where he stood beaming and rubbing his hands.

Maud picked up his coat. It felt damp and it smelled of the fen. She handed it to Ivy. 'See that it's dried and bring the Master a glass of elderberry wine.'

'Yes, Miss.'

In the library Father had flung up a window sash, letting in the loud, jangling harmonies of the bells. His hair was tousled and there was a hectic brightness in his eyes. Maud wondered if he was ill.

Then she noticed water dripping from his cuffs. It was making little dark spots on the rug. 'Oughtn't you to change into dry things?' she said carefully.

'Not till I've had my wine,' he replied with that strange fixed grin.

'Father, do you think you might have caught a chill?'

He threw back his head and laughed. 'What makes you say that? I've never felt better! Oh look, it's snowing, isn't that splendid? I do love snow! It's so pure, it makes everything *clean*!'

Maud was right. Father had fallen ill. Shortly after one o'clock in the morning he collapsed, and Jessop and Steers carried him upstairs. By then he was delirious, laughing and mumbling. Maud could make out nothing of what he said.

She sent Jessop for Dr Grayson, but two hours later Jessop returned without the doctor, who'd been detained in Carrbridge at a difficult confinement; he had sent a message that he would come as soon as he could. Daisy diagnosed pond fever and gave Father a mixture of calomel and spirits of hartshorn, which he promptly brought up. Maud took turns with Ivy and Daisy to sit with him. The doctor still didn't come.

At eight in the morning, after a few hours' broken sleep, Maud dressed, went downstairs and rang for tea.

The breakfast-room was cold, for the fire had only just been lit. As Maud sat yawning at the table, the bells of St Guthlaf's began to toll. Unlike the joyous peals of midnight, they sounded slow and subdued. Someone must have died in the night. Maud counted nine peals. That meant it was a man. Had it been a woman, there would only have been six.

A death on New Year's Day, she thought blearily. That didn't bode well for the coming year; the servants would be discussing this for weeks.

Daisy rustled in with the tea. She looked grim but not grief-stricken; clearly the death hadn't affected her personally. No doubt she already knew all about it, but she wouldn't say a word unless Maud asked.

There was silence while Maud sipped her tea and Daisy tended the fire.

Finally, Maud relented. 'So who died?' she asked.

With an air of importance, Daisy straightened up. 'I allus said it'd happen sooner or later. Not to speak ill of the dead, but what's he expect when he was allus drunk?'

'Who was it?'

Daisy replaced the poker in the stand and got to work with the bellows. 'Jubal Rede,' she said over her shoulder. 'He went and fell in the Lode and drownded.'

Thirty-three

D R Grayson diagnosed a dangerous case of enteric
fever and called in a special nurse from Cambridge.
For the first eight weeks, Maud barely saw her father. When
she did he was delirious.

She told herself that he couldn't have had anything to
do with the drowning. It had to be coincidence that his
coat-sleeves had been wet and that he'd smelled of the fen.
Or perhaps he had found Jubal in the Lode and had tried
to save him.

But even if – *even if* one entertained the possibility that
he had played some part in Jubal's death – that still left the
question of *why?* Jubal posed no threat to him. If Jubal had
shouted Lily's story from the rooftops, no one would have
believed him. He wasn't *worth* killing.

All this churned endlessly in Maud's head. One moment
she was convinced it was impossible. The next, she circled
back to her first appalling thought when Daisy had told
her the news on New Year's Day: *Father did it. Father
killed Jubal.*

Father was out of danger by the beginning of March, although still fearfully weak. Dr Grayson ordered two months' bedrest at least.

Surprisingly, Father seemed to enjoy this. He proved a model patient, and Nurse Lawson fell in love with him. She was a pretty, capable redhead who seemed not to care that within days she had antagonised the whole staff. Daisy hated her for fumigating Father's rooms with burning pastilles. Cook hated her constant orders for milk pudding and mutton broth. Ivy hated her because she wouldn't let her near Father. Nurse hated her for pointing out that as Quieting Syrup is a mixture of black treacle and opium, it is hardly advisable to give it to a four-year-old.

Somehow, Maud kept the peace. She had been running the household before Father fell ill and she went on running it now. The only difference was that these days when she ran short of money, she asked the rector to help her obtain more from Father's bank.

This gave her an idea. For years she had typed Father's business correspondence, so it was easy to imitate his style and signature. Now she typed two letters in his name: one to his attorney Mr Whittaker and one to Mr Davies the engineer. In them she ordered both to cease all activities concerned with draining the fen.

To her delight they replied by return, acknowledging their client's instructions with varying degrees of polite surprise. They also enclosed their notes of charges, which Maud hid at the back of her handkerchief drawer to deal with later.

For now, she had saved the fen. If Father recovered, she would think up something else. If he died, then well and good. The fen would be safe for ever.

March gave way to April. In a few weeks, Maud would be sixteen: the same age Maman had been when she'd married Father.

Maud now felt that she was living two separate existences. The first was as mistress of Wake's End, supervising the yearly spring-cleaning: the beating of rugs, the sweeping of chimneys, the replacing of sooty winter curtains with muslin ones for summer. In her second and parallel existence, her suspicions about Father were true and she was living with a killer.

The gulf between these two existences was vast. There was no in-between. Either he was a murderer, or he was not.

As Father remained in bed, Maud now spent part of her day in his room, reading *The Times* to him out loud.

One afternoon she was reading a report about a boy who had drowned in the Thames. At the end she glanced up. 'Did anyone ever tell you, Father, that the night you were taken ill, Jubal Rede fell in the Lode and drowned?'

Without opening his eyes, he turned his head on the pillow. 'Who?'

'Jubal Rede.'

He frowned. 'Do I know him?'

'He lived in the fen.'

'Ah, yes,' he said without interest. 'Well. No doubt he was inebriated.'

'Yes. I daresay he was.'

Soon afterwards, Maud muttered an excuse and left the room. She ran to the end of the passage and stood with her hands on the sill and her forehead against the window-pane. She was shaking. Jubal's death had been an *accident*. Father had had nothing to do with it.

In early April he was allowed downstairs for two hours a day on the drawing-room sofa.

By now he had ceased to be a model patient. He was silent and morose, prone to savage outbursts if his egg was overcooked or his tea lukewarm. Sometimes he wanted Maud to read *The Times* from cover to cover, sometimes he said it was bosh and waved her away. Often he complained that Felix made too much noise in the grounds. Maud took to accompanying the child on his walks and bribed him to silence by letting him hold her dragonfly pendant.

Throughout all this, Nurse Lawson remained her usual imperturbable self. She was pleased with Father's progress; she said ill temper was a sign of recovery. Dr Grayson patted her cheek and agreed.

With Father downstairs for a few hours a day, Maud finally had a chance to check his notebook in the dressing-room. She knew that he would have had little opportunity to write during his illness, so she wasn't surprised to find that the last entry was still the one at Christmas, when he'd had 'the most appalling idea'.

She found that she no longer cared very much what that idea might have been. Father's bizarre behaviour over Christmas – the stuffed bats, the salt – now seemed as unreal as a fairytale. Maud decided that at the time, he must already have been coming down with enteric fever.

By the 1st of May, Father was strong enough to spend an hour a day in his study, on the strict understanding that he did no actual work, merely light reading. He was still morose and bad-tempered, and Maud continued to check his notebook. It remained untouched.

One afternoon when she was pouring his tea, he said abruptly, 'What did they do with the body?'

She was so startled that she nearly dropped the teapot. 'Whose body?' she faltered.

'That fellow who drowned. What did they do with him?'

'He's in the churchyard, Father. I believe the parish paid for the grave.'

'Yes but where?' he said brusquely.

'The north side. I believe that's where they buried him.'

Maud had paid for Jubal's funeral out of the housekeeping money. She had attended it too. Unlike Maman's funeral, there was no one to tell her that she couldn't because she was a girl. A distant cousin from Brandon had also been present, and Maud had paid him two guineas to find Jubal's dog Nellie and take her home with him. The only other mourners had been Clem and his younger brother Ned. Maud had nodded to the lad and pretended to ignore Clem. It was the end of January. A year ago almost to the day, she had slipped on the church path and he had steadied her. Only a year.

A week after the funeral, Maud had paid her respects to Jubal in her own way. Crossing the foot-bridge into the fen, she'd gone to his hut and set it on fire.

She had said no words of farewell; he would have hated them. 'Moonshine,' she told the vast, empty sky.

Father was making such good progress that Dr Grayson allowed him to look over his correspondence. Inevitably, the subject of draining the fen came up.

'I wonder that Davies hasn't yet begun,' he said tetchily.

'Do you, Father?' replied Maud, who had prepared herself for this. 'But you wrote and cancelled. Don't you remember?'

'I? What on earth are you talking about?'

'I took dictation from you. Your instructions were very clear, and they both wrote acknowledging receipt. Shall I fetch their letters?'

Irritably, he waved that away. 'But how extraordinary. I have no recollection of that whatsoever.'

A few days later, he dictated letters instructing Davies and Mr Whittaker to resume their work. Maud duly typed them and promised to have them posted, then burned them in her room. When next the matter arose, she would blame the postal service.

It was very far from being a permanent solution, but it would keep the fen safe for now.

One night in the middle of May there was a violent lightning storm. It brought down one of the elms in the avenue, and next morning the grounds were littered with fallen branches.

Nurse Lawson told Maud that the patient had passed an exceedingly bad night. Despite that, Father insisted on getting up and spending his permitted hour alone in his study – where he promptly fainted.

Ivy heard him fall, and she and Steers helped him upstairs. Lawson took charge while Maud observed from the doorway.

'I'm perfectly fine,' snapped Father. 'A fit of giddiness, nothing more. Leave me *alone*!'

Maud noticed an inkstain on his right thumb. Something clicked in her brain and suddenly she knew why he'd written nothing in his notebook since Christmas.

Rushing downstairs on the pretext of sending for the doctor, she searched Father's desk. Everything was in order. Whatever he'd been writing in before his collapse, he'd had time to put it away.

Ivy had found him on the rug by the window that overlooked the church. Maud could find nothing there.

Nothing except that ledger on top of the bookshelf. Stupid, stupid, she berated herself. Why didn't you think of it before?

The spine of the ledger was embossed with the word *Accounts*, exactly like all the other ledgers in the top shelf of the bookcase. Father bought them by the dozen and used them for recording his financial affairs. It was the perfect hiding place: hidden in plain sight and safe from prying housemaids, because neither Daisy nor Ivy could read. Presumably Father didn't think that Maud would dare intrude on his privacy. Or perhaps he thought she lacked the imagination.

The first entry in the ledger was dated 24th December 1912, the week before Father fell ill. It began: 'At last I know the truth. It is as I feared.'

This was why he hadn't anything written in his notebook. Because he'd started a new one.

Thirty-four

From the Private Notebook of Edmund Stearne – Vol. II
Christmas Eve 1912, 8 p.m.

At last I know the truth. It is as I feared.

I realise now that it is not by chance that I have come by this knowledge on Christmas Eve. There is much of the infernal in this terrible affair, yet I also perceive the Hand of God. Years ago, He sparked my desire to find *The Book of Alice Pyett*. In June He caused Hibble to send me *The Life of St Guthlaf* 'in error'. Now Pyett and *The Life* have led me to the truth in all its naked horror.

This is why I've begun a new notebook: because, though I am assailed by terrors such as few men would have the strength to endure, I am also granted insights not vouchsafed to any but the chosen few. It is my *duty* to keep this record. I *must* set down the truth. My sufferings shall not be in vain.

First, to relate how the idea came to me.

It began with that passage in Pyett which states that her husband 'paid twelvepence for a new candlebeam in

Wakenhyrst Church, and threepence to the priest for certain prayers to be said over the carter who was possessed.'

With female impulsiveness, Maud suggested that the
candlebeam might have been the Doom; a conclusion I
would soon have reached myself by more logical means.
The timing fits. Jacobs dates the Doom to the 1490s, and
though I despise the fellow, I can't fault his scholarship. In
the 1490s Pyett would have been in her forties, and her
parish – this parish – was afflicted by the Devil.

So much I knew when Maud made her suggestion. What
happened next startles me still. The notion that Pyett's
husband may have commissioned the Doom instantly put
me in mind of a passage in *The Life of St Guthlaf*. Last night I
turned it up. That was when I had my appalling idea.

I told myself I must be mistaken, so I re-read *The Life*
from the beginning. To my horror, it only *reinforced* my idea
– for the parallels between myself and St Guthlaf are too
striking to be mere coincidence. I list them below, as they
lead inexorably to the truth.

'*Guthlaf was tall in figure and very handsome in countenance,
and he grew up pure in his ways...*' The monk who penned
those words might have been describing me!

'*There is in Britain an immense black fen with foul streams, miry
pools and desolate reeds. In the midst of this fen, Guthlaf went to
live on an islet especially remote, which none dared inhabit, as that
place was the haunt of an accursed spirit.*' I have always known
that Guthlaf's Fen was once the abode of the saint. But
I'd forgotten about the accursed spirit. The Anglo-Saxon
phrase for it is *awyrigeda gæst*. How ugly that looks on the
page; one can't say it without a grimace! The Latinate term

'spirit' evokes an airy, insubstantial being. The word *gæst* is earthier, more brutally corporeal. I fear that the monk who wrote *The Life* knew whereof he spoke.

'*Guthlaf was disquieted by the loneliness of the wild wilderness, and much tormented by the mischief of a magpie that lived nearby.*' The correspondence is remarkable. It is Maud's wretched bird.

'*Guthlaf's hut being surrounded by brambles, it happened that his hand was pierced by a thorn. And so strong was its point that he was grievously afflicted and could hardly write.*' I too scratched my hand in the churchyard on the very day I found the Doom! At the time I was struck by a passage in Corinthians: 'There was given to me a thorn in the flesh, the messenger of Satan to buffet me.' Now I turn to Revelations 13:16, concerning the mark of the beast: '... and he causeth all... to receive a mark in their right hand...'

'*One day as Guthlaf prayed by the stream that flowed behind his hut, he remembered the sin he had done, of which he could not be cleansed...*' This needs no explanation. L.

'*Then a demon came sliding out of the fen. It was most filthy and horrible, with squalid countenance and jagged teeth like those of a horse...*' I have seen such a one in my dreams. And there's something else I've only just realised. The Anglo-Saxon word for 'demon' is *feond*. The stream that flows around Wake's End is named Feon Lode. That is a corruption of Feond Lode: Demon Stream. All this time the Devil has been hiding in the name.

'*Guthlaf being much affrighted, he prayed to St Bartholomew, and the accursed spirit vanished like smoke before his face.*' Some small comfort here, I think.

MICHELLE PAVER

'*But in the stillness of the night, the foul spirit came again, creeping through the cracks in the wattle of Guthlaf's hut and under the door of the chamber where he slept. And the demon carried Guthlaf up on its creaking wings to the cloudy sky, then down through the noisome waters of the fen to the very jaws of Hell. There Guthlaf beheld the blackest torments and heard the endless screams of the unrighteous. And the demon said to Guthlaf: For thy sin, Hell's door openeth before thee.*' I too have been visited in my sleep. I too have dreamed of the icy waters of Hell.

The rest of *The Life* contains much that has no parallel in my own experience, for Guthlaf is saved by St Bartholomew and granted healing powers, &c &c. *However.* One of Guthlaf's miracles struck me most forcibly. In fact, it sparked my whole dreadful idea: '*It happened that the accursed spirit entered into the body of a boatman who lived in the fen, so that he was possessed, and wounded himself and others with an axe. Then Guthlaf prayed over the sick man and blew in his face, so that the evil one flew out of his mouth. And Guthlaf trapped the evil one in a flask and flung the flask containing the demon into the deepest part of the fen. And after that the boatman came into his right wits again. And the accursed spirit troubled the fen no more.*'

The '*flask containing the demon*'. The Anglo-Saxon phrase is *flaxan mid deofol gefulde.*

Can it really be only a matter of hours since I first saw those words? It feels as if they have haunted me for years.

This morning I went to church and made the necessary enquiries. I had forgotten that today is Christmas Eve, but I prevailed upon a grumpy and 'extremely busy' Broadstairs to let me examine the parish records.

First question: Did Pyett's husband in fact commission

the Doom, as his wife says? Answer: yes. In 1492, one Adam Pyett is recorded as having paid twelvepence for a new candlebeam.

Second question: What was the *purpose* of the Doom? According to Pyett, she stood accused of being possessed, so her husband commissioned the painting to save her. As well as commissioning the Doom, he also – and this is crucial – '*paid threepence to the priest for certain prayers to be said over the carter who was possessed.*'

The importance of these 'prayers' cannot be overstated. *They are nothing less than a veiled reference to an exorcism. That is* what Adam Pyett paid for. He paid the priest to banish the demon from the carter – thereby exonerating his wife from 'false blame'. *And the Doom was part of the exorcism.*

Why, one might ask, doesn't Pyett's Book explicitly mention this exorcism? I think she was afraid, for she lived in perilous times. In the past she had nearly been burned as a Lollard; but later, this part of Suffolk became a hotbed of Lollardism – and it was a movement that denounced exorcism as necromancy. Pyett must have been unsure where people's sympathies lay, so she took refuge in vagueness – hence the reference to 'certain prayers' being said over the possessed man. But clearly the exorcism worked, for 'the evil spirit plagued the parish no more'.

There is one further piece of evidence which confirms that an exorcism was performed. On Pyett's first pilgrimage she went to North Marston in Buckinghamshire. That is the shrine of the well-known pseudo-saint John Schorne, who is said to have imprisoned the Devil in a boot. In Pyett's time his cult was widespread, and people afflicted

MICHELLE PAVER

by demons often visited his shrine. Doubtless Pyett went there to give thanks for her deliverance. Perhaps she was accompanied by the carter who had been possessed.

But to return to the Doom. Having concluded my perusal of the parish records, the vital question remained: *how* was the exorcism carried out – *and in what way was the Doom involved?*

This brought me back to Wake's End around midday, for I hoped to find the answer in my own volumes on mediæval beliefs.

I turned out to be right – but not in the way I had anticipated.

Thirty-five

Christmas Eve, 10 p.m.

I must set down everything before I go to Midnight Mass.
I must not shrink from my task, however dreadful.

The question before me when I returned to Wake's End
was this: *How* was the Doom involved in the exorcism? In
short, how would Pyett's parish priest have rid the carter
of the demon in 1492?

The casting out of demons has been well known since
long before Christ, and by Pyett's time it involved both
spoken and written prayers, the use of certain herbs,
and bizarre and often fatal 'treatments' meted out to the
afflicted person. I already knew much of this, and naturally
my extensive collection of volumes on the period contains
a good deal on the topic.

To my surprise, none of it helped in the least. Assistance
came from a most unlikely quarter.

My father's younger brother Octavius was a keen folk-
lorist. Papa always ridiculed his hobby as unscientific, but
he was fond of his brother, so he preserved the latter's

collection of local folklore after Octavius' untimely death. It was among those papers that I found a volume amateurishly bound in blue American cloth, entitled *The Folk-Lore of West Suffolk* by one Enid Gurdon. It was published by The Folk-Lore Society in 1882. The chapter on exorcisms proved startling.

The form of exorcism local to this part of Suffolk derives from both Anglo-Saxon and Old Norse practices brought over by the Vikings. In essence, the priest reads the Bible 'at' the evil spirit or the possessed person, thus progressively shrinking the spirit until it is small enough to be overcome. The priest then imprisons the tiny, furious demon in some sort of receptacle: a box, a jar or a bottle. This receptacle is then either placed under a boulder, or flung into a pool (as in *Guthlaf*) – *or secured behind a monument in church.*

People in Suffolk have long memories. They think nothing of telling stories rooted in the Middle Ages. In her book Miss Gurdon includes one such tale about an exorcism which she took down from an old ploughman in Wakenhyrst in 1878. According to the old man, the exorcism occurred 'in the years arter the Great Death'. In other words, in Pyett's time.

I reproduce his tale in the vernacular in which Miss Gurdon recorded it: 'They duh say that the passon read that sperrit daown small into a bottle, and he tied its stopper about with reeds. Then they put that bottle agin an owd beam in the church, and arter that the sperrit worn't heard no more for ivver so long, for that owd beam han't been interfered with sence.'

When I read that, I was physically sick. I knew at once that the church was St Guthlaf's, and that the 'owd beam' was the Doom. This is why I've always hated it. It isn't the painting that frightens me. *It is what was trapped behind it.*

The old ploughman said that the spirit – the demon – had never been heard of since, because the beam (i.e. the Doom) had remained undisturbed. Doubtless that was correct at the time he told his tale to Miss Gurdon. But now the Doom *has* been disturbed. Last year I gave orders to strip the chancel arch of those whitewashed planks. *All this is my fault.*

Later

I was too overcome to go on, but a little brandy has given me strength. I still have a few minutes before Midnight Mass, and I must finish. *It is my duty.*

Once I had found that description of the exorcism in Miss Gurdon's book, I could have stopped there – but I had to know for sure. Accordingly, around three o'clock I hurried back to church and collared the sexton. Old Farrow wasn't best pleased to be questioned on Christmas Eve, but when he saw that I would not relent, he capitulated.

Like most locals he is intensely superstitious, and he only told his story with the utmost reluctance. He confirmed that last year, while he was supervising the work of removing the planks from the chancel arch – those very planks which were later found to comprise the Doom – something fell from behind them and shattered on the flags. Close examination showed it to have been a small flask of greenish glass, which had been stoppered and bound with a kind of string made of dried reeds. This flask had been fastened to the back of the Doom, in the angle between a baton and one of the planks. When the planks were torn from the wall, the flask had fallen and smashed to pieces on the stones.

I didn't ask Farrow whether he'd ever heard the ploughman's tale of the exorcism. I knew that he had when he told me that he'd preserved the bottle's remains: 'not liking to destroy it'. In other words, out of fear.

Those shards lie before me now on my desk. The glass is thick, greenish, and in places smeared with an oily black residue that smells most foul. Nothing would induce me to touch them with my bare hands. I even fear to look at them too closely, lest I glimpse not my own reflection, but something worse.

Later

Farrow gave the remains of the bottle into my keeping with undisguised relief. I wrapped them in my handkerchief. Then I made him give me the key to the room in the tower, and I forced myself to go in and confront the Doom.

By then it was past three in the afternoon and the light was beginning to fail. The devil leered from its corner. It knows all about me. It knows everything. It is a creature of the swamp and it squats among the reeds, mocking and obscene. Since I first saw its eye in the grass, I have hated and feared this painting. At last I know why.

I think some part of me sensed from the beginning what lay behind it. And tonight, on Christmas Eve, I am sure: whoever painted that picture painted the demon from life.

The devil in the corner is real. For four hundred years it was imprisoned behind the Doom.

Now it's loose.

Thirty-six

Christmas Day 1912, 3 a.m.

For Midnight Mass I wore my limmell stone under my shirt along with my crucifix. I hoped it would make me feel less alone.

Never before have I realised how isolated one can feel in a throng of people. Everyone around me was singing and praying, unaware of what is happening. They have no idea there's a devil in their midst. I'm the only one.

At last I know the true nature of the threat. I suppose that's something. It's always better to know.

It's also startling to look back to when it all began: to that day in the churchyard when I saw the eye in the grass. The signs were there from the very beginning. The sky was overcast, and now I remember (although I didn't before) that in the east I saw thunderclouds and a distant bolt of lightning. There was lightning at Blythburgh too, in the great tempest of 1577 when the Devil attacked the church of the Holy Trinity as a monstrous dog. And lightning attended the Devil in the Bible. Luke 10:18: 'I beheld Satan as lightning fall from Heaven.'

As I made my way towards our pew, I felt as if I'd gained an extra sense, or a third eye; isn't that what the Hindoos call it? I felt the stone demons on the corbels peering down at me.

Then I saw those toads carved on the oak chest against the wall. They too were staring at me: *We know what you did.* It came to me suddenly that this chest was made in the same century as Pyett and the Doom, and that it was fashioned from what locals call 'black oak'. *It came from the fen.* Pyett called the demon 'the thing that cries in the night'. Whoever carved those toad-like faces on the chest did so 'from life'. He had seen the thing that cries in the night.

After coming to this realisation, I couldn't endure to be near that chest, so I decided to move to another pew, much to the consternation of old Broadstairs and the wonderment of the congregation. Well, let them talk. I knew where I had to be: on the other side, by the door to the tower.

The demon comes and goes at will. When all is quiet, it slithers out from behind its erstwhile prison, the Doom, and slips under the door. At other times it slinks back and conceals itself once more. I could feel it there now. And I sensed that it knew that it was perceived – but that it would not show itself while I was there to keep watch. It is a creature of shadows. It hates to be observed.

As the congregation embarked on another carol, I had a second astonishing idea. Covertly, I turned up the passage in Revelations where the angel comes down to earth and seizes the Devil. And there it was as plain as day. It might have been written for me! The angel 'bound him a thousand years, And cast him into the bottomless pit, and shut him up... And when the thousand years are expired, Satan shall be loosed out of his prison.'

It all fits, *all*. At the beginning of the world – that is to say, a little over four thousand years ago – the angel caught the devil and bound it and cast it into the bottomless fen. Then after a thousand years, the devil was 'loosed out of his prison'. Who knows for how many centuries it roamed at large? But eventually St Guthlaf trapped it in the flask and flung it back into the deepest part of the fen.

There the devil lay imprisoned once more; this time not for millennia but for seven hundred years – until in Pyett's time the cycle began again. The devil was loosed. It haunted the fen as the thing that cries in the night. Then Adam Pyett paid a priest to 'read it down' into a bottle – which bottle was secured behind the Doom. And there the devil lay trapped for over four hundred years. Until last September, when I ordered those 'planks' torn down – and I set the demon free.

The entire pattern flashed before my eyes as the congregation sang the last verse of 'O Come All Ye Faithful'. One might have thought I would be appalled at the cosmic battle in which I am caught up, but instead I felt the most enormous surge of power – for in grasping the pattern, I also perceived the working of Providence. First, St Guthlaf fought the demon. Then came the turn of Adam Pyett. Now the flaming sword has passed to me.

I have been chosen for this task by God.

Later

I've been sipping brandy and watching dawn break on the morning Our Saviour was born. No snow. Not even a frost to brighten the outlook. And yet I feel so blessed.

My whole life has been leading up to this. It is for this that I took honours at Cambridge. For this that I laboured for years to find *The Book of Alice Pyett*. Only I, with my unrivalled knowledge of Pyett and her time, could have read the clues and deciphered what is really happening.

People in ancient times believed that the world was a battleground between God and Satan: two vast cosmic forces fighting an endless struggle for men's souls.

Pyett and her contemporaries would have regarded that view as wicked, since it denies the omnipotence of God. She was right. The truth is, God rules *all*. He sends devils to test us. By sending them, He shows His great love for us – for how else could we perceive His ineffable goodness, save through the presence of the blackest evil?

It is *God* who put into my mind the notion of renovating the chancel arch. It is *God* who made me order the Doom to be torn down, thereby setting the demon loose. And now it is *God* who commands me to go into battle.

I know what I have to do, and I shall not shirk my appointed task.

I must hunt down the demon and destroy it.

Thirty-seven

Christmas Day, Later

The question is: *how?* Draining the fen will merely destroy its hunting-ground. Besides, once Guthlaf's Fen is gone, it will take refuge in North Fen – and that's common land, I could do nothing about it.

Moreover the threat is more proximate than the fen. *It can get inside the house.* I haven't forgotten those noises at my bedroom door, or those eyes at the foot of the stairs. Priorities, Edmund. First, find some way to keep it outside. Once the house is secure, proceed to the exorcism. My expertise as an historian makes me well suited to undertake the necessary research about the latter. I may also need to enlist the help of the Church, although I shall consider carefully before taking any steps in that direction.

I feel better now that I've devised a strategy. It is pragmatic and rational. It makes sense. I know that if I remain strong, I can bring this horror to an end.

26th December

Excellent progress. I have already put in place a preliminary
measure of protection that seems highly effective.

The answer was simple, I found it in *The Life of St Guthlaf*:
'*And there came to Guthlaf a man whose eyes were dimmed by the
white speck. And Guthlaf took salt and blessed it, then sprinkled
the hallowed salt in the blind man's eyes, and the dimness was
banished and the man could see.*'

Today after the service I remained in my pew. Once the
church was empty, I went to the cupboard in the vestry
where the rector keeps the sacramentals. I took the blessed
salt and decanted the oil of chrism into the bottle I'd hidden
earlier, replacing what I'd taken with plain salt and oil I'd
obtained from the pantry. Old Broadstairs won't know the
difference, and my need is greater than his.

Using a modicum of cunning, it didn't take long to
anoint all points of ingress into the house. Doors, windows,
chimneys, even the ventilation grilles in the back offices;
all now have their measure of hallowed oil or salt.

The effect was immediate. As soon as I'd anointed my
study, I felt clearer and calmer. I was even able to do a little
work on Pyett.

27th December

Much better. Having taken particular care in anointing my
bedroom and dressing-room, I enjoyed my first unbroken
night's sleep in weeks.

I've made excellent progress with my research on
exorcism, too, and have chanced upon another powerful
protective measure. Mediæval sources including *Wolfsthurn*

tend to deal with exorcism in the context of demonic possession – that is, when a demon has entered the body of a human being. That is different from the present instance, when the demon is free to roam without taking human form. However, the same measures obtain in both cases.

Having found numerous references to 'the Herb of Solomon', I braved the frost and consulted Cole in the glasshouse. He told me that Herb of Solomon is the old name for an herbaceous perennial, Solomon's Seal; and greatly to my delight, he said that a large clump of the plant flourishes in the flowerbed outside the library! Can that be mere chance, or do I once again detect the workings of Providence?

At this season the plant is of course leafless, but Cole admitted that in summer he habitually dries a quantity of leaves for Biddy Thrussel to use in her potions. He also retains a supply for his personal use. I expressed an interest from an historical perspective, and now carry a pocketful of dried leaves always on my person.

Later

This afternoon I drove to the Rectory and sought help from old Broadstairs. I didn't tell him explicitly that I wish to perform an exorcism, I mentioned the subject in the context of my work on Pyett. I said that I desired to know his views, as a twentieth-century man of the cloth, so that I might draw comparisons with the beliefs of the fifteenth century.

To my surprise, the old fool became positively uncomfortable, huffing and fidgeting in his chair. When I pressed him he reluctantly conceded that 'there are those' in the Church with expertise in dealing with 'these matters'; but he said that he himself has no knowledge, nor has he any idea to whom I might apply. He practically hustled me out of the Rectory. His parting shot was that there would be no point in my seeing the bishop, for his advice would be the same.

So now I know: no assistance to be had from that quarter.

28th December
My adversary knows that I am fighting back. All morning I have felt watched. I tried to continue with my research, but in the end I had to ring for the blinds to be drawn. Daisy gave me an odd look – as well she might, for it was only just after noon, and the winter sunlight was still bright.

Even with the blinds down, I could feel the demon's presence in the grounds: watching, waiting. It wants to stop me. *It shall fail.*

Later
Before luncheon I forced myself to take my usual walk outside, and was rewarded with another excellent idea.

I was very much struck by the extent to which the house is encroached upon by shrubberies, and is itself thickly clad in ivy. The shrubberies provide excellent cover for my adversary's approach, while the ivy affords a means of ingress, enabling it to crawl up the walls and slip over my bedroom sill.

Well, *no more.* As I write, Walker and a gang of men from the village are hard at work tearing every scrap of ivy from the house. I've also told them to grub up the shrubberies, so that no cover remains within twenty feet.

By my express orders, they are leaving untouched the Solomon's Seal.

Later

Events are moving fast. Once I'd completed the above entry, I ordered the dog-cart and drove to the village to interview the wisewoman Biddy Thrussel.

I gave her a simpler version of what I'd told the rector, namely an academic interest in folkloric charms against the 'evil eye' (I didn't mention demons). Of course I had no need to explain myself at all to such as she; the shilling I paid her would have sufficed. However I thought it best, in order to forestall gossip.

Most of what the wisewoman said was nonsense, yet there was one nugget worth hearing. It turns out that she herself has performed one or two exorcisms. There was much confusion in what she said between the evil eye and witchcraft, and I'm well aware that imps such as rats, bats and toads are more commonly associated with witches; but I was struck by one of her stories, which took place some years ago.

A young labourer had fallen gravely ill, and as the wisewoman knew that he was possessed, she embarked on an ancient charm to expel the demon. First she boiled the patient's urine with nine nails from a horseshoe, then began muttering the charm – having warned the skivvy who was tending the fire that on no account must she look behind her during the spell.

Of course the foolish chit forgot herself and glanced over her shoulder. She uttered a piercing shriek, for she beheld 'a little black thing escaping through the keyhole'. In the uproar that ensued, the 'little black thing' was seen to return and re-enter the mouth of the sick man – whereupon he died.

Representations of such demon imps are common in the art of the Middle Ages, *viz* numerous woodcuts, illuminated manuscripts, those frescoes of Giotto, &c &c.

This gives me much to ponder.

I wish I could stop there, but I have a duty to tell all.

The drive back from the village did me good. The sun was out and the frosty Common glittered attractively, so I was in tolerably high spirits when I reached Wake's End. I can't have been paying attention, for on ascending the front steps, I slipped on a patch of ice. I managed not to fall by gripping the baluster, but as I recovered my equilibrium, I distinctly heard a low chuckle in my right ear.

It couldn't have been one of the men at work on the ivy, they were all at the back of the house. Besides, the laugh was not behind me or anywhere around, it was *in my ear*.

When as I say I'd regained my equilibrium, I hastened inside and rang for Walker. I told him to scatter quantities of grit and coarse salt over the front steps. I felt steadier after that. Practical measures definitely help.

Nevertheless, I find myself reverting again and again to that laugh. It was a most horribly sly, mocking sound. In my fancy, I hear it still.

Later

I have just realised what caused those nightmares about

Lily a few months ago. *They were the work of my adversary.* My adversary brought back those memories in order to distract me: to prevent me from hunting it down.

And now that I think of it, perhaps its malign influence was also at work years ago when I was a boy. Perhaps when Lily and I made our way to the Mere that day, some vile emanation from the demon trapped behind the Doom poisoned the atmosphere around us, thus clouding my judgement and making me panic and flee.

At the time, I believed that God would save her. That's why I didn't tell anyone where she was. Then she was brought in and it was too late. Her flesh was torn where the glaves had hooked her. I remember thinking that Nurse Thrushie's warnings had come true. 'Don't you never go near the Mere, or the ferishes 'ull hook you into the water.'

I don't remember much after Lily was brought in. Merely snatches. Father turning into an old man overnight. Mother's scream. She only screamed once. It must have been when she saw the body. I wasn't there but I heard it. I had never thought Mother could scream like that. She didn't sound human.

Later

Do you see how insidious my adversary is? Once again it seeks to distract me – by making me dwell on that time!

It won't work. In fact, the reverse, for by thinking of it I finally understand that what happened when I was a boy *was not my fault.* I didn't kill Lily. It was the demon.

MICHELLE PAVER

29th December

I'm not sure that the salt and the oil of chrism have worked.

I was making my descent to breakfast when I heard movement in the downstairs passage. It was very faint, but I know that I heard it, although it had ceased by the time I'd reached the foot of the stairs.

As I was about to enter the breakfast-room, the noises began again: small, furtive, like claws scrabbling on glass. But how could this be? Apart from the fanlight above the front door, there are no windows in the passage, and hence no glass. And surely my adversary cannot reach as high as the fanlight? It slinks too low to the ground.

Yet I distinctly heard those noises. Not a shred of verdure now remains on the exterior of the house, nor any shrubs that might afford cover to my adversary. Every point of ingress has been anointed with oil and salt.

So how has it got inside?

274

Thirty-eight

29th December – Later

All morning I've been tormented by that scrabbling. I never know when it's going to begin, and it stops the moment I step out into the passage. Sometimes if I'm quick I sense movement behind me, but no matter how swiftly I spin round, I see nothing there. As soon as I turn my back, the noises begin again.

It is taunting me.

Later

I know what it is. It's the glass dome on the side-table. I've always hated those bats. As a boy they gave me nightmares. I used to fancy they were giant spiders. They were Father's pride and joy – and of course Lily adored them. She used to pester him to tell her their names and about their 'behaviour'.

I was in my study when I heard the noises again. This time I opened the doors silently, and was quick enough to catch a flicker of motion. In the dome I distinctly saw one of the bats stealthily draw in its wing. It was all I could do not to cry out, but I knew that I *must not* let them know they'd been observed. Feigning indifference, I withdrew to my study. I pretended to shut both sets of doors, but kept the outer ones very slightly ajar and remained in the gap, listening with bated breath.

It wasn't long before the scrabbling began again. This time I was ready, I caught them at it. For the blink of an eye I beheld a heaving mound of leathery wings and misshapen bodies scrabbling and clawing at the glass, like the very imps of Hell. They spotted me and scrambled back into place, the last one twisting its tiny monstrous head and hissing at me.

So now I know. As my adversary can no longer gain entry to the house, it has found a new way to torment me.

It makes dead things move.

6 p.m.

I feel much calmer now that I've destroyed those loathsome creatures. I should have done it years ago. I can't imagine why I didn't.

The smell of burning drew Maud from the library. She stood sniffing and staring. I wanted to slap her stupid face. She is such a typical *female*. That animal inquisitiveness. They're all alike. All daughters of Eve, whose curiosity caused the Fall of Man.

Lily was the same. Always asking questions. She was the one who insisted we go to the Mere that day. She wanted to see the dragonflies. She brought it on herself.

276

God how I loathe them all.

I have just summoned Ivy and vented copiously. Recently she has begun to protest about marrying Walker. She still harbours an absurd idea of becoming mistress of Wake's End. I told the chit that she must do as I say or be dismissed. She continued to protest, but turned pliable when I named a sum. They're all the same. All whores.

30th December

My research into exorcism continues. Unfortunately the measures related by Pyett are somewhat barbaric. Also, since the demon was erroneously believed to be within her, her *Book* provides no guidance on how to summon a free-roaming spirit, such as I have to contend with here. This brought me briefly to an impasse. How can I exorcise the demon when I can't find it?

Then I remembered that Father – before he decided that we are all descended from monkeys – was for a time beguiled by the works of Cardinal Newman. Amid his volumes of Catholic writings, I found a passage on demons.

Such a relief to see them rationally discussed: their existence accepted, their effects pragmatically described. Apparently they are known to cause various kinds of obsessive disorder, including pederasty and onanism.

My course of action is now clear. Since the Church of England has declined to assist me, I must apply to the Church of Rome. I have telegraphed to Father Hillier in Ely, requesting an urgent consultation. I have also telegraphed to the White Hart, reserving rooms for two nights. I have told Maud not to expect me back until New Year's Day.

Jessop suggested that as there is snow on the way, he ought to drive me in the covered carriage; but I prefer to go alone. Fresh air is just the ticket, as Grayson would say. I shall set off as soon as the dog-cart is ready.

New Year's Eve. Ely

Father Hillier refuses to help. He was suspicious from the start. Why, he wondered, should a lifelong Protestant who openly scorns Catholicism suddenly seek his aid – and in such a matter? Nothing availed. Why, the arrogant young fool practically threw me out.

So now I know. I am alone in my battle against the demon. I can't say that I'm surprised. It is the will of Providence that I should fight unaided.

However, my visit to Ely has not been in vain, for at Hibble's I purchased two volumes that may prove useful.

I also take much comfort from *The Life of St Guthlaf*: *'Blessed is the man who endureth manifold troubles, for whereas he is tried, then shall he receive everlasting reward.'*

New Year's Day 1913, 2 a.m.

It is finished. God has granted me the strength to destroy the demon of the fen.

I write this in pencil, for I have a fever. The servants are watching me, but I insisted on using the bathroom unaided, having secreted this notebook under my nightclothes. I'll have to get Ivy to take it down to the study and put it back in its hiding place.

Marsh fever. What else could I be afflicted with, given

the nature of my adversary? I'm shivering, I can hardly hold the pencil. Just now I saw eyes peering at me from under the bath. I *must* gather my wits and record what happened.

On leaving Ely and wishing to avoid the New Year revelries in Wakenhyrst, I drove home via Harrow Walk. The willows bordering the Dyke stood deathly still. No moon. All was dark and silent, save for the creak of the dog-cart and the clop of hooves. In my mind's eye I saw shadows behind, slinking on to the road and creeping after me. I dared not look over my shoulder.

At last I beheld St Guthlaf's, and my courage returned. It was then, as I drove the last few hundred yards along the Lode, that the demon rose before me.

I tried to grasp my limmell stone but my hand would not obey. Until that moment, I had pictured the demon as it is in the Doom: a small hunched thing, very low to the ground. *It never occurred to me that it could take human form.*

Now I beheld it in the guise of a *man*. Very foul he was, and ragged, and he stank of the swamp. He was just as Guthlaf describes: '*most filthy and horrible, with squalid countenance and jagged teeth like those of a horse...*'

The thing rushed at me and seized the reins. In the murk I made out its loathsome toad-like features. 'I know what you did,' it rasped. 'If you drain the fen, I'll tell.'

What happened next is as broken in my mind as splintered glass. I remember uttering a cry and leaping from the dog-cart to the ground. I remember the thing coming at me. I think I pushed it. Certainly I heard ice crack. Then

I was gripping that matted head and pushing the demon under. It fought with unspeakable strength, but God lent me supra-human power and I held it down.

It is finished. The demon is dead.

Thirty-nine

MAUD shut the ledger and stared out of the window. A wasp bumped against the pane, then veered towards the flowers by the front steps.

Mechanically, Maud put the ledger on Father's desk and went out into the passage. Daisy was climbing the stairs with a tea-tray. Maud heard Nurse Lawson tell the housemaid that it was only a dizzy spell and the Master felt better already.

It took Maud a moment to remember that Father had fainted in his study and been carried up to his room. The time is all mixed up, she thought. Am I standing here on a hot morning in May, or is it still New Year's Day, with the bells tolling for Jubal?

She opened the front door and the heat hit her like a wall. She walked down the steps and vomited into the flowerbed. Father killed Jubal. Father is a murderer.

Hoverflies floated over a clump of snapdragons, and a ladybird climbed up a stalk. Maud thought: He must have been out of his mind with fever. He didn't know what he was doing.

But he killed Jubal. He pushed him into the Lode and held him under.

A shadow appeared beside her, and Clem asked if she was all right.

'No,' she said, wiping her lips with her handkerchief. 'But I shall be.'

He watched her wistfully. She gave him a cold stare. Summer had put coppery glints in his fair hair, and his grey eyes were vivid and arresting. Maud noted this dispassionately, as if she were looking at a beautiful horse.

'I got to talk to you,' he blurted out.

'No, Clem. You really don't.'

'There's summat I got to tell you—'

'Leave me alone. Don't ever talk to me again.'

She ran up the steps and Steers opened the door for her. 'When will you be wanting luncheon, Miss?'

The ledger. She'd left it on Father's desk.

'No luncheon,' she muttered. 'Just a cup of tea in the library.'

'Very good, Miss,' said the butler with weary forbearance. The Master had been ill for so many months that the staff were used to sudden changes.

Back in the study, Maud was about to replace the ledger on the bookshelf when something made her check the final entry about killing the demon: the one Father had pencilled on New Year's Day.

It wasn't the final entry. After four blank pages his account began again. This time it wasn't in that deranged pencilled scrawl but in ink, in Father's neat, cramped hand.

13th March
Now that I'm well enough to sit up, I'm rather enjoying my convalescence. I am discovering the delights of idleness. It's such bliss to do nothing except eat, sleep, and obey the commands of the excellent Lawson.

For a woman of her class, she has an agreeable appearance. Her only fault – if fault it be – is an intense dislike of Ivy. This means I've had to employ cunning to avail myself of this ledger without Lawson noticing. I waited until she was taking her meal in the kitchen, then had Ivy bring it up from the study. The girl makes the perfect courier, not only because she is illiterate but because she is jealous, and delights in deceiving Lawson. I've told her that the ledger concerns my investments, so she treats it with enormous respect.

The days are lengthening and the light is returning. The darkness and the horror – that's all in the past.

If indeed it ever existed. The Doom, the devil in the corner, my fantastic notions of a mediæval exorcism... I must have been ill for months and I never knew it. I find the sight of my scribblings embarrassing. I've no desire to re-read what I wrote. Perhaps I ought to rip it all out and burn it.

Later
Yesterday Maud took it into her head to mention Jubal Rede, of all people. The name evoked disagreeable memories from my boyhood. We were of an age, he and I; but Jubal was a great rough fellow, and I was scared of him.

4th April

The past fortnight has been fearfully damp. I'm finding it rather trying. And although the excellent Lawson keeps my windows securely shut, this room smells of the fen. Naturally I find that disturbing, for the fen is what made me ill.

It appears that at some stage during my delirium, I dictated letters to Whittaker and Davies, cancelling my instructions to drain it – and Maud actually had the ill-judgement to post them. Today I wrote instructing Whittaker and Davies to recommence their preparations for the drainage with all possible haste.

6th April

Last night I was woken by the wind in the passage rattling the bedroom latch. Being only half-awake, I fancied that it was not the wind, but something attempting to get in. I tossed and turned for hours, and dreamed of the episode in *The Life* when the demon slips into Guthlaf's hut and carries him off to Hell. Finally I rang for Lawson, who brought me a cup of beef-tea and read me a chapter from St Mark.

Needless to say, by morning I had fully recovered. I've eaten a hearty breakfast, and Lawson has devised a means of silencing the offending latch with a wedge of folded paper, which she promises to employ whenever the wind is high.

23rd April

It has been the wettest spring I can remember. Doubtless that's contributing to my low spirits. Also, Lawson says it's natural for the patient to feel moody as he regains his strength.

I blame Maud too. Confound the girl for mentioning Jubal Rede. For some reason he has become linked in my mind with my collapse on New Year's Eve. Of course I don't remember anything of that night, I was too ill. I don't *want* to remember. I simply wish I could stop thinking about it.

2nd May

Maud tells me that they buried the body in the north side of the churchyard. An odd coincidence, for that's where I saw the eye in the grass.

Although it's appropriate, I suppose. The north side of the graveyard is the Devil's part.

17th May

That storm last night gave me the most dreadful nightmare. I dreamed that I stepped into the Doom.

I was aware of a great cacophony and confusion all around, and I knew that St Michael and the hosts of Heaven were far away, and that I was perilously near the Jaws of Hell. My ears rang with the screams of the damned, and I breathed the biting stink of sulphur. Then in a clump of reeds I beheld the devil in the corner. I tried to run, but I felt as if I were wading through sand. The devil hooked me by the shoulder with the prongs of his glave and dragged me into Hell, and Hell was wet and cold and it reeked of the fen. The devil pushed me under. Filthy black water roaring in my head, my lungs about to burst. I was yanked to the surface. Desperately I gasped for air – only to be pushed under and drowned again. And again and again.

I woke wheezing, drenched in sweat. It was hours before my trembling ceased. Even now, with the sun blazing down from a cloudless sky, I'm not myself.

This was no nightmare. This was real.

Hell is real. Hell exists.

'Your father is making excellent progress,' Dr Grayson told Maud the day after she'd read Father's final entry. 'Nevertheless, we would do well to regard yesterday's fainting spell as a warning. He must not *think* of resuming his work for another two months at least. Do I make myself clear?'

'Perfectly, Doctor.'

He gave her a considering look, and tugged his nose. 'What you must understand is that a relapse would have grave consequences. Extremely grave.'

'Yes, Doctor.'

She opened her mouth to say more, then hesitated. Now would be the perfect opportunity to show the doctor her father's ledger. 'Here is the evidence,' she would say. 'It's all written down in Father's own hand, and it proves everything I told you at Christmas. You must act now. You must restrain him.'

But she knew that the doctor would either refuse to read a gentleman's private writings – or if he did, he would dismiss them as the ravings of a delirious mind.

And after all, Maud reflected, perhaps Dr Grayson would

be right. Perhaps everything Father had written was a phantasy, because he was ill. Perhaps he didn't kill Jubal.

And when one thought about it, of what had he written since he'd started getting better, except a couple of bad dreams?

Forty

From the Private Notebook of Edmund Stearne – Vol. II
18th May

What a brouhaha over nothing. Yesterday I fainted in the study. I was standing at the window when I fancied I saw something slip through the hedge and make its way towards the house. But it was *nothing*, merely the shadow of a bird! I'd had a bad night because of that wretched storm, and it disordered my nerves. I'm perfectly fine now.

Later

I wish my thoughts didn't keep returning to New Year's Eve. What troubles me most about that night is that I acted on impulse. I didn't plan or prepare for what I did, so I had no time to marshal the correct prayers or make the other observances.

Now I can't help wondering whether I did in fact achieve what I thought I'd achieved. *Can* my adversary be destroyed simply by drowning?

And will it stay dead?

24th May

Horror, horror, horror. I'm shaking so hard I can scarcely hold my pen. But it is my duty to keep this record.

I write this on a hot summer's dawn in the silence of the sleeping house, but the dread is still with me. It happened a couple of hours ago, around three o'clock in the morning. I woke to find that I couldn't breathe. The air had been sucked from the room. There was a darkness over me, incorporeal, yet pressing horribly on my chest. I caught a stink of the swamp. I felt thin leathery arms squeezing me with appalling strength. Above me, almost touching my face, I saw – no no, words cannot describe it. When my adversary takes human form it is very horrible, but this – this was its true form, and it was fluid and ever-changing, infinitely worse. This was 'darkness visible'.

I woke with a cry. The room was sunk in gloom, but I sensed that dawn was near. Beyond my feet I saw that the blind was up and the sash raised. The curtains were flapping. I inhaled the stink of the swamp. With a groan I rolled on to my stomach and pressed my face to my pillow. My lips touched something slimy and wet. With a cry I drew back. There on the pillow lay a long thin strand of waterweed.

Later

I'm calmer now. I can face the truth. This last encounter has confirmed my fears beyond doubt. What I did on New Year's Eve didn't work. My adversary is not dead. By drowning it, I merely sent it back to its own element. I made it stronger.

25th May

It is vital that I make believe that all is well. I don't care about Maud or the servants, it's not for them that I maintain this pretence. *I must not let my adversary become aware that I know.*

I must never betray myself, not by the smallest gesture. I must watch what I say, how I look, what I do. I must show no fear. I must never, never let down my guard.

This means that my research must be carried out *sub rosa*, so that my adversary suspects nothing. Perusing those volumes from Hibble's, consulting others borrowed from Dr G.; all must appear to be in furtherance of my historical research.

26th May

I feel my solitude keenly. There is no one to help me. Pyett survived because her husband had the assistance of the Church and could thus commission the exorcism. Guthlaf survived because he was a saint; and because a saint came to his aid. He 'prayed to St Bartholomew, and the accursed spirit vanished like smoke before his face'.

St Bartholomew is the patron saint of exorcists. I have prayed to him, but to no avail. Perhaps that's because his feast day is three months hence.

St Michael is the Prince of Spiritual Warfare, but he hasn't heard my prayers either. His day is even further off, at the end of September. *I know now that I cannot wait that long.*

Later

Perhaps God is with me still, for at last I know the appointed Day.

27th May

This morning I made my first visit to church since falling ill. I was aglow with piety, and for a while I felt that all shadows were banished. But after the service, some impulse made me ask the rector for the key to the room in the tower. Why did I need to see the Doom? I've no idea. I only stayed a moment, but it was enough. The devil in the corner winked at me.

Of course it didn't *really* wink, that was merely fancy. But I was shaken.

How I wish the Day would come. This constant pretence is proving an enormous strain. But I must *not* let down my guard, not for an instant.

Later

I've just realised that I've overlooked a crucial aspect of the nature of demons. *How* could I have forgotten, when it is so familiar? Revelations, Milton; it's plain for all to see.

This is what I must remember: my adversary could be anything or anyone. It can take *any* form.

28th May

The worst has happened. Once again, it has taken human form. *I have seen it.* And it's far closer than I thought.

But I must take courage. At last I know what I have to do.

Forty-one

'BUT my dear Miss Stearne,' said the rector with an incredulous smile. 'Surely you appreciate that I couldn't possibly read a word of what your father has written? Why, I should be intruding on his private thoughts. That's something no gentleman would ever do. I confess I am shocked, profoundly shocked, that you have seen fit to do so yourself, when you must have known that he never meant these notes to be seen by another living soul! Why, he has written as much on the first page: "Private."'

Shutting the ledger, he stared at her over his half-moon spectacles. He had a naturally high colour which made him appear permanently angry. Right now, the anger was real.

'I only read them after a great deal of agonising,' lied Maud. 'But Father's behaviour has been so very bizarre—'

'Your father was delirious with fever! Surely that entitles him to sympathy and forbearance, especially from his own daughter.'

'Yes, indeed, but—'

'Besides, why come to me? If you genuinely believe there's

something amiss, why did you not consult Dr Grayson?' He noticed her hesitation. 'Ah, then you have spoken to him.'

'I tried.'

'May I ask when?'

'Shortly before Christmas.'

'From which I infer that the good doctor very properly declined to assist.'

In the silence that followed, the rector drummed his fingertips on the ledger.

The door opened a crack. Miss Broadstairs peeped in and asked in a hushed voice if they wanted tea.

'Thank you no,' snapped the rector.

Miss Broadstairs withdrew, shutting the door without a sound. The clock on the chimney-piece ticked. Maud sat with her hands clenched in her lap.

The rector heaved a sigh. 'You come to me with some nonsense about "demonic possession". You tell me that someone – you've no idea who – is in imminent peril. You say that *your father* – a gentleman of considerable standing in the parish, whom I myself have known and respected for decades – poses some kind of "threat". My dear Miss Stearne, what on earth am I to make of all this?'

He was right. It made no sense. Maud didn't know who was in danger, or when the blow would fall. All she knew was that on some unspecified day, Father would kill again.

'At last I know what I have to do,' he had written yesterday. She had read it this morning. She hadn't waited to tell Jessop to prepare the dog-cart. She had run the three miles to the Rectory, arriving dusty and dishevelled while Mr Broadstairs and his daughter were having breakfast.

'How old are you, Maud?' he said in a kindlier voice.

'Sixteen,' she muttered. Her birthday had been three days ago. On the same date, Father had ascertained what he called 'the appointed Day'.

'Sometimes I forget how young you are,' said Mr Broadstairs. 'You've been a great help to your father in his work, but I fancy it's been too much for you. You've become confused. You've garbled things in your mind. No, don't interrupt. You see, Dr Stearne himself has spoken to me on this very matter of "demons" – *but as part of his research!* He laughs at it as nonsense, he once told me "it's all bosh"! My dear, his only interest is in the context of his *work!*'

'I see that now, Rector.' Maud rose to her feet. 'I've been most frightfully foolish and I'm sorry to have taken up your time. Now if I might trouble you for Father's—'

'Oh no, my dear. I must return these to him myself.'

She stared at him in horror. 'But you can't. Then he'll know I've read them.'

He stood smiling down at her. 'Our actions have consequences, my dear. My duty couldn't be clearer. I must hand these volumes to him in person. And obviously I shall have to tell him how they came into my possession.'

After weeks without rain, the Common was a scorched brown wilderness of dead grass and brittle gorse. Maud walked home amid clouds of white dust. Soon Father would know that she knew everything: the Doom, the devil in the corner, Lily. Jubal.

She reached Wake's End around noon. Father was

upstairs lying down. Maud took off her outdoor things and washed the dust off her face. Then she sat in the library and waited.

An hour later, the rector arrived on his cob and was shown upstairs to Father's room. Mr Broadstairs was there for ten minutes, after which he left. Maud went on waiting.

The expected summons never came. She saw nothing of Father for the rest of the day. Lawson told her that the excessive heat had given her patient a migraine headache, and he would take his dinner on a tray.

That night for the first time in her life, Maud locked her bedroom door. She didn't sleep, and next morning she went downstairs feeling hollow with dread.

Father was waiting for her in the breakfast-room with the rest of the household. It was the first occasion since his illness that he was taking morning prayers. He was immaculately dressed and he greeted her with every appearance of good humour. He led the prayers in the same way he always had. Maud could see no sign of anything amiss, except that while he was giving the reading, his left arm hung at his side and he rubbed his thumb and forefinger ceaselessly together.

After prayers he ate breakfast with her – again for the first time since his illness. Maud ate nothing, but he consumed a hearty meal. He frowned and tutted at his newspaper as he'd always done, and treated her with his usual distant courtesy. Apart from asking for a second cup of tea, he spoke no word to her. That was also entirely normal.

She was on her way out when he called her back. 'I nearly forgot,' he said. 'I have a small commission for you.'

'Yes, Father,' she croaked.

He held out a piece of folded notepaper. 'I wonder if you would be kind enough to take this to Ely? It's rather an urgent order and I don't care to entrust it to the servants.'

'Yes, Father.'

'Aren't you going to read what it says?'

'No.'

He looked amused. 'Then how shall you know to whom you ought to take it?'

Shakily, Maud unfolded the paper and read the hand-written lines: 'One ice-pick; one geological hammer, its leading edge to be sharpened in the manner of a chisel.'

'The blacksmith ought to be able to provide both items,' he told her. 'Oh, and there's one more matter. Yesterday I had a visit from the rector.'

Maud's stomach turned over.

'He was kind enough to return to me certain volumes of notes.'

'Yes, Father.'

'You see, Maud,' he said gently. 'There are things in this world which pass your understanding.'

'I know, Father, and I'm so dreadfully sorry – and truly, I – I didn't understand a word!'

To her astonishment, he smiled at her with great sweetness. 'Of course you didn't. How could you possibly? Now run along, I want that order placed as soon as you can.'

She hesitated. 'When shall I say you need the items by?'

'Oh, no particular date. If they can't give them to you at once, just tell them to send them as soon as they can.'

'Yes, Father.'

From the doorway she watched him fold his newspaper with his usual precision. He sat in a shaft of sunlight, and his face was as handsome and serene as the alabaster knight in church.

It came to Maud suddenly that this was all an act: that he was straining every sinew to appear normal, so as not to give himself away.

She remembered something he'd told her once: that the female, being the weaker vessel, was more susceptible to demonic possession. Was that what he believed? That the demon had taken female form?

He raised his head and his pale eyes met hers. 'Run along, there's a good girl.'

She felt as if she was falling. It's me, she thought. Dear God he thinks it's me.

Forty-two

MAUD nearly made Clem drive her to Ely. But even if he wanted to help her, what could he do?

Instead she had the boot-boy drive her. Billy was new to Wake's End, and slightly simple. He would do what she told him without asking questions.

They set off in the dog-cart shortly after ten, but by then the sun was relentless. Blossom was already drooping, so as they started up the slope towards the Common, Maud got out and walked.

She knew there was a train station at Ely; perhaps she could escape to London, or Norwich, or Edinburgh. She had a sovereign and three shillings in her purse; would that be enough? She'd never travelled on her own. She didn't even know how to buy a ticket. Besides, wherever she went, Father would find her.

She glanced back at Wake's End shimmering in the heat. She had always loved this view from the Common. From up here one could see how the fen wrapped its arms around the old house to protect it. But who would protect the fen?

I can't run away, she thought. If I do, he'll destroy it. He is right. I am his adversary. It's either him or me.

Tuthill the blacksmith didn't have the hammer or the ice-pick, but he said he could send them in a few days. He asked what Dr Stearne wanted them for, and Maud replied that she had no idea.

After giving Billy sixpence to buy himself something to eat, she told him to meet her on the corner of the Market Place and the High Street at half past three. Then she found a bench on St Mary's Green and sat down to think.

She knew no one in Ely who would help her. Priests, aldermen, physicians, attorneys: to a man, they would declare that she was ill and send her back to Father. The police were also out of the question. Maud had only the vaguest notion of what policemen actually did, but she knew that her sort of people never had anything to do with them.

Besides, who would believe her without the ledger? Without it, all she had was some wild story about devils which no one would believe. Especially not from a girl.

Despite her sun-umbrella, the heat was unbearable. She was covered in dust and her underclothes were soaked. Her new long corset made sitting uncomfortable, and as it reached almost to her knees, it impeded walking. Her damp stockings chafed her thighs and her button boots pinched her feet. Everything she was wearing seemed designed to prevent escape.

To her surprise, she discovered that she was ravenous.

She decided to do what she always did when she was in Ely: she went and had luncheon at the White Hart. Mrs Palmer put her in the private dining-room, where Maud ordered asparagus soup, roast lamb with watercress and new peas, ginger beer, and gooseberry tart with cream. She demolished the lot, and felt a little clearer in her mind.

There *was* something she could do. Those books Father had bought at New Year: if she knew the titles, she might be able to find them when she got home. They might tell her how and when he intended to kill the 'demon'.

Phrasing it like that reduced it to a puzzle she had to solve. Her mind shied away from the fact that Father was planning to kill *her*.

Mr Hibble was proud of his record-keeping, and delighted to be of service to the daughter of his most valued customer. He insisted on personally copying the details on a sheet of notepaper: *Late Mediæval Art and Iconography* by A.J. Stanbury; and *Rituale Romanum*, revised by Pope Benedict XIV in 1752.

Neither title meant anything to Maud, but at least she knew what to look for when she got home. She felt a little stronger. Instead of simply watching and waiting, she had something to do.

During her absence, Wake's End had undergone a startling transformation. Since the heat wave had begun, many of the windows and doors had stood open, but now Father had ordered the servants to drape them with bedsheets soaked in lime-water to keep out the bad air.

Maud had read of such measures in Maman's book of household management, but they'd never been employed at Wake's End. First Father had stripped the house of its protective ivy. Now he had blinded it.

To her intense relief, Lawson told her that the Master was upstairs lying down, and intended to remain in his room for the rest of the day. So at least it won't be today, she thought.

This gave her the courage to look for the volumes on Hibble's list. She started in the study. The servants had already covered the windows, and she found herself in a shrouded dimness amid the eye-stinging smell of lime.

She found both books almost at once in the bookshelf and bore them off to the library. The windows in here hadn't been done, but no sooner had she settled in an armchair than Ivy bustled in with a basket of damp sheets.

'Not now,' said Maud.

'Master's orders,' snapped Ivy.

'I said not now! And don't talk back. You might think your position is secure, but you're a servant. One day I'll be mistress of this house.'

Ivy snorted. 'You're just jealous 'cos I got Clem.'

'You're not exactly shouting it from the rooftops, though, are you?'

Ivy climbed on a chair and hung a sheet over the curtain rail. 'Thass up to me and Clem,' she smirked. 'Next week he's buying me a ring at the Fair.'

Maud stared at the housemaid's hourglass figure. That's what men want, she thought.

As never before she felt the corrosive force of jealousy.

She wanted Ivy dead. Preferably from some painful disease that destroyed her looks slowly, while she was still alive. Smallpox would be ideal.

And she realised too that if by some miracle she was wrong and Father didn't believe she was possessed, but instead thought it was Ivy – then she, Maud, wouldn't lift a finger to help. If Father 'exorcised' Ivy, she would be glad.

It would solve both her problems at one stroke, because then both Ivy and Father would be out of the way. It would kill two birds with one stone.

The *Rituale Romanum* contained certain rites of the Catholic Church, including the rite of exorcism. It was in Latin, and Father had marked several passages: *Exorcizamus te, omnis immundis spiritus, omni satanica potestas, omnis incursio infernalis adversarii, omnis legio, omnis congregatio et secta diabolica…*

It went on for pages and it told Maud nothing about how he intended to destroy the demon – although she was pretty sure that he meant to do a lot more than pray.

Tucked inside the volume was a pamphlet containing a comprehensive list of Catholic saints' days; Maud guessed that this was where he'd looked up the feast days for St Bartholomew and St Michael. Unfortunately, he hadn't marked any other dates. And since there were dozens of saints for practically every day of the year, again it told her nothing.

The text of *Late Mediæval Art and Iconography*

contained only glancing references to devils, but plate after plate depicted Hell with a sadistic inventiveness that made the tortures in the Doom seem positively humane. In picture after picture, an entire demonic fauna inflicted endless torments on the damned. Bird-headed monsters stuffed naked sinners into meat-grinders, and skewered them on spits over burning coals. Men had red-hot horse-shoes nailed to their feet. Women were sawn in half between their legs, or thrust like pallid moths into giant blazing lanterns.

Maud was familiar with such images from Father's books on medieval art, but she was unable to determine in what way this book was different. Why did he regard it as so important?

Her final lead was the reference in his notebook to Milton. She'd never heard the name before, but Mr Hibble had told her that Milton had been a poet. The bookseller had sold her two weighty volumes, *Samson Agonistes* and *Paradise Lost*. She started with the latter because she liked the title, but soon gave up in despair.

How could she find anything when she didn't know what she was looking *for*?

Even after sunset, the heat did not abate. Maud tied back the lime-soaked sheets that Daisy had draped across her bedroom windows, and raised the sashes as far as they would go. She'd already locked her door and put her knife under her pillow. That was all she could do to protect herself.

Lying on her side with her knees to her chest, she waited for the moon to rise. Images of torture flitted before her eyes.

Sleeping in moonlight was supposed to turn you mad. Was Father mad? In his speech and general demeanour he did not appear deranged. And he had found reasons for everything he did.

She thought about that time last year when he kept finding his bedroom windows open. She had always believed that he must have done it himself, in his sleep; or perhaps it had been Ivy, playing tricks. But what about the waterweed on his windowsill, and on his pillow? He couldn't have done that in his sleep. And it didn't sound like Ivy. Besides, Ivy didn't know about Lily, so she couldn't know how profoundly waterweed would affect him.

The night was airless, with not a breath of wind. Maud longed for the barn owl to come and perch on her windowsill, as it had done when she was little, before everything went wrong.

She woke to stifling heat and a smell of meadowsweet.

Drowsily, she became aware that someone had untied the sheets across the windows. They hung motionless and faintly aglow.

Something was moving on the ceiling above her head. Through half-closed lids she made out shifting bands, like waterlight.

It can't be waterlight, she thought. Not unless the fen has crept up to the walls. But that's in Father's dream, not mine.

Her nightgown stuck to her back. Rucking it up around

her waist, she moved to a cooler patch of the bed. The smell of meadowsweet grew stronger.

As she lay panting on her side, a small grey shadow appeared in the middle of the sheet that covered the left-hand window. The shadow grew steadily larger and darker.

It's a head, Maud thought with a jolt.

She sat up. The head pressed against the linen. Maud made out a face with mouth agape and blind, sheeted eyes.

A cry rang out. Now Maud was truly awake, standing in the middle of the room. The sheets were tied back from the windows, as they had been before. The cries were coming from next door, where Felix slept.

Fumbling to unlock her door, Maud lurched into the passage and collided with Nurse. Maud felt the heat off the woman's solid flesh and inhaled the sour smell of her scalp.

'He's hot, poor lamb,' muttered Nurse. 'Go back to bed, I'll see to him.'

Maud locked herself in and padded to the window. The dream had shaken her. It had felt so real.

The fen lay still and silent in the moonlight. She loved it for its starlings and dragonflies, its rustling reeds and glinting pools – but these things were all on the surface. She'd never thought about what lay beneath.

The fen was deep: people said that there were places where you could never touch the bottom. The fen was old: it had endured for thousands of years. Who knew what had haunted it since long before the coming of men?

Despite the heat, Maud felt cold. For the first time since Father had found the Doom, it occurred to her that his wild imaginings might be true.

Forty-three

Next day dawned hotter than ever. Maud dressed in her lightest combinations and muslin day-frock and slipped her knife in her pocket. She hadn't worn her corset since Ely. She wanted nothing to impede her movements.

Lawson was waiting for her in the breakfast-room. She told Maud that Father had spent an uncomfortable night and would be keeping to his room all day. Maud took this in silence. Either it meant that today was not 'the Day', or else he was trying to put her off her guard.

It was hard to believe in demons with Daisy grumbling about her heat-rash, but by now Maud was used to living in parallel worlds. Having cancelled morning prayers, she ate a substantial breakfast of a veal cutlet with two coddled eggs, two slices of thickly buttered toast and marmalade, and three cups of tea with plenty of cream. She hadn't forgotten how much sharper she'd felt after luncheon at the White Hart.

And there was something else she could do to protect herself. Cramming on her hat, she headed out into the grounds.

The heat was intense, not a breath of wind. Beyond the Lode the reeds stood motionless. The buzz of crickets was very loud.

She found the Solomon's Seal in the flowerbed outside the library doors. It was a large, vigorous plant with greenish-white, bell-shaped flowers. She remembered a medieval woodcut in which a monk clutched a single arching stem like a shepherd's crook. The leaves were a vivid glossy green, and as she stuffed them in her pockets her fingers became sticky with sap. She didn't believe they had magical powers, but Father did. It might help her fight him off.

Clem appeared on the path with a wheelbarrow. When he saw her he stopped. Let him stare, she thought savagely.

As she was picking her way out of the flowerbed, he left his wheelbarrow and cut off her retreat. 'I got to talk to you,' he said urgently.

'Out of my way, *Walker*,' she snapped.

'Just *listen*, will you? I don't want her. I don't even *like* her!'

'But you're still going to marry her, aren't you?'

With his thumbnail he dug at a cut on his palm. 'I can't afford not to.'

'Oh what a hardship, I quite understand.'

'No you don't. How could you? If I dun't do as he says, I'll not get another place. Then what'll I do? There's only me and Ned now. What'll we *eat*?'

He was three years older than her, but he looked younger. Young and miserable and out of his depth.

Cole was coming through the orchard.

'Clem,' she said suddenly. 'The Master's not well. Stay out of his way.'

'What d'you mean? He was all right the other day.'

'He's not himself. And Clem... It doesn't matter about Ivy. Do what you have to do. I understand.'

The day crawled by – and then another. And still Father kept to his room.

Maud re-read *Late Mediæval Art* and tried again with *Paradise Lost*. Once or twice, she felt she was almost on to something, but it slipped away. She redoubled her efforts. If she could find out what he was planning, she might be able to beat him at his own game.

In the evening she discovered that while she'd been in the library, the ledger and the notebook had been quietly replaced in the study bookshelf. She made herself re-read the final entries in case she'd missed something: 'I've overlooked a crucial aspect of the nature of demons. How could I have forgotten, when it is so familiar? Revelations, Milton; it's plain for all to see... *I have seen it...* At last I know what I have to do.'

Father had written this on the 27th and 28th of May. Today was the 1st of June. The remaining pages were blank.

Maud pictured him writing one final entry after he had killed her. 'It is finished. The demon is no more.'

She woke very early next morning to the certain knowledge of what she had missed.

'It's all bosh,' Father had told the rector. Except that wasn't quite what he'd said.

It was five o'clock and the household was still sleeping. Flinging on her clothes, Maud went downstairs. The heat was as oppressive as ever, but a strange hot wind was stirring the apple trees beneath an ominous red sky.

Late Mediæval Art was not in the bookshelf where she'd left it yesterday evening. It was on Father's desk, on top of a neat stack of medical monographs that bore the *Ex Libris* stamp of Dr Grayson. Father must have crept downstairs in the night, while everyone was asleep.

Had he meant her to find these papers? Or perhaps he no longer felt that he needed to conceal what he was doing.

She took *Late Mediæval Art* into the library and found what she was looking for almost at once. She was right. Father hadn't told the rector 'It's all bosh'. He'd said: 'It's all *Bosch*.' Hieronymus Bosch, c.1450–1516, 'whose minutely realised works with their unique, often nightmarish iconography vividly depict the Seven Deadly Sins and the torments of the damned.'

But the picture Maud turned up wasn't one of Bosch's depictions of Hell. That was why she'd overlooked it before. It was a smaller, quieter work, showing a surgeon in an odd conical cap and a long pink robe drilling into the top of a man's skull.

'*The Stone Operation*,' she read, 'depicts a procedure to cure seizures &c by excising the stone of folly from the brain. Some historians believe that this operation was actually performed at popular gatherings and country fairs, while others assert that it was only a metaphor. The latter seems more likely. Had it been performed, it would undoubtedly have proved fatal.'

Forty-four

MAUD heard Daisy clomping downstairs with the servants' slop-pail. Soon the housemaid would unbolt the back door for Billy, who would empty the pail in the outside water-closet, then set about his morning tasks of trimming the lamps and cleaning the boots.

Maud waited until she knew Daisy would be in the scullery. Then she tiptoed into the study and retrieved Dr Grayson's monographs from Father's desk. There were three of them, all dating from the previous century and all with slips of paper between the pages, bearing neat annotations in Father's hand.

The first was a review of a procedure called 'trepanation', defined in the introduction as the removal of a circular piece of bone from the skull. Maud learned that the technique had been known for thousands of years, and that medieval apothecaries had used it to cure seizures and relieve pressure on the brain. Father's note said simply: '*vide* Fig. 13.'

Figure 13 was an engraving from the fourteenth century.

It showed a woman lying on her back, looking remarkably calm, given that her head was clamped in a large vice and a man with an augur was drilling into her forehead. A tiny black demon was flying out of one of her eyes.

The second paper was a translation of a work published in 1892 by one Gottlieb Burckhardt, who had experimented on lunatics by excising sections of their cerebral cortex (Maud gathered that this meant he'd cut out parts of their brains). Two of Dr Burckhardt's patients had died, two had developed epilepsy, and one had committed suicide. The sixth had undergone repeated excisions of brain tissue, which had transformed her from a noisy and 'particularly vicious' female to a 'more tractable' one, albeit with some loss of intelligence. Despite this, Burckhardt had declared his experiment a success.

Maud couldn't make out Father's annotations except for the phrase 'orbital aperture'. She didn't know what that meant.

By the sound of it, Ivy was sweeping the top of the stairs and working her way down. A clank came from the breakfast-room as Daisy put down her cleaning things. Once she'd set it to rights, she would lay the table, and Ivy would do the hall. After that the other servants would file in and await the Master and Miss Maud for morning prayers.

The final monograph was by an anatomist named Dr Paul Broca, who had made a study of trepanation through the ages, as well as trying out various techniques on the skulls of dead people. He concluded that drilling was the quickest means of penetrating the skulls of adults, while for the softer skulls of children, one only had to scrape the bone for a few minutes with a sharp-edged instrument such as a chisel.

Father's note was brief: 'Cut, or scrape?'

Maud had four pounds, six shillings and sevenpence from the housekeeping to finance her escape. She wore the dragonfly pendant Maman had given her and put the viper skin and the porcelain wing in her pockets. She would get Clem to drive her to Ely and take the first train out. Then she would find a way to contact Great-Uncle Bertrand in Brussels.

In the downstairs passage she met Lawson, who told her that Father would not be down for breakfast. Maud noted the distinction: he had said nothing about the rest of the day. She sent Lawson to tell the other servants that there would be no morning prayers, then hurried into the breakfast-room, where she crammed two bread rolls with bacon and stuffed them in her hand-bag.

She was grabbing her hat from the hatstand when Father appeared at the top of the stairs. He was fully dressed and his cheeks were scrubbed and shining. 'Ah, so you've already breakfasted,' he said with an absent smile.

'I – I wasn't hungry,' she faltered. 'The heat...'

'To be sure, the heat, the infernal heat.' As he descended, he tapped a rhythm on the banister. 'I wouldn't go into the grounds if I were you, it'll be no cooler there.'

Her mind went blank. 'I – need to see Cole. About the strawberries. For tea.'

His glance passed over her as if she didn't exist, and as

he entered the breakfast-room he chuckled to himself. 'Yes, I think we *might* attempt a little light work on Pyett... *If* the excellent Lawson permits.'

'Where's Walker?' cried Maud when she found Cole.

'It's his half day, Miss,' said the old man. 'He won't be in till noon.'

She blinked back tears. She'd been counting on Clem, and now he was three miles away in Wakenhyrst. It would be no use telling Jessop to drive her to Ely, he would refuse. He would tell her that he couldn't answer for the horses in this heat.

'You're not displeased with Walker, are you, Miss?' said Cole.

'What?'

'Only I seed you having words with en yesterday, so I thought you might of heard about that toad.'

'*Toad?* What are you talking about?'

'No need to take on, Miss Maud, I'm sure.' He launched into some rigmarole about Clem finding a toad under a flowerpot and the Master making him kill it. 'Walker didn't want to, Miss, knowing your feelings for the animiles. So I thought mebbe...'

A dreadful thought occurred to Maud. 'When was this?' she said sharply.

'When?' The old gardener tugged his ear-lobe. 'I dunno. Three days since. Mebbe four?'

'The twenty-eighth of May.'

'Thereabouts, Miss.'

On the 28th of May, Father had written: 'Once again, it has taken human form. *I have seen it.*'

Cole was squinting at her curiously.

'When the Master was talking to Walker, how did he seem?'

'Seem, Miss? I don't know as I—'

'How did he *seem*? Was he startled or brusque or what?'

'Oh, no, nothing like that. He wor his usual self.' He grinned. 'He did give Walker a bit of a look when his back wor turned, but I'm sure he meant nothing by it...'

The pieces of the kaleidoscope shifted, and Maud knew that she'd got it all wrong. Father hadn't been feigning indifference to her, his indifference was genuine. He didn't believe she was the one possessed.

At last she understood the entry in his ledger about having overlooked a crucial aspect of the nature of demons. '*How* could I have forgotten, when it is so familiar? Revelations, Milton; it's plain for all to see.'

It was indeed in Revelations: a well-known passage which she also knew well. 'And there was war in Heaven... and the great dragon was cast out, that old serpent, called the Devil, and Satan... he was cast out into the earth, and his angels were cast out with him.'

That was the aspect Father had remembered: that demons were fallen angels. They weren't always ugly.

Demons could be beautiful.

Like Clem.

Forty-five

'... for the devil is come down unto you, having great wrath, because he knoweth that he hath but a short time.'
Revelations 12:12

Saints' Feast Days for 2nd June: St Ada, St Adalgis, St Blandina, St Bodfan, St Erasmus, St Eugene, St John de Ortega, Sts Marcellinus & Peter,* the Martyrs of Lyons, St Nicholas of Peregrinus, St Pothinus.
* also known as Petrus Exorcista, or St Peter the Exorcist

*T*HE track over the Common seemed endless. The sun was a strange angry red and a hot wind was whipping up blinding clouds of dust. It was nearly ten o'clock. Maud was still a mile from the village.

At last the Rectory rose into view, and beyond it the cottages of Wakenhyrst. But in front of them Maud made out a cluster of tents flapping in the wind, and pedlars' barrows and people holding on to their hats. It was the day of the Fair. She'd forgotten all about it.

To avoid it she took the path that led behind the Rectory and came out into the High Street, not far from the Walkers' cottage. Clem wasn't there. His younger brother said he'd gone eel-babbing the night before and was camping in the fen, so that he could go straight to work.

Maud stood blinking the dust from her eyes. Her boots hurt and she was drenched in sweat. It was nearly eleven o'clock and she was three miles further from Clem than when she'd started. Ignoring Ned's frightened offer of a cup of buttermilk, she ran back to the Fair. She collared the carter and offered him a guinea to take her to Wake's End and stay with her till she'd found Clem. The carter dursn't risk his horse in this heat, not if she promised him ten guineas. She started back to Wake's End on foot. Clem was bigger and stronger than Father. If she could warn him in time, he'd be all right.

She thought of Father's neat annotations on Dr Grayson's monographs. Drilling was the quickest way to pierce the skulls of adults, while for the softer skulls of children, you scraped the bone with a sharp instrument like a chisel. *Cut, or scrape?* Father must have written that because Clem was young.

And the tools he intended to use had already arrived. Before leaving the house, Maud had ascertained from Daisy that Tuthill's boy had brought them the day before – Father having telegraphed the blacksmith to send the items by the 2nd of June without fail. 'One ice-pick; one geological hammer, its leading edge to be sharpened in the manner of a chisel.'

It was half past noon when Maud finally reached

Wake's End. She shouted for Clem, but he didn't appear. The grounds were deserted. The house stared at her with blinded eyes. In the orchard the trees were thrashing and groaning. Across the Lode the reeds were hissing, as if the fen itself was angry.

No one opened the front door for her and she found nobody in the library, the drawing-room or the breakfast-room. Father's study was empty, his desk orderly and undisturbed. But the ledger was gone.

She ran out into the passage. 'Hulloa?' she called. 'Anyone?'

The green baize door opened a crack, and the boot-boy peered at her with frightened eyes.

'Where is everyone?' she cried.

'Master sent en off to the Fair, Miss.'

'What, everyone?'

Billy ducked his head. 'There's only me, Miss. An Ivy upstairs with Master Felix.'

'Where's Walker?'

'I dunno, Miss, I an't seen en.'

'Where's the Master?'

'I dunno, Miss. I'm to stay out back. Did I do wrong?'

Maud picked up her skirts and ran upstairs. Ivy wasn't in the nursery, but Felix was fast asleep. He was flushed and breathing heavily through his mouth. On the nightstand, flies clustered on a spoon and a bottle of Rawlinson's Quieting Syrup. Ivy must have drugged him and slipped off to the Fair.

Maud ran down to the bathroom. Her reflection in the looking-glass was wild-eyed and spectral with dust, the skin of her face as taut as if someone had pulled back her scalp.

Down the passage a door slammed. Peering out, Maud saw that the doors to Father's bedroom were shut. They'd been open before. Taking her knife from her pocket, she crept along the passage.

No sounds from within. But downstairs, the study doors softly closed. He'd been up here and he'd slammed these doors. Then he'd stealthily descended to the study.

Noiselessly, Maud turned the handles. Father's bedroom and dressing-room were stiflingly hot and smelled sharply of lime. Sheets hung motionless across the windows, bathing the room in a strange, fiery light. On the side-table by the chaise longue lay a pen and a bottle of ink. On the chaise longue lay the ledger. It was open.

Wincing at every creaking floorboard, Maud crossed to the chaise longue. Father had started a new page with the heading: 'The Second of June – The Feast of Petrus Exorcista.' Beneath this he'd drawn the head of a child.

The drawing was in black ink and executed with the clarity and precision of an anatomical diagram. Above the child's left eye, a neat triangle of scalp had been sliced and partly peeled back to expose the skull.

The blood soughed in Maud's head. The child was a boy about four years old with a luxuriant mop of curls and a chicken pox scar on the bridge of his nose. Felix.

Beneath the drawing, Father had written a Bible reference, Mark 5:9. Maud grabbed his Bible from the nightstand and rifled the pages.

St Mark, 5:9: 'And he asked him, What is thy name? And he answered, saying, My name is Legion: for we are many.'

It took her a moment to grasp what this meant. Even then she couldn't believe it. Did Father think the demon was in Felix *and* Clem?

My name is Legion: for we are many.

Forty-six

THE study doors creaked open, and Maud heard Father calling for Billy. He sounded vexed, but bizarrely calm.

'You wanted me, sir?' the boot-boy said timidly.

'Which is why I rang,' chided Father.

'Sorry, sir.'

Maud couldn't make out what Father said after that, but a minute later she heard the study doors close. Billy trotted back down the passage. Maud went to the top of the stairs and stood twisting her hands. It sounded as if Father was opening drawers in the study and talking to himself. She couldn't leave Felix to be slaughtered. But what if Clem came in from the fen and Father attacked him?

She thought of that drawing of Felix's head, with the scalp peeled back. She thought of Clem. Clem was strong. He could defend himself. Felix was four years old. She turned and ran upstairs to the nursery.

Felix was still asleep, whiffling into his pillow. Maud locked him in and slipped the key in her pocket.

She'd just descended to the first floor when she heard the front door shut. Through the round window at the end of the passage, she peered down on to Father's fair head. He stood on the steps, looking about him. In his right hand he held an ice-pick and in his left, a hammer with a long thin head of grey steel that glinted in the sun. As Maud watched, he straightened his shoulders and started down the steps.

Abandoning stealth, she clattered downstairs, yelling for Billy. 'The Master's gone mad! Run as fast as you can and fetch help! Go on, *run*!'

Pushing the terrified boy through the scullery door, she rushed into the boot-room. The gun-cupboard was locked. She darted into the scullery and grabbed a cleaver, ran back to the boot-room and tried to prise open the cupboard. She couldn't do it. Besides, she'd never held a gun in her life, she was wasting *time*. Still clutching the cleaver, she burst through the back door. Her stomach turned over. Propped against the pump was Clem's eel glave. He must have come in from the fen and stopped to have a wash before going off to start work.

Flinging down the cleaver, Maud grabbed the eel glave and raced round the corner to the orchard.

Father was kneeling in the long grass under an apple tree. His hands and shirt were scarlet with blood and he was bending over Clem, who lay on his back.

Clem must have been tired after his night's eel-babbing. He'd left his pail of eels in the shade to keep cool, then folded his jacket under his head for a pillow and lain down and gone to sleep. In an instant that would stay with Maud for ever, she saw the shiny mahogany handle of the ice-pick sticking out of his left eye. She saw where Father had sliced away part of Clem's scalp and hammered a hole in his skull. She saw splinters of white bone, and the glistening red and grey sludge that had been Clem: his thoughts and hopes and loves.

As she stood on the path, Father yanked out the ice-pick and put it in his pocket. Then he pressed a shard of green glass into Clem's ruined eye, and lifted the lid of the other eye and did the same, after which he prised apart Clem's lips and stuffed more glass into his mouth and a handful of leaves. Throughout all this he'd been muttering in Latin, but now he sat back on his heels and frowned. 'But where did it go?' he exclaimed.

Catching sight of Maud, he waved her away. 'Go back inside, there's a good girl. Can't you see I'm busy?' Rising to his feet, he cast about, as if looking for something in the grass. With a sigh he gave up the search. Taking the hammer from one pocket and the chisel from the other, he started for the house.

'Get back,' said Maud, barring his way with the eel glave. 'You can't have Felix.'

'But it *isn't* Felix,' he said irritably. 'Now give me that thing before you hurt yourself.'

'Get back! I won't let you kill Felix!'

'I told you,' he said with the weary pedantry of someone correcting a grammatical error. 'It's not Felix, it's the adversary.'

He stood ten feet away from her, a tall, powerful man.

She was a girl of sixteen. She thought fast. 'You won't find him in the nursery,' she lied. 'Ivy took him to the Fair.'

'Now we both know that's not true. I saw Ivy run off on her own. It's in the nursery. Its mortal body is asleep, I saw it myself. Now get out of my way.'

'It went down the well,' she blurted out.

He looked at her.

'It's true, I saw it! What you were looking for just now, a little black imp? I saw it fly out of his – out of his eye, when you pulled out the ice-pick! It went down the well. If you don't catch it, it'll get away!'

The well was behind him. He couldn't resist moving towards it and glancing in. Maud rushed at him with the glave and shoved him in the back.

He didn't utter a sound, he just fell. Maud heard an echoing splash. She held her breath.

'Why on *earth* did you do that?' Father sounded angry, but weirdly rational. 'Run and fetch Billy *at once* and get me out of here before I catch my death!'

She had hoped that the fall would break his neck. She wondered if she had the courage to kill him. She wondered how to do it. The prongs of the glave were curved, so she couldn't stab him. Perhaps if she steeled herself she could claw open his throat, or—

A gasp behind her made her turn.

Ivy stood on the path with her mouth open. 'You *pushed* him. I *saw* you.' Picking up her skirts, she ran to unwind the rope and let down the well-bucket.

'Leave it!' shouted Maud, warning her back with the glave. 'I mean it, Ivy. Don't you touch that rope!'

Ivy stared at her. She hadn't yet spotted Clem's body. The well was in the way.

'Ivy, is that you?' called Father. 'Be a good girl and let down the rope!'

'Don't touch it,' repeated Maud. Jabbing with the glave, she moved in front of Ivy and peered into the well.

Father stood ten feet below, waist-deep in filthy black water. He was smeared in blood and slime, and his face was pale and furious. 'You *lied*! It isn't in here! Now put that thing down and help me out!'

It was no use. She couldn't bring herself to do it. Casting aside the glave, she stumbled off to fetch Clem's pail. It was full of fat black eels, and so heavy she had to carry it with both hands. As she staggered to the well, the eels began to writhe.

'This is for Clem,' she told Father, hefting the pail on to the wall. Then she tipped the eels on to his upturned face.

'Don't you dare let down that rope,' she said to Ivy as she flung the pail in the grass.

She was dimly aware of Billy bursting round the corner with two labourers.

As she walked past them towards the house, Father started to scream.

Forty-seven

*D*EATH freezes everything. Whatever you did or didn't do, whatever you said or left unsaid: none of that is ever going to change. You have no more chances to say sorry or make things right. No more chances for anything except regret.

If Maud had called Clem's name a little louder when she was running towards the house, or if she'd searched the orchard instead of rushing inside, he would have been awake when Father came looking for him and he wouldn't have died.

Maud taught herself to believe that he couldn't have felt the ice-pick going in: that he'd simply fallen asleep under the apple tree and never woken up. But was that true? Or had the last thing he'd felt been a blaze of unimaginable pain?

She paid for his funeral out of the housekeeping. She attended it with Cole and put flowers on the grave. She never visited it again. Clem wasn't there. He was out in the fen. That was where she'd been closest to him.

People were disconcerted by her silent, unblinking stare.

They took it for lack of feeling and they were right. Inside, she was frozen. She couldn't feel anything. She couldn't understand that Clem was never coming back. She kept expecting to see him pushing his wheelbarrow about the grounds. She kept having to remind herself that he was gone.

The evening of the murder, the weather broke and Miss Broadstairs moved into Wake's End. She stayed for three weeks, by which time a housekeeper and a governess had been retained.

Great-Uncle Bertrand had arrived two days after the killing. Maud liked him because he left her alone; unlike Miss Broadstairs, who expected her to be devastated and was shocked when she was not.

Great-Uncle Bertrand became trustee of the estate and guardian of 'the children'. It struck Maud as bizarre that this term included herself, as her childhood felt impossibly remote. But Great-Uncle Bertrand was affable and worldly, and he readily agreed to cancel Father's plans to drain the fen, which he considered a waste of money. So in that Maud succeeded. She couldn't save Clem, but she saved the fen.

Great-Uncle Bertrand also protected Maud from the newspaper men and the day-trippers who came in char-à-bancs to peer over the hedge. But he couldn't protect her from the police.

She answered their questions with as much truth as

she thought appropriate, which meant that she made no mention of the demon or the Doom. Neither Dr Grayson nor the rector had believed her, so why should the police? They would think she was mad, and lock her up.

For days she lived in dread that Dr Grayson would reveal what she'd told him when she'd sought his help, but before they could question him, he had a stroke from which he never recovered. That was a weight off her mind.

She also worried that Mr Broadstairs might tell the police about the notebooks; but apparently he'd decided that that would be ungentlemanly. At any rate, he didn't mention them at the trial; nor did anyone refer to Father's odd behaviour in the months before the murder. Presumably no one cared to admit that they'd done nothing about it.

Father himself hardly spoke. He'd abruptly ceased his dreadful screaming on being hauled out of the well. 'I did it,' he declared. 'But I did nothing *wrong*.' That was all he ever said.

The notebooks were never found because, within minutes of the murder, Maud hid them. While Billy was going for the police and Ivy and the labourers were guarding Father, Maud slipped quietly into the house. There she wrapped both notebooks in oil-cloth and concealed them in her room, behind the wainscot where she'd hidden her viper skin when she was little.

She left Father's translation of Alice Pyett on his desk. If it had gone missing it might have aroused suspicion; and Maud guessed (correctly, as it turned out) that the police would regard the life of a medieval mystic as irrelevant to their enquiries.

They would probably have thought the same thing about *The Life of St Guthlaf*, but Maud decided not to risk it. So *The Life* joined the notebooks behind the wainscot.

The governess, Miss Birch, was a brisk Scotswoman who to Maud's intense relief was more interested in remedying the gaps in her education than in interrogating her feelings.

Miss Birch liked Maud because she knew her Bible, while Maud took pains to make herself agreeable, being well aware that she would be under the governess's thumb until she was twenty-one. She also reasoned that if Miss Birch approved of her, she would tolerate the occasional instance of odd behaviour.

One such occurred on the day Father began his life sentence in Broadmoor Criminal Lunatic Asylum. While Miss Birch was talking to the housekeeper, Maud crossed the foot-bridge into the fen. On reaching the Mere, she took out her scissors and chopped off her hair, stuffed it in a pillowslip with a stone, and threw it into the water.

And that was the start of her long atonement for Clem.

Thereafter, Maud's sole aim was to hide. She never visited Wakenhyrst again, and it was only to propitiate Miss Birch that she attended church once a week.

Great-Uncle Bertrand sensibly abandoned his idea of taking her to Brussels. He took Richard and Felix and left Maud with Miss Birch and a small staff comprising Mrs Entwhistle the new housekeeper, Cook, Ivy, Jessop, and

Jessop's brother Daniel, who saw to the grounds now that Cole had retired. At Maud's request, Daisy, who since the murder had had fits of hysteria, was pensioned off. Maud also arranged for Clem's brother Ned to fulfil his desire of joining the Navy. And she had Daniel plant ivy all around the house.

The Great War went almost unnoticed, except that Miss Birch saw that Wake's End did its duty by allowing Jessop and his brother to enlist and be slaughtered at Ypres. Ivy had married Daniel Jessop a few months before. She was pleased with her war widow's pension, and black suited her, although she was beginning to grow rather stout.

Maud's one complaint about Miss Birch was that she conceived it her duty to keep her informed about Father. He had a private room in Broadmoor's Block Two, which housed the better sort of patient (Miss Birch never called them prisoners). His doctors had diagnosed 'homicidal monomania with delusions', and treated him with ice-baths and rhubarb laxatives. To these Father objected violently; but a year into his sentence he asked for painting materials and a magnifying glass, and once he was given them he became a model patient, so the doctors left him alone.

Public interest in the art of the insane had been aroused by Bethlehem Hospital's exhibition of *Work by Mad Artists*, which featured paintings by, among others, Richard Dadd; but Father only started painting in 1915, and by that time interest had waned. He spent the rest of his life working on his canvases, which his physicians viewed as clinically irrelevant. His only other expenses were claret and sweets, his favourites being barley sugar and acid drops. Miss

329

Birch told Maud all this until she perceived how much her charge hated it, whereupon she stopped.

Her attempts to educate her charge met with more success. Maud liked history, literature and nature studies, which she used as a pretext for daily walks in the fen; a habit she continued all her life. For the sake of good relations, she tolerated Scripture and never revealed her lack of belief. She loathed geography. All those countries. All those people who knew about the murder. It confirmed her conviction that she must never leave Wake's End.

Her education proved a welcome distraction, but the most vital lesson was the one she taught herself on the day the trial ended. She taught herself never to think about Father.

She put him in a corner of her mind and slammed the door.

On Maud's twenty-first birthday, she came into a small annuity from Maman. She parted with Miss Birch on good terms, grateful to the governess for not having tried to be her friend.

Three years later, Richard attained majority and inherited the estate. Having taken rooms in London, he'd contrived to live down Father's notoriety. He never returned to Wake's End, and agreed to let Maud live there if she did so at her own expense. She dismissed Mrs Entwhistle and Cook and retained a skeleton staff comprising Billy, a girl from the village, and Ivy.

She would have loved to have dismissed Ivy too, but that was impossible. They were bound together by lies.

Ivy had been outraged by Clem's murder. 'Now I got *nothing!*' she spat. 'Well not if I can help it, I'll tell em you pushed the Master down the well. I'll tell about the eels.'

'I'll tell them you left Felix on his own to go to the Fair,' retorted Maud.

'I'll tell about you and Clem.'

'I'll tell them myself.'

'Not about Clem you wun't, you're too ashamed!'

She was right. Maud couldn't transcend her class. People of her sort did not fall in love with under-gardeners. So in the end, Ivy told the police that Maud had volunteered to watch Felix, while Maud corroborated this in return for Ivy's silence.

Maud never discovered how Ivy had found out about her and Clem. All she knew was that Ivy was enraged that he'd preferred Maud. And since Ivy believed that the Master had killed him to stop him 'carrying on' with his daughter, she blamed Maud for everything. In Ivy's mind, Maud had deprived her of the husband who would have made her respectable and of the Master who would have kept her in luxury. 'You owe me a living,' she said succinctly.

Maud found it hard to disagree.

During Maud's thirties, she thawed a little. She had Billy drive her to Ely, and wore a thick veil as a disguise. She ventured further afield to Peterborough and Cambridge.

Then in 1939 Father ended years of impeccable conduct by strangling an orderly. No one ever found out why. Maud retreated into her shell. She reduced her book-buying sorties to once a year. She barely noticed the outbreak of war.

The doctors tried in vain to control Father's increasingly erratic moods, and in 1941 they sought the family's consent to a new treatment. Transorbital leucotomy, or lobotomy, involved introducing an ice-pick under the eyelid, breaking the eye-socket with a hammer, and severing parts of the frontal lobes. In 1941 there was no more reason to believe that this would work than there had been in the fifteenth century, but all three of Father's progeny gave their consent: Richard and Felix after some hesitation, Maud with none at all. The lobotomy was a failure, and Father died six months later. He was sixty-nine.

The asylum wrote to Maud enquiring what should be done with the paintings at which he had laboured for twenty-six years. It was the first she'd heard of them. By this time Felix was dead, so with Richard's agreement she told the asylum to sell them, which it did for a nominal sum to the Stanhope Institute of Psychiatric History.

As with the Great War, so the Second World War passed almost unnoticed at Wake's End – except when Felix was shot down over Crete. He died without ever knowing that Maud had saved his life. It would only have embarrassed him, and they'd never been close. Richard died of oesophageal cancer in 1953, and as he had no children, Maud inherited Wake's End.

Richard and his wife Tabby had squandered most of the Trust, but Maud didn't care. The pattern of her life had been set. She had no need for gas or electricity, and she grew her own fruit and vegetables. Apart from her yearly visit to Hibble's, she ordered her books via the post from a shop in the Charing Cross Road.

Like the magic thicket in the fairytale, the hedge that protected Wake's End grew ever higher, and behind it, Maud continued to hide.

For decades the world forgot about the murder. Then in 1965 an art historian named Dr Robin Hunter found three dusty paintings in a tea chest, and an unscrupulous journalist named Patrick Rippon concocted a story about witches.

And suddenly everyone wanted to solve the mystery of Edmund Stearne.

1967

Forty-eight

'AND the rest you know,' said Maud Stearne in her cut-glass accent. 'Now, Dr Hunter. D'you think this will raise enough money for my new roof?'

Robin held her breath. 'Does that mean you've decided to publish?'

'I've no idea what I shall do. I find the thought of everyone knowing quite intolerable. However, I need *money*. I don't intend to let this house fall down around my ears and I won't see the fen given over to pigs.'

Her narrative lay on the footstool between them, on top of her father's notebooks. Despite Robin's entreaties not to entrust anything to the Royal Mail, Maud – as Robin privately thought of her – had insisted on posting the typescript to her in instalments, along with the notebooks at judicious intervals. Robin had sat up until three in the morning, reading the final pages. Today she'd brought everything back to Wake's End.

To keep the typescript together, she'd put it in a lever-arch file. As she watched Maud lean forwards and turn the file face down, she realised her blunder. The file's cover bore the famous detail from Painting No. 2. The face that had been leering up at them was that of the devil in the Doom.

Robin was mortified. 'Miss Stearne, I am *so* sorry.'

'It's of no consequence,' Maud replied stiffly.

They were sitting in armchairs on either side of the library fire. Robin had dressed with care, swapping the infamous white vinyl boots for sober brown ones, and her mini-skirt for a midi. Maud wore the same shapeless slacks and twin-set as before.

Today was only the second time that Robin had seen her. At their first meeting back in November, Maud had been icily defensive. Four months later, she was worse: brusque, suspicious, haughty and frightened. Her fists were clenched in her lap and her deep-set eyes avoided Robin's, gazing into the distance and moving restlessly from side to side.

The clock on the mantelpiece ticked. The silence lengthened.

Robin cleared her throat. 'There may be a way for you not to publish at all – but still make enough money for your new roof. You could sell Wake's End to the National Trust. On condition, of course, that you'd go on living here for the rest of your life. That way, your house and the fen would be safe for ever.'

Maud blinked. 'What is the National Trust?'

'Um – it's a charity that looks after places for the nation. Stately homes, nature reserves, that kind of thing.'

Maud grabbed a poker and attacked the coals. 'Good Heavens. But would they – it – really pay that much?'

'For the ancestral home of Edmund Stearne and one of the last stretches of undrained fen? Oh, yes, I think they would.'

'Good Heavens. Then I wouldn't have to "sell my story" to anyone.'

'Quite. You could do what you like with the typescript. You could tell Hollywood to get lost.'

Maud barked a mirthless laugh. 'My sister-in-law would be incandescent. It would be worth it simply for that.'

Robin nodded unhappily. 'Naturally, I'd much prefer it if you did publish. I'd love to work with you, Miss Stearne. I mean, on the editing and so on.'

'Naturally,' Maud said drily. 'So why did you suggest this – National Trust? Surely enabling me *not* to publish goes against your own interests as an historian?'

'You can say that again,' said Robin. 'It's just – well. I can see how much the idea of publishing upsets you.'

Maud looked startled.

'So what do you want to do?' said Robin.

'I don't *know*,' snapped Maud.

Cook lumbered in and they waited while she gathered the tea things. Watching her waddle out again, Robin tried and failed to see traces of Ivy the beautiful housemaid under all that fat.

There was another silence after she'd gone. Robin wondered how she was going to persuade Maud to answer her questions, *and* admit what she'd left out of her narrative, *and* agree to publish.

'At the end of your account,' she began carefully, 'you mention "atonement". But I don't understand why you blame yourself. Surely what happened was mostly just chance?'

'Ah yes, *chance*,' Maud said acidly. 'If it hadn't rained that night in 1911, Father wouldn't have seen the eye in the grass and the Doom would have gone up in smoke. Oddly enough, that has occurred to me over the last fifty-four years.'

Robin felt herself flush. 'And if Hibble's assistant hadn't made a mistake – if he hadn't included *The Life of St Guthlaf* in that parcel of books – your father would never have got the idea that there'd been an exorcism in Pyett's time.'

Maud turned her head and stared out of the window. 'One could go back a good deal further than that. If my grandmamma hadn't given Father a book of Greek myths when he was a boy, he wouldn't have taken it into his head to play Perseus and Andromeda with Lily. All this I *know*, Dr Hunter. What happened was still my fault.'

'Why?'

'Because I didn't prevent it.'

'Is that the only reason?'

Maud's gaze remained fixed on the window. 'Dr Hunter, you are living up to your name. You're making me feel like a cornered beast.'

'I'm sorry.' Robin studied Maud's profile. A harsh, bony face; but age had brought out its resilience and strength. 'There's something else I don't understand,' Robin ventured. 'You didn't show the notebooks to the police. But then why keep them at all?'

'Because of Lily,' Maud said impatiently. 'And Jubal.

Surely you've grasped that without the notebooks, there'd
be no proof of what really happened to them?' She shifted
in her chair. 'Lily died a dreadful, lonely death. She doesn't
deserve to be forgotten.'

'Is she the figure at the heart of the paintings?'

'She was ten years old and he painted her as a grown
woman. That was unforgivable.'

'Why do you think he did that?'

'To make her easier to blame, I should imagine. Somewhere in the ledger he says it was her fault. That's what he
did all his life: it was Lily's fault, or the demon's. Never his
own.'

'Perhaps he couldn't bear the truth.'

Maud twisted her hands in her lap. '*He* was the devil in
the corner. He left Lily to drown. That was what he could
never bring himself to face.'

'So he ended up painting devils.'

'"My name is Legion",' quoted Maud.

Robin thought about that. 'That bit in his medical
records: "He is terrified of the tiny beings he feels compelled
to paint, and yet he seems quite unable to desist."' She
paused. 'He went on doing that for twenty-six years.'

They were silent. Robin wondered if Maud was thinking
of the paintings. That swirling vortex of demons with the
diminutive woman at its heart: a grown-up Lily in a long
black dress, her fair hair hanging loose.

'Which reminds me,' Maud said abruptly. She rose and
fetched an envelope from her desk. 'I'd forgotten this. It's
from the physician in Broadmoor. He wrote to me after
Father died, but I never read it attentively until this morning.

I thought you might care to hear what he says towards the end.'

Putting on her spectacles, she read aloud in her clipped accent: '"One day I overheard him" – he means Father – "muttering to himself while he was painting. 'You must paint them down fast,' he kept repeating under his breath. 'Fast, before they get away. Paint them down thick, thick, so they can never get out.'"'

Taking off her spectacles, Maud pinched the bridge of her nose. 'The doctor never thought to mention that in his case notes. Which is why the odious Mr Rippon never came across it.'

Robin's mind was racing. 'That's why your father filled his canvases with devils. They were all around him. Always.'

'Yes,' said Maud. 'He was trying to trap them. One might almost say that he was creating his own Doom.'

'So the typescript,' said Robin in her quiet, inexorable way. 'What would you like to do with it?'

'I told you, I've no idea!' Maud scowled at the file on the footstool. She had turned it over again, for she was finding 'The Three Familiars' oddly fascinating. The creature known as 'Air' had a nebulous beauty, marred by a scar that twisted one eye savagely out of shape. 'Water' was androgynous, its features impossibly slanted, as if distorted by unseen forces emanating from the grown-up Lily at the painting's heart. And then there was 'Earth', with his grin and his lascivious wink.

Sitting back, Maud squared her shoulders. That file

contained her life. Well, more or less. She wondered if Dr Hunter – Robin, as she was beginning to think of her – had any notion of what had been left out.

Beneath the file lay Father's notebooks. Robin had carefully re-inserted the page which Maud had torn from Father's notebook and sent to her last year. It was the sketch of a magpie: crouching, its head lowered as if it was just about to fly off. Father had caught the bird's wariness with breath-taking skill. He'd even drawn the scar down one leg which Chatterpie had acquired on the day when she'd rescued him from the well.

It still hurt to remember. I am nearly seventy years old, thought Maud. And yet inside I'm only sixteen.

Suddenly she couldn't breathe. 'Come along, let's walk. Can't stay cooped up inside all day.'

It was a bright, freezing February afternoon and the fen was at its wintry best, glittering with frost beneath a limitless sky of dazzling blue. Maud took the path at her usual lope, leaving Robin to keep up. No birds. The geese were off foraging in the fields, and Maud had seen no sign of the starlings for days.

She realised that she was twisting her hands. She'd been doing that a lot, and her eczema was worse. Writing her account had forced her to re-live everything: the grief, the guilt. Especially the guilt.

'You know,' panted Robin behind her, 'I do understand why you blame yourself.'

'No you don't,' snapped Maud over her shoulder.

'Actually, I do.' Robin halted. When she didn't move, Maud felt compelled to halt too.

Dr Hunter wasn't pretty, but she had the cast of features that Maud would have wanted for herself: narrow and vulpine, like a female Voltaire. It was an agreeable face, and Maud admired the girl's red hair against the frost-spangled reeds. She envied Dr Hunter, who was clever and self-possessed, and who – while belonging to a class decidedly below Maud's own – had achieved everything she had not: a university degree, an occupation. Freedom.

'You told me you didn't show the notebooks to the police because they wouldn't have believed you,' said Robin with gentle persistence. 'But there was more to it than that. If they'd seen the notebooks, they would have found out about *The Life of St Guthlaf.*'

Maud looked at her.

'They would have known that it was *The Life* which sparked your father's ideas about exorcism and made him think there was a devil behind the Doom. They might also have found out the truth about why Hibble's sent it. You see,' Robin added apologetically, 'Hibble's still have all their records. It didn't take long to find the entry for the twenty-fourth of June 1912. That's the day when you and Clem went to Ely—'

'I remember the date,' cut in Maud.

'And you'll be aware that Hibble's assistant didn't include *The Life* in your father's parcel by mistake.' She paused. 'They showed me the record. I had them photostat the page. "*The Life of St Guthlaf*, 2 shillings and sixpence: to Miss Maud Stearne."' She bit her lip. 'You bought it. You planted it among your father's books for him to find.'

Maud turned and stared at the ice on the Lode. 'I didn't

even read it,' she said. 'I flicked through and saw something about demons and a magpie. Good, I thought. That'll scare him. I wanted vengeance for Chatterpie.' She paused. 'I never even saw that passage about trapping the demon in the flask. I never *imagined* it would make him think there was a real devil trapped behind the Doom.'

'No one could have foreseen that. And even if you hadn't planted that book, he'd probably have got the idea from somewhere else.'

'You don't know that. All you know is what happened. And that was my fault.'

'You were a child. You can't go on blaming yourself for what you did then. Besides, you saved Felix. You saved the fen.'

Maud nodded wearily. 'Yes. But I couldn't save Clem.'

They reached the Mere. It had snowed in the night and the ice was netted with the tracks of wild creatures. Maud felt tired, but oddly at peace. 'I'm glad that you know,' she told Robin. 'It's a relief.'

The younger woman stood hunched in her duffle coat with her chin buried in her scarf. 'Did your father never suspect that you planted *The Life*?'

Maud snorted a laugh. 'Heavens no, it never occurred to him. I am devoid of imagination, remember?'

'Ah.' Robin frowned. 'Forgive me for asking, but do you still hate him?'

Maud considered that. 'Writing it all down has been a trial. At times I've hated it. But I no longer hate him. I think

345

I feel sorry for him.' With her eyes she followed the trail of a fox. 'Sometimes,' she said, 'on quiet nights, I fancy I can hear her crying.'

'You mean Lily?'

Raising her head, Maud squinted at the sky. 'I've decided to publish.'

Robin audibly gasped. 'Do you mean that?'

'I said it, didn't I?'

'What made you decide?'

'Lily. I want people to know the truth.'

Forty-nine

*T*HE following year, on a misty October evening, Maud apologised to Schubert and turned off the wireless in her bedroom.

Picking up Robin's postcard with its picture of dancing cranes, she re-read the message on the back, which made her smile. Then she replaced it on the windowsill between the lump of bog oak propping up the sash and the porcelain wing she'd stolen from a Brussels graveyard sixty-two years before.

In the sky above the Mere she made out a wavering blur, and her spirits rose as they always did when she saw the starlings. Cold air drifted in from the fen, dispelling the lingering smell of paint. Despite Robin's best efforts, Maud had insisted on keeping her old mahogany furniture, but she had consented to have her room re-painted. The brown stains on the ceiling were gone. In the morning as she lay in bed, she enjoyed gazing up at the pristine white distemper.

The sale of Wake's End to the National Trust had finally gone through and the estate's future (and hers) was secure.

MICHELLE PAVER

Every day when she set off for her walk, she admired her new roof. It looked a trifle stark without the softening effect of lichen and houseleek, but that would come in time.

'All in good time,' she would tell Robin as she batted away the young woman's latest suggestion: central heating, learning to drive, a telephone, a dog. 'I'm enjoying the peace now that the roofers have gone.'

They both knew that what she really meant was Ivy. Maud's book had been published at the end of last year, but she had sent Ivy packing months before. Once the truth was known, Ivy's hold on her was over. With indescribable relief, Maud had watched that great smouldering lump of resentment clamber into a taxi and disappear.

And yet it wasn't only relief that Maud had felt. It was shame. How was it Ivy's fault that she was what she was? In all her life she'd never been out of Suffolk. She would have said that she didn't want to thank you very much; but she'd never been taught any different. From childhood she'd had to fight to get enough food, while fending off the groping attentions of men. Later she had used her good looks to get what she wanted. She and Maud had both had to fight to survive. Ivy had used sex, Maud had used her brain. Why could they not have found some common ground?

Too late for that now. According to Robin, Ivy was in Bury, blighting the existence of one of her many relations. She was also 'in talks' with Patrick Rippon about a memoir of her life at Wake's End.

Well, let her do her worst. Astonishing how the truth really did set one free.

Besides, not even Ivy knew the whole truth.

'Why don't you change your mind and come with me to Tokyo?' Robin had said on her last visit. 'They wouldn't expect you to speak at the conference, but they'd be over the moon if you came.'

'All in good time, Professor,' Maud had said, and Robin had laughed.

That had been one of their most agreeable evenings. Maria the new cook-housekeeper had surpassed herself for supper, and the weather had been warm enough for them to eat on the library terrace.

Robin had been amusing about her tribulations as 'historical adviser' on the forthcoming film. 'Be warned, they've ignored everything I said. It won't bear any relation to the truth.'

'I should hope not,' Maud had replied.

Apparently, the cinematic version of herself was to be played by a stunningly beautiful actress rendered 'Hollywood plain' by a plastic nose; already there was talk of an Oscar. To appeal to the American market, Maman had become an heiress from New York, and there was some kind of ancillary plot about witches, with 'flash-backs' to Salem. The writers had added a happy ending in which Maud married Mr Broadstairs' handsome nephew. They'd also given the whole story an unequivocally Christian message. 'You may be sure,' intoned the rector in his rousing final speech, 'that it was *not* by chance that Edmund Stearne discovered the Doom in the churchyard – it was by the Hand of God. For God shows us devils in order to make us believe in angels.'

Robin thought this was hilarious. Maud didn't find it

quite so amusing. This she did her best to conceal, but the ever-observant Robin noticed and was contrite. 'I'm sorry,' she said, touching Maud's shoulder. 'I shouldn't have made light of it.'

'Why ever not? I shan't go and see the wretched thing. Now make yourself useful and pour some more wine.'

It was a beautiful evening. The last of the sun gilded the long grass in the orchard, where blue tits squabbled at the bird-feeders hanging from the well. A magpie swooped from the roof and strutted about the lawn. Maud thought of Clem's slow, shy smile when she'd questioned him about Chatterpie's perch.

'One thing still bothers me,' Robin said quietly.

Maud sighed. 'I thought I'd heard the last of remarks like that.'

Robin smiled, but her face wore her determined look. 'Waterweed,' she said.

'What about it?'

'The waterweed on your father's windowsill. And on his pillow. You've always said that's the one thing you can't explain.'

'Well, I can't,' Maud said evenly.

Robin turned her wine glass in her fingers. 'Your father believed there was something in the fen. Do you?'

'My dear Robin. I was frightened and alone and I'd lived for months with a monomaniac. It would have been odd if I *hadn't* believed there was something in the fen. That doesn't make it real.'

'So how do you explain the waterweed?'

Maud paused. 'I don't.'

Robin nodded slowly. 'It's just that I've often wondered… Why do you always keep your bedroom window
open?'

Maud took another sip of wine, then calmly met her
eyes. 'I like fresh air. Let's leave it at that.'

'They don't need to know *everything*,' Maud told herself
as she ran her hand over the lump of bog oak propping
open the sash. She had found it by the Mere on that dead,
windless afternoon in October 1912, just after Father had
decided to drain the fen.

In her typescript and in her book, Maud had written that
as her courses had come unexpectedly that day, she had
squatted by the Mere and rinsed the blood off her hands.
That wasn't true. Her courses hadn't come for the past
three months. It wasn't menstrual blood she had washed
off her fingers. It was from the pathetic lump of flesh which
had been her child and Clem's.

Their daughter, as she liked to think of it; although
thanks to Biddy Thrussel's herbs, one couldn't really tell.
Maud had wrapped it in a pillowslip and committed it to
the Mere. Shortly afterwards, Jubal had found her there
and told her about Lily.

'Of course I keep my window open,' said Maud, giving
the bog oak a little pat. 'How could I ever shut her out?'

Above the Mere, the starlings were gathering. From her
window, Maud watched more birds flying up from the

reeds to join the great dark cloud that swept and wavered over the fen.

'Dear Maud,' Robin had written on her postcard. 'The conference is fun & despite appalling jet-lag I'm enjoying the enthusiasm for your father's work – but I wish you were here! I thought you'd like this picture of cranes. As you probably know, in Japan the crane is a symbol of love & fidelity because they mate for life & dance in pairs. But I'm told – & this made me think of you – that sometimes, for reasons no one understands, a single crane dances alone.'

With a last glance at her postcard, Maud headed downstairs to begin her walk. It was time to be out in the fen with the starlings, and to feel the rush of their wings, as if she were flying.

Author's Note

Like Maud, I saw my first murmuration of starlings when I was alone in a Suffolk marsh one autumn evening. It began with a few birds skimming the reeds as they rushed past, and I stood transfixed as the murmuration grew and grew.

That was in early November 2015, and I was in Westwood Marshes near the coastal village of Walberswick, on the other side of Suffolk from where I eventually sited Wake's End. I'd been thinking about writing a gothic story set in the fens for some time, but I'd never had a strong enough idea – until a few weeks before I saw those starlings, when three had come along in a matter of days.

One idea came when I'd picked up a battered copy of *The Book of Margery Kempe* in Oxfam. I'd never heard of the fifteenth-century mystic, and her writing struck me as bizarre, narcissistic and oddly pitiable. Her voice brought the times she lived in vividly to life.

Another idea was sparked by Carl Watkins' marvellous

book *The Undiscovered Country* about beliefs on death
in the Middle Ages. In it I read the astonishing story of
the Wenhaston Doom, a medieval painting of the Last
Judgement which was whitewashed by the Puritans, then
nearly chucked on a bonfire by the Victorians when they
were renovating the church in 1892.

Finally and also by chance, my mother and I visited an
exhibition of the paintings of Richard Dadd at the Watts
Gallery near Guildford. As you may know, Dadd was a
Victorian artist who murdered his father with an axe, and
spent the rest of his life in Broadmoor, where he devoted
years to painting obsessively detailed canvases of tiny,
otherworldly creatures. As my mother and I stood before
one particularly seething painting, we speculated about the
feelings that might have prompted Dadd to create it. 'Fear,'
suggested my mother. That interested me: the idea of a man
being terrified of what he created, but unable to stop. On
the train home I jotted a few notes: 'He's scared of what
he paints… Does he believe they're real … Any link with
Wenhaston Doom?'

I made up Wakenhyrst and its Doom, as well as Wake's
End, Guthlaf's Fen, St Guthlaf's Church and the family of
Edmund Stearne. But all of them are anchored in reality.

Guthlaf's Fen is based on my visits to marshes and fens over
the years both before and during the writing of *Wakenhyrst*,
including Wicken Fen, Dunwich and Walberswick Marshes,
Rainham Marshes and others. Similarly, the hamlet of
Wakenhyrst and St Guthlaf's Church are based on the many
English villages and medieval churches I've visited over the
years. One of the great pleasures of an English country walk

is diving into the nearest old church, and deciphering the tombstones in the graveyard. You never know what you're going to find.

The Wakenhyrst Doom is of course based on the Wenhaston Doom, which I visited during the same trip when I saw the starlings. The church was open but empty at the time, and I spent a peaceful hour sitting unnervingly close to the Doom's giant green Satan with his enormous bat wings and ragged knee-breeches.

The Life of St Guthlaf is based on the life of the Anglo-Saxon saint Guthlac of Crowland, who was either a saint, or merely a delusional young man afflicted by malaria, home-made opium and loneliness. It depends on what you choose to believe.

The Book of Alice Pyett is of course based on *The Book of Margery Kempe*. Like Alice, Margery Kempe was married in her teens, had an unconscionable number of children, and ended up longing for chastity. This led to some truly bizarre visions of Jesus and lots of crying. She also had a sin on her conscience that she wouldn't even reveal to her confessor. Nobody ever found out what it was.

I didn't invent the folklore and customs of the Wakenhyrst villagers, or what they believed about the spirits that haunt the fen. Ferishes, Jack-o'-Lanterns and Black Shuck are all part of East Anglia's rich folklore. My only invention is 'the thing that cries in the night'. Similarly, the Norfolk 'pseudo-saint' John Schorne also existed and is indeed said to have imprisoned the Devil in a boot. And although I made up the Stearne family, a real seventeenth-century John Stearne was a 'witch-pricker' and helped Matthew

Hopkins, the infamous Witchfinder-General, at the Bury St Edmunds witch trial of 1645.

I'm afraid I also didn't invent the idiosyncrasies and/ or idiocies of three medical men mentioned in the story: Jean-Martin Charcot, Gottlieb Burkhardt and Paul Broca. Only Dr Grayston and Dr Buchanan are fictional, but I based Dr Buchanan's *Plain Words for Ladies and Girls* on advice in real nineteenth-century publications. I mention all this as I think it's important to remember that these things were once perpetrated in the name of science, and some quite recently: lobotomies were still going strong in the 1950s.

But the heart of the story belongs to Maud, and aspects of her tale have a much more personal source. They were sparked by the reminiscences of my Belgian mother and aunt over the past few years (although I'm glad to say that neither my mother nor my aunt went through what Maud or Maman did).

Their mother, my Belgian grandmother, seems to have had a pretty tough childhood. Her father was a man who 'didn't like children, but liked making them'. He was also violent, and as a child she was so scared of him that she used to hide under the table when he came home. Her mother (my great-grandmother) was nicer, but she had a very hard life with an abusive husband, frequent pregnancies, and three children lost to illness. Being too poor to buy dolls for her small daughter, she used to 'rescue' porcelain angels in an Antwerp cemetery and knock off their wings with a hammer. (She was careful only to take angels from neglected graves; and although she was a devout Catholic, she felt it was the least God could do to turn a blind eye, after the trials he'd sent her.)

When my grandmother grew up and got married, she almost never signed her own name, but instead wrote Epse P. Van Mensel. That means: 'Epouse [wife] Pierre Van Mensel'. I think that says quite a lot.

And all that was just my grandmother. There was also the male relation who was such a womaniser that not even his own daughter-in-law was off-limits. And finally, the tale of the family doctor who was overheard quietly counselling yet another male relative not to have sex with his wife *every* night. In Flemish the advice translates roughly as: 'Once in a while, skip a night, eh?'

All this was well within living memory. It makes me particularly glad to live where and when I do.

On a happier note, I rescued Chatterpie myself. One June afternoon in 2014 I was reading in my study when I heard a strange panicky splashing in the alleyway alongside my house. Rushing downstairs, I found a young magpie drowning in two feet of rainwater which I'd stupidly allowed to collect in a garden urn. Having fished him out, I wrapped him in a tea towel and hurried off to a wildlife sanctuary where they cleaned him up and pronounced him none the worse for his ordeal. I'll never forget the strength of his claws as he clutched that tea towel, or his total lack of hesitation when I set him free the next day on Wimbledon Common, where I live. He flew straight to a nearby oak, which promptly erupted with the magpie equivalent of outraged parents demanding to know where he'd been.

While I was writing *Wakenhyrst*, certain books were particularly helpful, and I acknowledge them with thanks. For the Wenhaston Doom and lots more besides: *The Undiscovered Country: Journeys Among the Dead* by Carl Watkins (The Bodley Head, London 2013); also the excellent booklet in St Peter's Church, Wenhaston, by Judith Middleton-Stewart (2006). On eel-babbing and country life in East Anglia: *The Rabbit Skin Cap* by George Baldry (Boydell Press, Ipswich 1974, first published 1939); *I Walked by Night*, edited by Lilias Rider Haggard (Boydell Press, Ipswich 1974, first published 1935); *Life as We Have Known It* by M. Llewelyn Davies (Hogarth Press, London 1931); *Fenland Chronicle* by Sybil Marshall (CUP, Cambridge 1980, first published 1967). For East Anglian folklore and customs: *County Folklore – Suffolk* by Camilla Gurdon (1893); *The Folklore of East Anglia* by Enid Porter (Batsford, London 1974); *Folklore and Customs of Rural England* by Margaret Baker (David & Charles, Newton Abbot 1974); *The Penguin Book of Scandinavian Folktales*, translated and edited by Jacqueline Simpson (Penguin Books, London 1994, first published 1988).

Also: *The Book of Margery Kempe*, translated by B.A. Windeatt (Penguin Books, London 1985); *The Anglo-Saxon Version of the Life of St Guthlac, Hermit of Crowland*, translated by Charles Wycliffe Goodwin (London 1847); *Richard Dadd: the Artist and the Asylum* by Nicholas Tromans (Tate Publishing, London 2011); and *Madness in Civilization: A Cultural History of Insanity* by Andrew Scull (Thames & Hudson, London 2015).

Lastly, I need to thank some people. First, my marvellous publisher and editor Fiona Kennedy at Head of Zeus, who from the start responded to the story with her characteristic insight, imagination and enthusiasm; my editor Helen Francis, for her perceptive comments and always helpful suggestions; Jessie Price, Art Director at Head of Zeus, for her gorgeous cover design for the book, and Stephen McNally, illustrator, for creating its splendid magpie image and the beautiful chapter illustrations; and finally to my hugely talented agent Peter Cox, for his unfailing optimism and support, even during the years when I wouldn't even tell him what this story was about.

MICHELLE PAVER
LONDON